BRUTAL KING

RAVENWOOD ELITES BOOK ONE

NIKITA

To anyone who has ever second-guessed themselves before,
Push through because you can do it!
You just have to believe in yourself more.
xoxo Nikita!

AUTHOR'S NOTE

This is the first book in the Ravenwood Elites Trilogy, and it does end in a cliffhanger.

Though it is not as dark as my debut novel, there are some scenes that sensitive readers may find triggering, which includes bullying and non-con.

PROLOGUE

Winter

Winter 10, Mason 12

THE SOUNDS of screams and giggles coming from the bouncy house are so loud I had to roll my eyes at the antics of everyone in there.

Riley's backyard was transformed for her tenth birthday, which is today, and everyone seems to be having a good time. I am too, but I have trouble making friends and I get uncomfortable around too many people.

I guess that's what happens when there are people always following your parents around with cameras. You sort of don't like the crowds.

The adults, aka the parents, are all lounging around by the pool and doing whatever parents do. So that leaves everyone to play wherever they want to. Half of them are in the bouncy house while the other half are just around the house.

Riley's brother, Beckett, is playing with his friends somewhere. He doesn't want to play with us today because he says we are babies, as if! I just roll my eyes at that thought because he acts like more of a baby than us.

Instead of the bouncy house, I go to the monkey bars Riley's dad set up at the back of their yard. There are even slides here! I wanted my own slide and monkey bars too, but my mom always got mad at me when I asked her for one.

Eventually I asked my father, and he built me a really cool treehouse instead. It was so awesome, and I spent most of my time there, I loved it so much.

I was content to play by myself until it would be time for cake. I really love cake and if I could eat that everyday then I would, but daddy says I can't. I was sad for a while until he said he loved me but cake every day would make me sick.

I try climbing up on the monkey bars to get to the top, but I slip and fall on my butt. It hurts so much, and tears instantly start streaming down my face. Hmmm, maybe I am a baby. I try to get up, but the pain in my leg is too much to move with, so I just sit there sobbing.

"Why are you crying?" a voice asks suddenly from next to me. I quickly wipe my eyes to cover the fact I've been crying, though I'm sure that can't be missed. My eyes always get super red whenever I cry. When I finally look up at the boy who came over to talk to me, I let out a gasp because he's the prettiest boy I've ever seen.

Now, I don't know if we should call boys pretty or not, but that word instantly came to mind when I first looked up at him.

His light green eyes drew me in as soon as I looked into them. It was at that moment, I knew that this was going to be the boy I married someday.

"I fell," I say to him, sniffling.

"Aw cheer up, my dad always tells me '*whenever I fall, no matter how much it hurts to get back up, I should always do it.*'

And you should definitely do that too," he says smiling at me.

"Wow, you're smart! I'll do it so that way we'll always have something we share with each other," I say, returning his smile. I couldn't remove the smile from my face even if I wanted to.

"I'm Mason," he says, and wow, even his name is nice.

"Mine is Winter," I say with a small smile.

"You want to go get some cake?"

"Duh! I love cake."

Okay, I changed my mind. I didn't know he would be my soulmate when I first looked at him, I knew it the moment he asked me if I wanted cake!

———

THAT WAS the day I met who I thought was the love of my life. From the day we met, we became friends and by the time I knew what a crush was, I was already crushing on him.

As we grew up together, we had to hide the fact that we were friends because our parents didn't approve. They said our families hated each other, but I couldn't fathom why.

When I thought of not being able to be with Mason anymore, it hurt and I wasn't sure what to do with that. Mason was two years older than me, so he knew what to do. We agreed to continue being friends secretly, and I was glad he didn't want to stop being my friend just because our parents said we had to.

At a young age, I didn't grasp what they meant when they said our families didn't like each other. I wasn't aware that things like hate existed in our family along with the Kings. Though I'd come to learn it wasn't simply hate for each other, it was something that ran much deeper than hate ever could.

I certainly couldn't have predicted that once I got older, I would know exactly what it meant to have the people you loved betray you in the worst possible ways you could ever imagine.

I'd also come to learn that blood doesn't always mean family, and the people who you considered family would do everything in their power to serve their own agenda before they ever thought about the effects their actions would have on you.

Life got so messy and uncontrollable, that at the time I had no idea if I would make it out alive because there were people who wanted everything I had because of greed.

Another hard lesson I had to learn was that not even love could survive everything thrown at it. The web of lies and deception was one that we never saw coming, but the most painful thing of all was when that love turned to hate as well.

The love of my life believed lies that tore us apart in a minute. He saw what they wanted him to see, and with that; it brought on the hate he developed for me.

The hatred he had inside of him built up into something that turned him into someone so cold I had no way of knowing if anyone could ever break his icy exterior. Even seeing him as what he became, I couldn't help but still love him deep down inside. Yeah, I know that makes me look stupid, but the heart wants what it wants after all, doesn't it?

I didn't know that when I returned to the place I once called home, he'd set out to destroy me. The place that I could have died without ever seeing again.

On most days, his hatred for me felt like it was something so visceral it did nothing but suffocate me until slowly he got what he wanted and I started to break, though if I had to admit the truth, I was already a little broken by the time I returned to California.

I tried to stay strong, just like my father used to tell me to be when I was growing up. But my monster was a brutal king in the place he ruled, and I was no match for him and his hatred. He just kept taking from me until I had nothing left to give him.

If there ever came a point in time where he asked for forgiveness for all the things he did wrong, would I ever be able to forgive him? I guess we'll all just have to wait and see.

Family wars, greed, hate and lies...

Those were the things that broke my already fragile being, but the only question is, by the end of it, would I rise again or would I fall just like our empires did?

ONE

Winter

I LIE on my bed with a sense of both dread and excitement that I can't contain. Dread because today is my last day here in Ravenwood. My father is a billionaire, and he owns his own company called Crowne Enterprises.

It's a large company and has a host of other small subsidiaries that operate under Crowne. Over the years, his company has gotten so big he's decided to move us all to London for a while to open a second headquarters there. He said the expansion overseas has gotten larger than he expected, so that's why he needs to make the move.

I have no idea how long we'll be staying there, but he assured me it wouldn't be over three years tops. Naturally, being the teenager I am, I was super pissed off when he sprang the news on us.

I love my father more than anything in the world, so I decide not to be a pain in the ass and just go along with it. After he had his affairs in order, we'd be moving back home according to him.

He has someone here who he appointed as his CEO while he'll be in London. I don't want to leave, but I have no other choice but to follow my parents' orders since I'm not eighteen yet and can't live on my own. Life is so unfair when you think about it.

I'm excited because Mason agreed to sneak over tonight so that we can spend some time in our special place, aka the treehouse in my backyard. This way I get to see him one last time before I leave for London tomorrow morning.

We've been best friends ever since he asked me if I wanted cake at Riley's tenth birthday party. See, even then I knew we were meant for each other, though I've said nothing to him yet because I feared he'd reject me. I'm not even sure if he feels anything for me other than friends.

Now that I'm older, I know that I've been in love with him since we met that day and I looked into green eyes that captured my soul. With the plans I have for tonight, hopefully that will all change, and we won't be just friends, but something more.

I have to admit I'm nervous about how he'll react, but I have to at least try before I leave. Who knows what will happen once tomorrow comes. If I leave without telling him how I feel, then I'll probably regret it in the coming days. Nothing sucks more than missed opportunities and regrets.

With the possibility of me being gone for at least three years, I risk him finding either a bitchy girlfriend or a gold digger and we can't have that. Ugh, I already hate his imaginary girlfriend.

I might die of embarrassment if this backfires in my face. Over the last few months, I've felt the subtle changes between us, and I'm hoping I haven't misread the signs and tonight isn't a total bust.

I can't bear the thought of losing him as someone I love and as a best friend. We both grew up in the same social circles and attended many of the same events. We would sneak off at events and find somewhere quiet to just talk and hang out until it was time to leave.

Sometimes his brother, Grayson, would hang out with us, but most of the time it would be just us while Gray hung out with his other friends. Gray and I were close, and he was like the brother I never had.

My best friends Riley, Avery, and Luna were always close by in case my parents ever looked for me. They never did, but it was nice knowing that my friends had my back.

They all knew about my long-standing crush on Mason, though we had to keep it on the down low. It was no secret in this town that both our dads hated each other. There's been a rivalry between them for years. No one is even sure how it started, but that's the way it's been.

I never let that fact bother me when it comes to being friends with Mase or Gray, and they haven't either, though we keep our friendship hidden from our parents as best we can.

We spend most days over at Riley and Beck's house since Riley is my best friend and Beckett is Mason's. I don't think either of our parents suspect anything because they never questioned me before. I don't think they know the boys are always over at Becks when we're there, so that's a good thing. Avery and Luna are always there with us too, so it's an easy cover.

I'm also not the only one in our group with a secret crush. Though none of them have admitted to theirs yet except for me. My best friends are the only people who know, and if I wasn't leaving, then I'd be too much of a chicken to tell him, unless of course he admitted to it first.

I finally get up, shower, and wait for the girls to come over to help me pick out an outfit for tonight. They all know Mason agreed to meet me in the treehouse and we're all excited.

Half an hour later, I'm in the kitchen eating breakfast when I hear the doorbell. I put my bowl in the sink before rushing to answer it.

When I pull it open, three faces are smiling back at me, each with a goofy expression on their face.

"Are you ready for tonight?" Riley squeals as soon as her ass passes through the door, followed by Avery and Luna.

"Shhh! Before my mother hears you! They're still home," I whisper-yell at her.

"Shit, sorry! I don't want to ruin this before you've ruined it yourself," she says seriously. She snorts a laugh.

"Gee, thanks for the vote of confidence, bitch!" I say, rolling my eyes at her.

"Come on, you have nothing to worry about," Avery pipes in. "Everyone can see how much Mase is smitten with you. I'm sure tonight will be fine."

"Gahh! I hope so, but I'm nervous he won't take me seriously or just laugh in my face. Can you imagine the embarrassment I would die from? I mean, he's drop-dead gorgeous. What would he even want with me when he could have his pick of experienced girls who know what they're doing?" I ask no one in particular while rubbing a hand down my face.

"Don't worry, it'll be fine. He's just as crazy about you as you are about him, even if he hasn't said anything yet. Why would he need some other bimbo when you're perfect for him?" Luna chimes in and the other two agree with her as we make our way up the stairs.

"Well, at least if things go south, I'm moving to London

tomorrow, so I won't have to see him around anymore," I say as we walk straight into my bedroom.

I'M LYING on my bed, scrolling through my phone when my Dad knocks on my door to tell me that they're leaving for the party they're attending. I look at the time and see it's seven p.m. which means I have an hour until Mason is supposed to get here.

Around seven thirty I decide to start getting dressed in the outfit the girls and I picked out today. Once I'm done, I check the time. I have ten minutes left, so I decide to wait in the treehouse for him.

As I walk out the back door and up to the treehouse, I can't help but look up at the place that has been my escape for as long as I can remember. This is definitely not your average treehouse. It has stairs that lead up to a wrap-around porch and the treehouse itself is like a mini house.

I walk up the stairs and into the house. It's spacious. I usually spend most of my free time here, so Dad spared no expense with building it.

The inside is like a studio apartment, there's the bed and then a couple couches off to one end of the room for when my friends are over. There's a bookshelf with all my favorite paperbacks. It has a bathroom and mini kitchen for snacks and then the entertainment setup for when we're watching movies.

Over the years, the girls and I have spent many nights having sleepovers in here. Thinking about it, I'll miss this treehouse the most because this is also where Mason and I spent a lot of time together.

The television is on as background noise and I'm staring

up at the night sky when I hear him come in. He walks over to the bed and I shift a little so that he can lie down next to me while we both look up at the stars. There's not a lot of them. We've spent countless nights just like this, but hopefully tonight will be different.

I turn my face toward him at the same time he does the same. We're now staring at each other, and I can't help but take in how absolutely beautiful he is. He has jet-black hair and thick eyebrows that frame his light green eyes. He's six foot three, lean and muscular, and towers over me. I secretly love it because one, I can still wear heels and two, tall guys are just somehow hotter than shorter ones.

His face is just pure perfection with a straight nose and square jawline and don't even get me started on how pink and kissable his lips are. You're probably not supposed to call guys beautiful but hey at least I upgraded from calling him pretty.

Whenever he's around, I can't help but just stare at him. I always end up getting lost.

"Hey, little Crowne," he says in a voice that drips of sex and sin. At least that's what I always think to myself whenever I listen to him speak. *Don't even try to tell me you've never been addicted to a man's deep voice that sounds like nothing but sin.*

"I'm so glad you came," I say while I grab his hand and wrap our fingers together.

"Wouldn't have missed it for the world. Besides, I don't know when I'll see your annoying ass again!" he says with a chuckle that's followed by a grunt because I punched him in the abs. Damn if the feel of his abs doesn't get me hot half the time I'm around him.

The reminder that I'll be leaving tomorrow makes a sob

rip out of me and I instantly launch myself into his arms. He lets out a grunt as he catches me with ease, and I cry in his arms. *Full-on crying, which is sooo not pretty!*

"I don't want to leave you!" I tell him while sobbing.

"We'll still talk on the phone and message each other and shit. I'll even try to come visit you, don't worry," he says, trying to reassure me.

When my tears dry, I pull back and look at him. I probably look like a drowned rat right now with tears all over my face. Before I have the time to second guess myself, I lean in and touch my lips to his.

There's a second of hesitation before he brings his lips closer to mine and kisses me with such force that I feel my head spinning with the intensity of it. This is not only our first kiss, but my first kiss as well. It's mind-blowing. Better than anything I could have expected. By the time we finally break off the kiss, we're both panting.

"Whoa, that was amazing," I whisper out in a ragged breath as a flush spreads over my cheeks. He goes to open his mouth to speak but I cut him off, "Before you say anything, I need to get this off my chest." I close my eyes, gathering my courage before opening them again.

"You can tell me anything, you know."

"I love you!" I blurt it out. "I know it's probably not the best time to be telling you this, but I just had to let you know before I leave. I've loved you for years and I didn't want to regret never telling you how I felt."

By the time I'm done bearing my heart out to him, I feel self-conscious. I'm not sure how he'll react since I just sprang this on him and waiting for a reaction from him is just about killing me. I'm a hundred percent sure he wasn't expecting this when he agreed to come see me tonight.

"I've had feelings for you for a while too," he finally says, putting me out of my short-lived misery with one of his breathtakingly beautiful smiles. "I just wasn't sure when it would have been the right time to tell you, especially with all the bullshit our parents have going on."

I almost squeal but catch myself in time before I embarrass myself further. I already cried on him tonight. I get up off the bed, telling him to give me a second before walking off into the bathroom.

Once I'm in the bathroom, I look at myself in the mirror, telling myself that I can do this because it's what I've wanted for a while. I've loved him for years and this is finally the time to show him.

Now I'm certain the time we spent together when I felt like there was more, I wasn't just hallucinating and there actually was an attraction on both our parts. I just hope what I have planned next won't have him running as far away from me as possible.

I'm just a big bundle of nerves right now. What if he doesn't want the same thing right now? Because of our history together, I feel it deep in my soul that now is the right time for us, and I wouldn't have it any other way. All those times together have led up to this.

I quickly take my pants and top off and look at myself one last time in the mirror. I have on the black lace bra and panty lingerie set the girls made me wear for tonight. Pushing all the nerves away, I walk out of the bathroom and back into the room. No matter what happens in the future, I want him to always have this part of me.

When I step back into the room, Mason is staring up at the stars again. I take a minute to just look at him and commit everything to memory. I move closer and when he looks over at me; I see the heat that flashes in his eyes.

"What are you doing so far away, babe?" he asks in a husky voice. It's deeper than it usually is, and it must have a direct link to my pussy because it clenches with need. I walk over to the bed closer to him and my entire body ignites with his lust-filled stare.

"I-I want to be with you tonight. I know you'll probably think it's too soon because we've just admitted our feelings for each other, but I feel like everything we've done together and all the time we've spent with one another has been leading up to this. I want you to have this part of me." I try to explain while looking down at my hands because I don't want to look at him. I'm scared to face him in case he rejects me.

I guess I was worrying for nothing because before I can even comprehend what is happening, I'm in the middle of the bed on my back, and Mason is laying between my spread legs. *Wow, he works fast!*

He gives me another soul-crushing kiss before we're moving against each other in a frenzy. I grab for his shirt, trying to pull it off him before running my hands over his chest and stomach, feeling his hard-as-rock abs. He's like an Adonis—pure male perfection that only serves to get me more turned on.

I grab for the zipper on his pants while kissing him. Somehow, we get both his pants and boxers off in one go. He turns his attention to me and strips me out of my bra and panties before placing a kiss on my neck.

He sucks the sensitive skin on my neck, and I let out a groan as he trails kisses further down my body before he stops for a second.

"Are you sure you want to do this, babe?" he asks, and I just nod.

"I've wanted to do this for years," I say as he dips his

head down and takes one of my breasts into his mouth and sucks on it hard.

His action causes me to arch my back, whimpering at the same time from how good his mouth feels on my body. A few minutes later, he switches to my neglected nipple. Wanting to feel him too, I grab onto his hard-on, paying it some attention. Wow, it's bigger and thicker than I expected and no, this isn't one of those cliche lines.

A flicker of uncertainty fills me because I'm wondering if that thing is going to even fit inside me. Pushing the nerves away, I grab onto it again and stroke. He lets out a groan of pleasure, which serves to turn me on even more.

He moves and rolls over onto his back, pulling me with him. "I need to feel those lips on my cock." he says, grabbing my hair into his fist and pushing me down.

He goes slowly at first, letting me get used to the feel of his cock in my mouth before he holds my head in place and shoves half his length down my throat. My gag reflex kicks in, but he doesn't let up on his hold up.

When it feels like it's about to be too much, he pulls his cock out of my mouth. It's not so bad, and I actually like the taste of him. Plus, I love the sound of him moaning my name. He looks at me like he can't wait to devour me, and a second later he's flipping me onto my back again.

"Looks like it's finally time for me to taste this untouched pussy of yours," he growls before he lifts my legs and places them over his shoulder. He buries his face between my thighs. I let out a scream as the pleasure takes over my body.

I've definitely been missing out if the pleasure I'm experiencing right now is anything to go by. The tingles grow throughout my body as he nips on my clit. The feelings intensify until they overwhelm me, and I explode. I can't help but let out a scream as my orgasm finally detonates into his waiting mouth.

After I come down from my high, he crawls up my body and gives me a searing kiss. It's weird tasting myself on his mouth, but it turns me on more.

"Are you sure you want me inside this pussy? Because once I take it, it's mine forever," he tells me.

I just nod before answering, "Yes, I'm sure. I've been waiting for you."

As soon as the last word leaves my mouth, he plunges his cock deep inside me in one long, hard drive. I let out a scream which he covers with his mouth on mine. He stops and remains still so that I can get used to his enormous cock.

A few minutes later, the pain eases up, and I move my hips under him. He takes the hint and starts to move slowly. It's not long before his thrusts speed up and the feeling of pleasure is more intense with him inside me, even if it still hurts a little. I never knew that sex could be like this.

I drag my nails down his back as the feelings inside me increase. The feeling of my nails dragging down his back must unleash something inside him because his thrusts speed up even more until he's pounding away at my already bruised pussy.

His thrusts become erratic before he stills and then explodes inside of me. He collapses on top of me. A few seconds later he pulls out and I wince a little. He looks down to where his dick was, just staring. I feel self-conscious and when I look down; I see it's the blood between my legs he's staring at and my cheeks heat even further.

He gets up off the bed and walks into the bathroom

while I just lie there, my mind spinning. First, I can't believe that just happened and second, I can't believe that it was Mason-freaking-King who took my virginity. I always thought that would be a dream of mine and nothing else.

Mason walks back out into the room and I see he brought a washcloth which he uses to clean me up. Once he's done, we change the sheets and then climb back into bed.

He lies on his back while I drape myself over his body and we cuddle until we both fall asleep in each other's arms.

We have sex two more times during the night. In the early hours of morning, we both get up so that I can sneak back into the house and he can go back home.

Once we both get dressed, he wraps me up in his arms, holding me close and dropping a kiss onto my forehead. I take in the kiss and just let it warm my entire body while I cling to him for a few moments more.

"I love you so much," I whisper into his chest before placing a kiss over his heart. He squeezes me tighter in his arm.

"I love you, too, little Crowne. Never forget that this pussy is mine. No one else gets to have it, and I'll make your life a living hell if anyone else touches you," he deadpans. I chuckle because I wouldn't even think about cheating on him now that he's finally mine.

"Always and forever my king," I say.

"Always and forever," he replies, placing another kiss on my forehead.

After that, we both leave the treehouse, promising each other forever before we finally leave for real this time.

Finally being with the boy I've always loved, like a

lovesick fool I had no idea that forever would have an expiration date and that the boy would turn out to be a brutal king hell-bent on leaving me a bleeding Crowne and us in a broken empire.

TWO

Winter

Winter 20, Mason 22

THE PAST FOUR years have been a blessing and a curse. A blessing because the relationship between Mason and I has never been better.

Somehow, we've made it work long distance, and I couldn't be happier. Mason has visited me in London a lot over the four years we've been here, and I literally couldn't love the guy more than I do right now.

It's been a curse because I've had some fights with my dad, though I'm not proud of those. The man said we wouldn't be in London for more than three years and look at us now, still in London way past the three-year timeline.

We should have moved back to the US already, but Dad said that he uncovered some unexpected problems that needed to be looked after, and that's why we're still stuck here.

Dad works hard, so I try not to be a spoiled bitch, but I'm salty. I miss Mason so much and he only comes when he can swing it. We still don't want our parents to know about us yet. I hate lying to my father, but it must be done if

I want to keep the love of my life. Hopefully it won't always have to be like this.

I'm still not sure what the issues are with his dad and mine, but even from thousands of miles away, they still hate each other. I'm not sure if Mason knows what the issue is, he's never said anything. Though to be fair, I've never asked.

But back to us, we've never been happier, and I can't wait for his next visit. I'm so glad I told him how I felt before I left because the time I've spent being with him has been amazing.

He treats me like a princess, and I always end up getting whatever I want. Yeah, can you say magical? Don't get me wrong, we've had tons of fights especially when he's being a possessive douche, but I can't stay mad at him for too long because it's kind of hot sometimes.

I come out of my daydream when I hear my professor say we're about to start and I get lost in classwork for this three-hour lecture. Gahh I hate those long ones, so boring.

As soon as two p.m. hits, Melanie and I rush out the class like our lives depend on it. The day is far from over and I already feel drained. I still need to head over to the lab and work on my project for a while before I even contemplate leaving campus and heading home.

I don't think I would've been able to go another day with school this week if it wasn't already Friday. So now I have the weekend to relax and thank God for that.

Even though I feel nothing but exhaustion, I keep going because I know it's everything my dad wants for me. I see the way he lights up when I do something to make him proud, and nothing in the world is better than that feeling.

You know the one, having someone who means the world to you be proud of you. He's the only one who encourages me to do everything that I set my mind to, and I honestly don't know what I would do without him.

He's my rock, my supporter and my biggest champion. I will forever be grateful to have someone like him in my life.

As soon as we get out of the classroom, I see Archie standing against the wall waiting on us and just like every day, Melanie runs straight to him and he barely catches her before they both fall onto the floor.

"Geez, babe, calm your tits! One of these days we'll take a tumble onto the floor if you don't stop running into me with full force," he says with mock annoyance.

He can try to act like whatever Mel does annoys him, but we all know he loves everything she does. Those two are inseparable and so in love, it makes me want to gag on most days.

They never pay me any attention whenever I tell them that because they know I'm just kidding around.

I roll my eyes at them. Melanie and Arch have been my friends since I moved to London four years ago, and I'd probably have gone stir crazy by now if it weren't for them keeping me sane on most days.

I don't really have a lot of friends except for these two and my three best friends back in the States. Come to think of it, those bitches are due for a visit soon and I can't wait to con them into it.

"Hey Win!" Archie says as I walk closer to them. They finally disengage from each other.

"Hey Arch the clinger, what's up?" I say. That's been my nickname for him since they became a thing. When they first got together, they were worse than they are now, in that they were always together every minute they could manage. He just ruffles my hair and I smack his hand away.

"Ugh, you're such a jerk!" I say, feigning anger because I can never stay mad at him for long.

"What's up is that we're partying tomorrow night at the Crowne Plaza!" he says excitedly.

"What do you mean partying at the Crowne Plaza? You know my father owns the place and would kill me if I went there to party, right?" I ask. Clearly, he's lost his marbles today.

"Before you even say no, this is non-negotiable!" Melanie chimes in oh-so unhelpfully.

"How did you guys even get a room there? You know it's super expensive, right? My father would probably have a coronary if he caught me partying it up there," I say to them as calmly as I can. "Besides, I have so much work I need to catch up on."

"Don't care, you need a night out to loosen up and he won't know if you sneak away! Besides, I don't think he'd care if you went out with your friends," Archie says.

"Fine, I'll think about it." I groan. "But back to the topic at hand... how are you even having a party there?"

My friends aren't exactly rich, but our hotel is very exclusive and expensive.

"You wouldn't believe me if I told you... but apparently, I won a weekend there. I thought it was a joke, but when I called the hotel, they confirmed that I indeed got one of the suites for the weekend!"

I've never heard of any promotions where people won weekend stays at the hotel so that must be new. I really need to pay more attention to the business if I want to know what is going on.

"This is going to be so much fun!" Melanie says excitedly.

"Yeah, because what better place is there to hold a party?" Arch says, wiggling his brows at me.

"Ugh, fine, I'll let you guys know by tomorrow night," I say before looking at the time and realizing I needed to get to the lab if I want to go home early today. "I need to get going, see you guys later."

As soon as I get to the lab, I put my stuff down on the table and decide to give Mase a call because I miss him.

I love him so much and even though the long-distance thing has been hard, especially on me, we've made it work. Whenever Mason comes here, I tell Dad I'm staying over at Melanie's. Since Dad has never had a reason to doubt me, he never calls.

So I get to stay with Mase and we make up for all the time we've missed while being away from each other. The phone rings once before he picks up.

"Hey, babe," he says as soon as his voice filters over the line. He sounds like he's still half asleep.

Oh shit! I quickly calculate the time difference from London time to Pacific time and realize that it's after six a.m. there and wince.

"Hey, baby, I'm so sorry for calling you this early. I always keep forgetting about this stupid time difference."

"It's fine, babe. You know I love hearing your girly voice." he says with a snicker.

"Rude much? I do not have a girly voice!"

"Sure you don't, babe."

"If you were here, I'd smack you in the dick!"

"Ouch! Geez, babe, don't say things like that. Besides, how would I fuck you if my dick were in pain?"

"I'd do it after you fucked me, obviously," I say and hear him burst out a laugh.

"Ha! So funny. I'm not letting you near my dick anymore!"

"Boo, you suck! What are your plans for the day?"

"I have a meeting with my dad later. No idea what he wants, but he said he needed to talk to me about getting more involved in the business. What about you?"

"I just got to the lab to work on my project for the day," I tell him with pride in my voice. I'm super excited to work on this project.

"I'm super proud of you, babe. I have faith that you'll work it out because you're a genius."

"Ha ha, not even close! But I am glad you have faith in me."

"Always. Okay, I've got to go, babe. I'll talk to you later!"

"I love you."

"Love you too." he says before hanging up.

Once I'm off the phone, I get started working on my equations and calculations.

Dad also owns a pharmaceutical company under a subsidiary of Crowne Enterprises, and developing a new medication for anxiety is what I'm hoping to work on.

It's not something that's widely known to the public, but I suffer from severe anxiety and sometimes the medication makes me feel like complete garbage. Hopefully, I can come up with something that doesn't cause any or a lot of side effects.

BY THE TIME Saturday afternoon rolls around, I've somehow forgotten about the party.

Last night when I got home, my dad told me he needed to go to New York for a business trip and that Mom would be here if I needed anything.

We both knew that if I actually needed something, I'd probably have to get it myself. My mother didn't care about me, and she'd most likely be out at some party instead of at home worrying about her daughter.

I told him I'd be fine on my own. Besides, I was twenty; I did not need a babysitter.

It's not until I get a call from Archie telling me to get my ass over to the hotel that I remember the party.

Both of them said that they'd come straight to my house if I didn't show up in the next hour and drag me there themselves. Since I know they weren't bluffing, I finally relented.

After I'm finished getting dressed, I ask our driver to take me to the hotel. There's no way I'm driving when I'll probably be drinking later tonight.

"Winter!" Archie yells for me as I get out of the car. I'm surprised to see that he's actually out here waiting for me.

"Hey," I say once I step closer to him.

"Hey, babe," he says, giving me a hug.

"Are you okay?" I ask. He has this weird look on his face that I can't quite decipher or place because it's one that I've never seen on his face before.

"Yeah, let's just party! Mel is already up there waiting for us. It's going to be a fun night!" he says.

"My dad will probably kill me if he finds out that I'm here!" I say laughing.

He throws his hands over my shoulder before walking us into the lobby and over to the elevator.

When we get to the room, the party is in full swing and I see Mel is already dancing away and having a good time. It's not a big party and from the looks of it, there can't be over thirty people in the room.

I hate crowds, always have. I have no idea if it's because

of my anxiety or if it's just a personality trait, but that's how I've always been. It's gotten worse since I moved here. I had a hard time fitting in because the environment is so different from the one back in Ravenwood.

After spending all week stressing about everything, I decide to let loose for a bit tonight. I deserve it. Archie hands Mel and me each a drink before we all head onto the little dance floor in the center of the living room.

An hour later we've danced and drank so much that my head feels fuzzy. Thinking that I must have drunk more than I realized, I stumbled into one of the rooms in the suite before I pass out.

THREE

Mason

I T ' S J U S T after six a.m. when I hear my phone buzzing from my nightstand. I feel around for it before grabbing it and seeing that it's Winter.

This time difference sucks balls sometimes, but I'd do anything for her because I fucking love that girl more than anything. I can't wait for her to get her pretty ass back in Ravenwood.

She's supposed to be back by now, but there's some issue her dad has to deal with that's kept them back in London for a while.

I can't fault her for that, but not being able to see my girl whenever I want to is a pain in my ass.

Even though we have a private jet, it's useless. Every time I've been to London in the past four years, I've had to take a commercial first-class flight because I don't want Dad to find out I'm going to London too often.

My father is not an idiot so if I took the jet especially to London, he'd know something was up. Of course, he knows Winter and her family are there, but I'd still rather keep that from him for now.

"Love you too," I say to Winter before hanging up the phone a while later after we've caught each other up on what we're doing for the day.

I lie in my bed for another hour before I get up to get my day started. *I have a meeting with my father this morning that I can't wait for,* I think sarcastically.

Around eleven a.m. when our meeting is scheduled for, I reach my father's home office and walk right in like I own the place. I'm ready to get this meeting over with. Not because I hate my father but because I just hate this bullshit world, he's made us a part of.

My father is the CEO of King's Corporation. His company deals mainly with real estate but there are also other small businesses that he owns. On paper, it's a legitimate business, but it's not all on the right side of the law.

My father is the owner of King's Corp, but Beckett, Nate, and Royce's dads all have shares in the company. They use the company as a front to conduct some of their illegal activities. This is the reason my friends and I hate being a part of this world. We've all have had to do things we're not proud of.

Plus, there are too many expectations, too many people wanting to know your every move but we all have a role to play when it comes to the business and what we show them. I know what my dad expects of me and sometimes I hate the fact that I was his firstborn, but then when I think about Grayson, I realize I would rather it be me than him.

My brother is a gentle and sensitive soul and I'd do anything to protect him, even if it means giving up my freedom so that he could have his.

I know how the world works, especially ours, and if he was the one who was in line to the throne as I like to call it, then it would eat him alive.

Not that I think my brother isn't capable, but there's too much shit going on behind the scenes that I don't want him to deal with.

Truth be told, he's actually glad that it's me and not him, He's made that known quite a few times. *Fucker!*

I love him with everything and he's definitely my best friend. I'm thankful that we don't have any bad blood between us. I know how it is for some people, especially when wealth, power, and status are the end goals.

Once I take over from our dad, I'll slowly bring Gray into the company. It is his birthright too. Even if I don't totally agree with it, I want my brother beside me. I sure as fuck don't want him in on the other side of things.

I walk over to the chair in front of my father's desk and plop down into it. He tells whoever he's on the phone with that he'll call them back later before he turns his full attention to me.

"Hey, Son," he says once he's off the phone.

"Hey, Dad, what's up? Why did you want to see me?"

"Can't a man just want to have a conversation with his son to see how he's doing?" he asks, raising an eyebrow.

"Any regular man, probably, but we both know that's not you," I say with a deadpan expression on my face. He chuckles.

My father loves Grayson and I both, but he isn't the talk-about-your-feelings type. We know we can come to him with our problems anytime and he'll back us up one hundred percent, but we never talk about our feelings with him. It's always business with that one.

"Yeah, yeah, smartass! Anyway, I have some business to discuss with you. It's about time I show you the ropes of the company so you can start working there. The first thing on our agenda is a trip to London," he says.

Okay, not what I was expecting. I thought I had another year before he started pulling me into the fold fully. Guess not. We've all had to do things for our dads but we weren't fully in the thick of things before.

But this is also not a bad turn of events because I could probably sneak a visit in with Winter.

Ever since we started dating, we've both kept it under wraps. We don't know how our fathers would react since they both hate each other. My father has a mean streak when someone crosses him and I don't know for sure how her father would react, but we don't want to chance it.

I don't know if my father's hatred for her dad would transfer to her. He must know that she's not her father, right? When the time is right, we'll tell everyone who needs to know about our relationship.

I just hope when that time comes, neither of our dads freak out. Though if they did, it wouldn't change anything between us because I love her, and nothing is going to change that.

If my father cuts me off because of her, we'll still live a comfortable life. I have millions in my bank account from the sizeable trust fund my grandfather left both Grayson and I when he passed away. My father also gives us money and it has added up. He always wanted us to be independent, so yeah, we could definitely survive if he decided to cut me off. I turn my attention back to him.

"When do we leave?" I ask.

"Around four," he says, and I nod my head.

"I'll go pack a bag," I say before walking out of his office and up to my room. We'll probably only be staying until Sunday, but I could probably stay until Monday so I can spend an extra day with my girl.

A minute after I walk into my room and start packing my bag, Grayson comes strolling into my room.

"Where are you going, Bro?" he asks after seeing that I'm packing a duffel bag.

"London," I answer, giving him a smirk.

"Use condoms! I don't even want to think about being an uncle yet," he says as he visibly shudders at the thought.

I grab a pillow off my bed and chuck it at his head. He catches it while laughing.

"I'm going on a business trip with Dad, asshole!" I say to explain the sudden trip.

"So, you're not going to see Winter?"

"Of course, I'm going to see Winter," I say with an eye roll.

"That's what I thought," he replies with a smug expression.

"Get out of here, you annoying kid!" I say with mock anger.

"Go fuck yourself, douche! Just because I'm two years younger doesn't mean I'm a kid," he says.

"Of course, it does!" I watch as a glint appears in his eyes before he answers me.

"Well then, give Winter to me since we're the same age, which that means she's a baby and you should not be dating a baby," Grayson jokes.

"Do you want me to punch your lights out, dickface?" I ask and he bends over, laughing at my murderous expression.

"It is too easy to wind your surly ass up," he says, still laughing. "Tell my girl hi when you see her!"

I move without thinking, and he rushes out of my room, still laughing. Ugh, younger brothers!

I spend the rest of the day relaxing until it's time to leave for our trip. At exactly four, we're on our private jet heading to London. When we get there, it's already midnight so I just shower and head straight to bed.

I'm jet lagged and just want to sleep it off. The next day we're busy with meeting after meeting. Dad said that I could do whatever I want to after the last one tonight.

The last one is a business dinner he said I needed to be at. We're meeting the guy at one of the restaurants that's opposite one of the Crowne hotels.

Dad chose outside seating, which is nice. It's not like regular outside seating; this one has more decor to it since it's a fancy restaurant, after all.

I didn't get to tell Winter that I was here yet, so I'm hoping to surprise her. I know she'll be excited. She never gets tired when I visit. If she could have her way, she'd probably have me living here with her.

We're sipping on our drinks, waiting for the guy to show up, when a loud shout from across the street grabs my attention.

"Winter!" some guy yells and I watch as Winter—my Winter—steps out of a car and walks up to the guy who called her name.

Once they get close to each other, I see the guy pull her in for a hug before they pull apart.

They talk and then a few minutes later, he throws his arms around her before they both walk into the hotel. *What the actual fuck?*

It takes a lot of willpower to not jump to the wrong conclusions, but I need to find out what the hell is going on.

I make a move to get up just as the guy we are waiting on shows up.

"I need to leave," I tell my father. It takes a lot for me to keep my voice controlled. I'm pretty sure he heard someone call for Winter because the guy was loud as hell, but hopefully he doesn't think that it's related to my current mood.

"You can't leave yet. This meeting is important for the company and the new project we're going to be working on soon," he tells me. "After we're finished with the meeting, you can do whatever you want. It shouldn't be more than an hour. You don't have to stay for dinner if you don't want to, but I need you here for the business part of it."

"Fine," I say settling back into my seat. If you asked me what went on and what they talked about during the meeting, I'd never be able to tell you because my mind was preoccupied with Winter, wondering why the hell she was going into a hotel with another guy.

As soon as the meeting is over, I scoot out my chair fast, barely muttering to my dad, "I'll be back later."

As fast as I can, I walk across the road and into the hotel. Once I get to the front desk, I ask for Winter. I'm sure all the staff here know her by now, so they know exactly who I'm talking about.

"Are you here for the party?" the lady at the reception desk asks me and I nod. Hopefully that will get me the answers I need faster. "Twenty-fourth floor, the suite at the end of the hall," she says.

I give her my thanks before I walk over to the elevator feeling better than I was before. This is obviously just a party, and that's why she came here with some guy.

As soon as I step off the elevator, the faint music can be heard coming from the end of the hallway. It's not loud enough to bother the other guests, but you can still hear it.

I'm surprised that her dad is letting her have a party in his hotel, especially when he's in New York on business. At least that's what she said the last time we spoke. Though if it isn't her party, you could throw a small one in any hotel as long as the price was right.

Once I get to the suite, I see the door is open, so I just walk right in. It's packed with people—some smoking, some drinking and the others dancing.

I stroll around the entire place looking for her but come up empty. After seeing her nowhere in the living room or the balcony, I decide to check the rooms before I leave. If she isn't here, then she could be anywhere in this hotel with that guy. That thought has anger brewing inside me. I didn't think she was the type to be disloyal in a relationship.

I walk to the place where I know the master bedroom usually is in these hotels, turn the knob and it's unlocked.

I push the door open and barely step into the room before freezing. The sight in front of me is one I never thought I would see, especially with Winter.

She's naked on the bed and a guy is positioned between her legs. Her arms are around his neck and he's busy kissing her. His face is blocking hers, but from the side profile, her hair, and the rest of her body that's visible, I know it's her. I've spent countless hours exploring her body to not know what it looks like.

From what I can tell, it's the same guy from downstairs that called out to her when she got to the hotel.

They're so busy and into what they're doing that they don't even notice that someone else is in the room with them.

I don't even bother letting my presence be known. I just turn around and walk out of the room. I bump into a girl on my way out, but I pay her no mind as I storm out of there.

My heart shatters into a million pieces as I walk out. It

hurts so fucking much. I never expected to fall for anyone, much less have them hurt me like this.

Betrayal has a nasty taste, and I can't believe I trusted her. She turned out to be like all the other bitches out there. *A disloyal cunt.*

When I get back to our hotel and into my room, I down a glass of whiskey as my father comes into my room. I fill my glass with another shot.

"Are you okay?" my father asks concerned.

"Yeah, I'm fine. When do we leave?" If he's surprised with my question, he doesn't show it. I'm sure he thought I would have wanted to stay here longer than the weekend because that's what I've done before anytime we've come to London together.

Though I don't think he ever knew why I wanted to stay. It doesn't matter anymore, nothing does. That bitch is fucking dead to me.

"In the morning," he finally responds after a minute of looking at me. I'm sure he's trying to figure me out, but I'm not telling him about this. It would be humiliating for him to know what she did. I know he probably hates her too just because of who her father is and now I'm glad that I never told him about her.

"I'll be ready," I say, and he nods before walking out of my room, deciding to give me the space I clearly need.

I fling my glass and it shatters when it hits the wall. After I've calmed down a bit, my feelings of anger and hurt turn into hate.

With nothing but hatred flowing through my veins, I make a promise to myself that if Winter ever steps foot into Ravenwood again, I will make her pay for ruining us.

FOUR

Winter

I WAKE up disoriented and have no clue what is going on. When I look around the room, I notice machines attached to my body as well as an IV bag attached to my wrist.

I'm guessing I'm in the hospital right now if the incessant beeping is anything to go by. I barely even remember anything. The last thing that came to mind was me going to the party and then dancing while drinking.

I didn't drink a lot. I only had a few so I have no idea why I can't remember anything at all.

A few minutes later, the door to my room opens and my dad comes in with a disappointed expression on his face.

"Hi, Dad," I squeak out. "What happened?"

He looks at me with an angry expression and I can't help but shrink back into my covers. I always hate it when my father gets angry at me.

He rarely gets mad at me so whenever it happens, I know it's got to be something bad that I did.

I have no clue what I did, Actually I'm still not sure how I ended up here.

"What happened?" he asks incredulously. "I'll tell you what happened! Do you not care about your fucking life, Winter?!" he roars out. Oohh, yep! Definitely pissed.

"What are you talking about, Dad? Why am I here and

how did you get here? Aren't you supposed to be in New York?"

"Oh, is that why you took it upon yourself to go to a party and get yourself drugged? Because I was in New York?"

"What do you mean drugged?"

"They did a toxicology screening when you first got here and found a high dose of Rohypnol in your system. You've been out for two days. The staff of the hotel found you passed out in the room where the party was held an hour after everyone left and they called the ambulance. Since you were fully clothed, they thought you drank too much before passing out. After you were in the ambulance the manager called me to let me know you would be here. What the fuck were you thinking?"

"I-I-I," I stutter.

"You knew I wasn't here, and you went without a body-guard? Do you know how fucking stupid that is?" he bellowed.

"I'm sorry," I cry out as tears stream down my face.

I don't think I've ever seen my father this mad before. I know that he is disappointed in me, and it's a feeling I don't want to feel again.

"Sorry doesn't cut it when you could have been hurt worse! You should be glad that you're still alive. Do you know how many people would hurt you just because of the name you carry?" he asks, sounding more disappointed. I feel even worse.

"Are Melanie and Archie okay?"

"I don't know who those people are, but they found you in that room alone, Winter."

"No, they were there at the party with me. They're my friends from school. You have to find them, Daddy! I need to make sure they're okay, too. I don't know what happened."

"Fine I'll look into it," he says. "Come on, get dressed. I've signed your discharge papers so you can go home now."

As soon as we get home, I try calling Mason, but he doesn't answer.

His phone keeps going straight to voicemail and that has me worried.

My dad will never let me out of his sight, so I know I'll have to sneak away. I book a ticket quickly and by the time I know he'll be sleeping; I slip out of the house and head for the airport.

I can't risk taking the jet because he'll be pissed as fuck. Just as the plane is ready to take off, I send him a quick message telling him that Riley had an emergency and I needed to fly to California, and I'll be back soon.

I'll face him when I get home. He'll either kill me or disown me but I need to see Mason.

I have a feeling in the pit of my stomach that something is wrong, and that's all the more reason to fly out there.

As soon as the plane lands, I get a taxi straight to his house. When I get there, I see tons of people there and wonder what the hell is going on.

Is his dad having another party, and that's why he couldn't call or text me? If that's the case, now I feel like an idiot for worrying for no reason.

God, I wasn't prepared for the hell he unleashed on me when I finally saw him.

When I get inside, I find out this is a wake being held for his mom. It makes my heart hurt for him so bad. No wonder he isn't replying to my message or taking my calls.

I look all over for him but can't find him, so I decided to look upstairs. Maybe he's in his room away from all the prying eyes.

I almost die when I go up to his room and find another woman riding him on his bed. It literally feels like my heart and soul are shattering from the inside out. I don't even know how to react.

"Mason! What the fuck are you doing?" I scream out.

His head whips around to the door where I'm standing, and I see a flash of something in his eyes before it's gone. He has a cold expression on his face directed at me. He's never looked at me like this before, and I have no clue what to do with this.

"Get the fuck out of here, Winter, because if you stay any longer, I won't be held responsible for what I do to you," he sneers at me, all the while that bitch is still riding him.

"What the fuck is wrong with you? How could you do this to us?" I scream at him.

I don't know if it's what I said that caused him to lose it, but he does. In an instant, he's shoving the girl off him and stalking over to me in all his naked glory. Tears stream down my face. He really was having sex with her.

"How could I do this to us? You have got to be the biggest fucking whore on the planet to ask me that when you know what the fuck you were doing back in London!"

"What the hell are you talking about?"

He grabs me by the neck and pushes me out of his room before slamming me against the wall. He squeezes my neck until my air supply is gone.

He yells, "Get the fuck out and never come back! I fucking despise you. I am so fucking stupid for giving my heart to someone as treacherous as you!"

"Stop acting like an asshole and tell me what the hell is wrong with you! You're throwing away four years of our relationship and more years in friendship, and for what? To fuck some slut?"

He pulls me closer to him and lets out a menacing growl before he shoves me back hard into the wall. My head collides into the wall and I see stars for a second.

"I'm not the one who threw all of that away first, you fucking whore!" he screams.

"Whoa, Mason! Let go of her!" Grayson says. "Don't do anything you'll regret later, Bro."

By now there are more tears streaming down my face. I don't know what's going on, but I've never seen Mason act like this toward me and it hurts so fucking much. Each one of his callous words lash at me, imprinting themselves on my soul with how vicious they are. I can't do anything but stand there and watch him turn into someone I didn't know existed right before my eyes. The pain is like nothing I've felt before.

It takes Royce, Beck, and Nate to get him to let go of me and hold him back. As soon as he lets go of me, I crumple to the floor and bawl my eyes out as I rub my sore neck.

Grayson walks over to me and helps me up. "Come on, you need to leave before he gets more pissed off."

"Don't fucking come back here, you whore. If you do, I'll make your life a living hell," I hear him say just before I walk off with Gray.

I'm too stunned to even say anything right now, so I just walk out in a daze and get into the car before asking their driver to take me to the hotel that's right next to the airport.

I call my dad and ask him to send our jet for me in the morning since that's more convenient than trying to find another flight. As expected, he's very upset when he answers the phone but agrees anyway.

I tell him I'll let him know everything when I get home and he reluctantly agrees. He can't really do anything when we're thousands of miles away from each other.

I'm in a daze by the time I get home the next day and just as I predict my father is royally pissed. He doesn't even wait for me to get settled before he yells at me again about going places alone. I can't take it anymore and break down in front of him.

"Jesus Christ, Winter! What the hell happened?"

"Ma-Mason ch-cheated on me," I say while sobbing. I don't have a clue if he even understands what I'm saying through the sobs.

"What do you mean Mason cheated on you? Were you two together?"

"Yes." I hiccup and then crumple to the floor with more vicious sobs wracking through my body.

"How long?"

"Four years..."

"Oh sweetheart, I'm so sorry," he says while wrapping me in his arms and holding me until I cry myself to sleep.

That was just the beginning of all my issues regarding Mason and my heartbreak.

FIVE

Winter

I'M LOST in my thoughts while the town car we're in makes its way through Ravenwood, California. *The place I hate most in the fucking world.*

The last time I was here in this town, it didn't end well. My heart was shattered into pieces and it left me so broken I didn't think I'd ever find myself again.

I hate Mason King. He promised me forever only to take it all away in the blink of an eye. Who knew forever meant only four years.

That's why I'm so hurt that my dad made it a stipulation in his will that I needed to move back here in order to take full control of his company. My father was the one there for me when I completely lost it, and I don't want to disappoint him by not following his orders.

The other reason I'm not too keen on being here is because Mason's words from the last time still haunts me, *Don't fucking come back here, you whore. If you do, I'll make your life a living hell.*

I've wondered so many times over the past two years

what he meant when he said I was the one to throw it all away first but as usual, I always come up empty. I honestly have no idea why he did what he did and after our last encounter with each other and all the hatred he spewed, there was never another opportunity to find out.

I have no idea if I'll ever be able to figure out what happened to us and that will always hurt.

I have no choice but to be here, so he'll just have to suck it up and deal with it. As much as I want to leave, there is no leaving because I need to do what needs to be done. This isn't just about me anymore.

The car comes to a stop and my mother gets out first. I make my way to follow her. Once I'm out of the car, I take a minute to look up at the mansion we used to call home. After six long years of being away from this house, it looks like it's going to be home again.

Somehow everything looks the same, and that causes a pang in my chest. It's not fair that this house, this town, and everything else looks the same when my life has turned upside down and has melded into chaos repeatedly. I wish I could go back in time to when I was a little girl, and my biggest problem was eating too much cake.

I have new responsibilities that are important, and the pressure has me on edge, more than the normal edge I'm always on. I'm here because I'm taking over as the new CEO of Crowne Enterprises, though no one knows about that yet.

But they'll all know soon enough since I already have the press conference scheduled for next Monday. I don't know what the reaction to the news will be, but I have to keep reminding myself that this is my legacy, and it doesn't matter what anyone else thinks.

Three months ago, my world imploded into chaos and

with the weight of everything happening around me, I wished I had my best friend beside me to offer his comfort but we're not in each other's orbit anymore.

Everything he ever promised me was just a big fat lie he wrapped up in a pretty bow with all the things I've ever wanted. It's funny how you never know how strong you really are unless it's all you have left to be.

I don't know if I'll ever be able to forgive him for his betrayal, not that Mason is the type to ever ask for forgiveness and since it's been two years already with no contact from him, I'm betting that's highly unlikely.

I can't believe that I was so fucking naïve and stupid for thinking that we actually had a future together. All he's done is bring pain and heartache into my life.

I guess when you're a teenager and your hormones take over, you don't know any better and your first love always feels like they're the world to you. He was my first everything, so that makes the pain ten times worse.

I'm glad I still had my best friends Riley, Avery and Luna by my side for my father's death and funeral, but the one person I wanted to be there was no longer a part of my life. I didn't even have Melanie or Archie by my side. Both had disappeared by the time I got out of the hospital.

I asked Dad to look for them so I could make sure they were okay too, but when he got the word back from his PI, he said that they were gone. Like they disappeared off the face of the earth and he couldn't find them anywhere.

I still have no clue what I did to make Mason flip a switch on us, and none of the girls know what happened either. I wish I had all the answers, but the whole Mason thing is just an unresolved mess. I'm not sure if I'll ever find any closure with that part of my life.

Thinking about him always makes me angry and sad,

but as soon as thoughts of him enter my mind, I have to force myself to push them away. He doesn't deserve any space in my head anymore. I'm here for business and nothing else.

As fast as my brain brought up Mason, it moves on to thoughts of running a multi-billion-dollar company. I'm nervous because those are some big shoes to fill. My father made it look so effortlessly but I know it's going to be a struggle to get used to the new normal.

I turned twenty-two a month after my father's death. The reading of his will was done that day and I learned the company is now mine.

I've always been rich, but this is a whole new level to work through. I didn't ask for any of this, and truth be told, I'd rather have my father here instead of having all this money to my name. Money means nothing when you're suffering inside.

I already know that I'll need to work extra hard just to prove myself because the first thing they'll say is I'm not capable of being a CEO. After all, this is supposedly a man's world and all that jazz.

I wish I didn't have to deal with any of this at such a young age. Dealing with the media, people in this town, and my mother, plus the daily fight to keep my mental health from tipping over to where I can't be reached anymore is hard and such a struggle that on most days it feels like I'm drowning and there's no way out of this vicious cycle.

I'm pulled out of my thoughts when I hear my mother calling my name. "Come on, Winter! Don't just stand there looking like an idiot!"

"I'm coming!" I yell out to her. Geez! Can't a girl just be in peace with her thoughts on how her life is about to change drastically again in the coming months? Not that my thoughts ever bring any sort of peace when I get lost inside my head.

I have to say over the past month my mother has taken it upon herself to let me know that I'll fail at being the company's CEO and how this company is rightfully hers and not mine. *Yeah, she's so not someone you'd want to have around if you wanted a self-esteem boost.*

She once told me during a fight when I was fifteen that I'd never make it in life. I mean, I knew that wasn't true, but her words have haunted me since that day. Every time I do something and fail, even though I get back up, the feeling of not being good enough is never far from my mind. I often wonder if it's because of her words coming to fruition. That was years ago, but it still fucking hurts to this day.

My thoughts go back to my father and his will. He planned everything to a T. I always have shivers every time I wonder if he knew he was going to die and that was why his will was so detailed. But you can't know when you're going to die, right?

While I was still in London, I had Chase, who is going to be my new assistant, help me enroll at Ravenwood University and get everything ready so that when I got here, I could get the ball rolling immediately. There's no time to waste.

School doesn't start until next week. Since today is only Tuesday, I have a few days to myself before I need to face the vultures, aka the high-society gremlins.

Chase has been the executive assistant to the current CEO for about two years now, so he'll be transitioning to my EA now that I'll be taking over. He sounded nice over the phone, so hopefully we hit it off. It will be a major step in the right direction to get all the help that I can. I have my work cut out for me.

Over the past few weeks, more often than not, my mind wanders back to my father. I don't know why I feel like I'm missing something important when it comes to him—well both my parents—but I just do. I'm not entirely sure what it could be.

Pain unlike anything I've ever felt before consumes me every single time he crosses my mind, especially when it hits that he's not here anymore.

I go back to the last day I ever spoke to him, and I feel the telltale sign of tears threatening to spill out.

I walk into my bedroom, having just showered when I hear my phone ringing. I go over to my bed and grab it, answering as I sit down.

"Hey, Dad, sorry I'm running a little late. Just give me about twenty minutes and I'll be ready."

"Actually, that's what I was calling you about," he says into the phone. "Change of plans, an important meeting came up and I have to take it today."

"What? Can't you get someone else to do it for you? Isn't that why you have employees?"

"Yes, smartass! That's why I have employees, but this specific issue requires my immediate attention. I'll take you into the office tomorrow instead to continue with your training."

"But—" I don't get a chance to finish because he cuts me off.

"Winter, I said I'll make it up to you soon, okay? Look on the bright side, your mom is in the States, so she won't be home to bother you today. I have to run, but I'll see you later tonight."

"Fine... I love you, Daddy."

"I love you too, sweetheart."

As soon as the phone cuts off, I flop down onto my back and stare up at the ceiling. So much for Dad always having time for me. I roll my eyes at myself because I shouldn't complain. He does make time for me.

Over the past few months, even though I didn't really want to, he's been taking me into the office, slowly showing me what he does every day. He said he wanted me to learn what goes on in the company since I'll need to work there after I finish school. It's only been a few days each month, so I haven't really learned anything yet.

I'm not all that excited because I feel like I'm giving up my life for something that I'm not even sure I want, plus there is so many expectations. I'm worried that I'll somehow fuck everything up.

I'll still do it though because I don't want to disappoint my father. I don't let him blowing me off today bother me anymore because there's always tomorrow for office training. As I lie there, our conversation filters back into my mind and I can't help the nagging feeling in the pit of my stomach that says something about my dad felt off.

He's never lost his patience with me like he did on the phone. Thinking back to the full conversation we had, he sounded distracted while he was speaking to me.

Come to think of it, he's been off for the past few months and I have no idea what's bothering him. He hasn't said anything to me yet. Knowing him, I figure he'll tell me what's bothering him when he's ready and not a moment before.

My father and I share a bond that's closer to the one I have with my mother. I don't know what, but something is definitely going on with those two. Lately she's been going to Ravenwood and my father has been acting cagey most of the time.

Deciding to just forget about all the problems my overactive imagination is trying to come up with, I spend most of the day relaxing at home.

It isn't until early evening when I get the knock on the

door that changes my life forever. I hear the doorbell ringing and walk out of my room and down the stairs to see who's here.

When I get to the foyer, I see our butler standing there with a police officer. That's odd... why is there a police officer here?

"Umm, hello, what can I do for you? My dad isn't here if you're looking for him."

"Actually, I was looking for you, Miss Crowne. My name is Officer Reginald."

"Uh, sure. What can I help you with?"

"I'm sorry to be the one to have to tell you this. Your father was in an accident this morning and—"

"What?" I shriek, not even letting him continue. "Can you take me to him?"

"Yes, that's why I'm here..."

I turn around to our butler and tell him to get our driver to follow me to the hospital. I'll need a ride back. I'm in no condition to be driving right now.

Once we get there, I rush through the emergency room and head to the nearest nurses' station before demanding to see my father. "I'm looking for Aiden Crowne," I say, out of breath from running all the way in here. I don't even know if the officer followed me in because as soon as the car stopped, I was out of there.

"Just give me a second to look it up for you," she says, and I nod. As much as I want to demand to see him right away, acting like a demented psycho won't help my situation.

"Umm, I need to call our chief to handle this," she says, giving me a sympathetic smile. That can't be good if she's looking at me with pity.

I'm sure everyone in this hospital already knows what happened with my father because he's a high-profile and well-known businessman. I'm also guessing it won't be long until the media gets a hold of this information and there will be a frenzy of fucking reporters in my face.

A few minutes later, a tall man in a tailored suit walks in the room and motions for me to follow him. Guess he already knows who I am. Even though I try to stay out of the media as much as I can, I've still been photographed millions of times.

"Is my father okay?" I ask while following the guy. He hasn't said a word to me yet, and that's putting me on edge even further.

"You'll see him in a few minutes," he responds in a professional tone. Ugh, I want to punch him just for that. I'm literally going out of my mind with worry here.

We pass door after door until we finally come to an elevator and we both get in. He presses the button to take us down. I'm no expert on how hospitals work, but shouldn't we be going up instead?

Suddenly my nerves are back full force and I barely keep it together instead of having a full-blown panic attack. The doors open a minute later and when we both walk out, I feel all the breath leave my body. The words on the door have me frozen in place.

MORTUARY...

I feel my heart stop beating for a second and think this must be a joke. My father can't possibly be in there.

No, no, no, nooo... please God... don't let my father be the one in there. That panic attack I tried to push away is fighting and clawing to reach the surface and explode. I'm barely hanging on by a thread here.

The douche finally speaks again, and I'm really feeling stabby where he's concerned at the moment.

"I know this isn't easy, but we need you to identify if this is your father. Though the sight is one that you might find disturbing since it was a nasty accident."

"When did the accident happen?" I ask. I need to know what the hell happened.

"About eleven a.m. this morning." Fuck! That was about an hour after I spoke to my father.

"Why the fuck did your hospital wait until now to call? Why wasn't it on the news? Does the media already know about this?" I'm practically screaming at him. I can't believe they waited hours before letting me know.

I probably still wouldn't have known about the accident if it was actually on the news, because who the fuck even watches the news?

"If that's my father in there, I'm going to fucking sue you assholes so hard, you won't know what hit you!"

"Please calm down Miss. I'm sorry but we've been trying your mother all day since she's his wife but we couldn't get through to her. We had to send officers to your home instead. I can assure you, this was a process that takes time." Okay his explanation kind of makes sense but I'm still a little stabby toward him.

How fucking convenient for my mother to be unreachable today of all days. I also can't fault stuck up over here because it's not his fault my mother is careless with her family.

"Let's just get this over with," I say with a sigh, rubbing my head like that will help take away the headache that's forming.

Stuck-up suit goes over to one freezer and opens it before pulling out the tray that has a man's body on it. I look up at the ceiling before taking a deep breath and putting my big girl panties on.

I blow said breath out and then walk forward to look at the body in front of me. I gasp because he's so pale he doesn't even look real and half of his face is disfigured because of the crash, I'm guessing. The rest of his body is filled with bruises and I can't help the sob that escapes me.

The other side of his face has some bruises, but there is no mistaking that it's my father lying here on this table.

"Yeah, it's... this is my father. His lawyer will contact you soon," I say before rushing out of the room. I can't bear being in there and looking at his body for a minute longer.

As soon as I exit the doors of the hospital, the flash of cameras is going off in my face and a bunch of questions are being thrown at me. Fucking reporters!

I feel someone's hand over my shoulder and look up to see our driver trying to shield me from all these people. He pushes our way through the crowd and gets us out of there as fast as possible. If you asked me how the ride was getting home, I wouldn't be able to tell you because I don't remember the drive there at all.

All I remember is rushing out of the car and into the house, then going straight into my room before sobbing my heart out.

When I finally calmed down for a bit, I grabbed my phone to make a phone call. It only rings once before she answers, and when she does, I break down completely again.

"Riles..." is all I get out before sobs wrack my body again.

"Winter? Babe, what's wrong?" she asks, instantly on high alert. "Talk to me so I can help you, babe. What's happening over there?"

"It-it's my dad, he-he's dead!" I barely get the words out before I'm crying again.

"Fuck!" I hear her voice on the other end of the line then I hear movement on her end. "Don't worry, babe, we'll be there in a few hours," she says, and I let the phone drop before crawling under the covers where I cry until I have no more tears to shed. I fall asleep under all the exhaustion.

When I wake up again, it's to the feeling of hands stroking my hair and soft whispers around me. When I open my eyes fully, I see my three best friends sitting on my bed surrounding me. When they notice I'm awake, they all crawl on top of me for a group hug, whispering how sorry they are about what happened. I instantly start sobbing again.

If I thought Mason leaving me was the worst thing to happen to me, I was wrong. Losing my father fucking took the cake. The pain I've felt since seeing his body is so excruciating it feels as though I'm dying too.

My mother came back the next day after apparently hearing the news, though I have no clue who actually told her. Over the next few days, I couldn't tell you what transpired because I was completely lost in my head and couldn't function on most days. I literally couldn't have gotten through those days without my best friends by my side.

What made the pain ten times worse was when I wished Mason were here to help me get through the pain. He always calmed me down whenever I was feeling too much and the fact that he wasn't in my life anymore—because he couldn't keep his dick in his pants—was like a shot straight to the soul.

The funeral passed by in a blur with me not having a clue of what occurred because I have been mentally checked out since the day I saw Dad on that cold metal tray. The only thing I remember is crying at the funeral home and then the screams that tore out of me when he was being lowered into the ground.

At that moment, I felt like a lost little girl. Now, I had no one else to love me anymore. The pain of losing a parent hit me so fiercely, my soul was being ripped apart from the inside out.

This hurt worse than anything I've ever experienced in my life, and I wouldn't even wish this on my worst enemy. Even Mason's betrayal didn't crush me like the death of my father did, and trust me, Mason's actions cut deep.

A month after his death and the funeral, on my twenty-second birthday, we got a call from my father's lawyer saying that he had my dad's will and was ready for the reading of it. Both my mother and I were to be present.

That was the day my life changed again, and it was not for the better. Funnily enough, this was the third major event that made an impact in my life, and none of it was ever anything good. The first being Mason's betrayal, the second being Dad's death, and finally the one I hated the most—I needed to move back to Ravenwood...

While my world was crashing down around me on most days, my mother didn't have the same issues. She was the epitome of calm, cool and collected, like the death of her husband didn't bother her at all. Just looking at her makes me mad as hell. She just goes on with her life like my father didn't exist for her and that makes my hate for her grow.

A WEEK AFTER THE FUNERAL, the girls came back to Ravenwood. I'm so grateful they were there for me throughout this whole ordeal. I wouldn't have been able to get through it without them.

When we walk into the lawyer's office, he didn't waste any time in starting the proceedings. "Mrs. and Miss Crowne, let me just start by saying how sorry I am about your loss. Aiden Crowne was an exceptional man, and the world is sad to see him gone."

I just zone him out because the thing I hate the most about this experience is people constantly saying they're sorry. Like what the fuck are you sorry for? And saying it just brings the memory that he's not here anymore back. I wish people would just keep their "sorrys" to themselves.

"I'll just start then... Mrs. Crowne, you have possession of the mansion back in the United States and you'll get an allowance of one hundred thousand dollars a month. Miss Crowne, your father has transferred Crowne Enterprises and all its subsidiaries into your name. Since you just turned twenty-two, you'll need to move back to the United States and immediately begin training as the new CEO. Your father has found someone here to run the offices, but they all answer to you. Moving back to Ravenwood is a stipulation your father put in place in order for you to inherit everything. You'll also need to complete your studies there as well."

Fuck! I sit there shell-shocked as all this information sinks in. One, I'm a billionaire. Two, why didn't my father leave his empire to my mother? She was his wife after all. And finally, three, the most disturbing of them all... I had to move back to Ravenwood.

I can't believe he would make that a stipulation because he knew what happened the last time I was there. Now I'm angry at him because I can't believe that he would do this to me.

When I came back after finding Mason cheating on me, I was a mess. I had to confide in my Dad. He wasn't mad that Mason was my boyfriend, but he was mad on my behalf that he would cheat on me. Maybe he wasn't mad because he saw how much I was already suffering and didn't want to burden me more. Yeah, he was good like that.

"What the hell?" my mother burst out. "That can't be right! There must be some mistake because he wouldn't leave everything to her!" she screams, pointing to me.

When I look up at her, there's hatred in her eyes, more than the usual. Great! I can already tell that she'll be making my life a living hell for this. She's looking at me like I made my dad put everything in my name.

"I can assure you, Mrs. Crowne, the will is one hundred percent correct. Miss Crowne is Mr. Crowne's rightful heir and as such, everything belongs to her," the lawyer tells her. She scoffs at him.

"I'll be getting my lawyer and we'll settle this soon!" she tells *him before storming out of the office. I rub a hand down my face just tired with this life. It's been an exhausting couple weeks already and now I have to worry about moving back home. I get up and move to leave when my dad's lawyer stops me.*

"I have a note for you. Your father asked me to give this to you in the event that he was no longer with us... it's for your eyes only. I suggest after you read it, you give it back to me for safe-keeping, so it doesn't end up in the wrong hands."

"Uh, sure," I say, and he gives me the folded note before leaving the room and closing the door behind him.

My dearest Winter,

First, I love you so much, my daughter.

If you ever get this, it means that I'm no longer around and the suspicions that I had of your mother are true.

Trust no one. I've left everything in your name as I'm sure you're already aware of.

This has always been your legacy, but I need to warn you, never let your mother get her hands on the company, though I have a feeling she'll try to take it from you.

I've made it so that she won't be able to take it via all the stipulations in the will. Don't worry, I've planned for everything.

I have faith you'll be able to run our company successfully.

I don't have all the answers yet, so I can't say what's going on, but know that I love you with all my heart.

I'm so sorry for leaving you, and I hope that someday you'll be able to forgive me.

Love always, Dad.

After reading the note my father left me, I give it back to his lawyer for safekeeping. That note leaves me confused because I wasn't sure what my father was talking about.

I shake my head to pull myself out of my thoughts. Since reading my father's note, I've tried to look at my mother's behavior, but she's been the same as she's always been. What did he even mean when he said he safeguarded the company? Sometimes I can't even believe that all of this happened only two months ago. It all feels like it's been going on for a lifetime.

After the will reading, it took me and my dad's lawyer a month to make sure all of our affairs was in order before I could leave London and come back to Ravenwood. *It took one month to wrap up my life in London, and that is just sad.*

The only good thing about this move back to Ravenwood is I'll have my best friends close to me again. I just hope I don't have to see *him.*

SIX

Winter

M<small>Y MIND HAS BEEN</small> an endless cycle of the same thoughts running through my head and apparently next on the agenda is the fact that I'll be the new girl at Ravenwood University or as I like to call it RU.

People transfer to different colleges all the time with no issues, but I know it will be different for me. I grew up here for a while and my family is one of the richest here. It'll be like I'm under a microscope, especially when the cat is out of the bag.

I'm in my last year of getting my bachelor's degree and then it will be on to my MBA. This is something my father has always wanted for me, and who am I to disappoint? Even though I know this is going to be a tough transition, I'll still get it done. I've always liked a good challenge.

Learning the ropes of a multibillion-dollar company while attempting to finish my degree? Check! Life can't get more complicated than this, right?

I can practically hear the gossip mill running and all the speculations that will follow once I claim the throne. Everyone will form an opinion on what I should and shouldn't do.

Every idiot in the business world will say that I can't possibly go to school while running such an enormous company. I might be inclined to agree if I wasn't so hell-bent on proving these assholes wrong.

I'm just hoping RU isn't anything like high school. I'd hate to deal with school drama on top of everything else because I literally won't have the time.

If I know anything at all, it's that these overprivileged assholes are savage as fuck and it will not bother their conscience in the slightest to be bullies. It's all the same old, same old with rich people. It's like a bad cliche everywhere you look.

No one here knows me except for my friends but everyone else will want to assume that they do. They'll want to be my friend—at least that's how it's always been —and when you don't want the same things that they do, they label you as the outcast. That's when you unfold their true colors.

I'm definitely not the same naïve girl I was when I left here. Now I know promises are nothing but things people break when it's convenient for them to do so. The girl who left here is lost and broken, even though she doesn't show it.

And I have to continue not showing it because as one of the richest families in this town—now that I'm back—I'm pretty sure the media and the nosy people living here will scrutinize my every move. It's always from one circus to the next.

My every move will now represent the company I'll be working hard to build up more by taking it to heights it's never seen before. So, I can't tarnish it or the memory and legacy my father left behind. *Big, big shoes to fill...*

The only other family that is under as much speculation as ours is... you guessed it, the Kings. I'm not sure how things will be now that we're back here... is there still a family feud now that my father is dead?

I'm not sure what to expect with their company and mine. Will they come after me now and try to crush me in the business world? There are literally so many unknown variables to consider, and I have no idea how I'm going to wade my way through all of them.

Just thinking about this aspect of things has a headache forming. Hopefully, my team and I will handle whatever is thrown at us in the business world because I know I can't do this alone without their help.

I don't think Mason's dad would do anything to sabotage the company now that my father is no longer running it... right?

This is just another everyday issue with the anxiety I suffer from. I overthink things way too much.

I don't care about wealth and status as much as my mother does and knowing that I have more than her with said wealth, I know for a fact that it's eating her alive. She always prided herself on being able to be the best. The best clothes, best parties and everything else that entailed being married to a rich man.

My father was the only one who gave a shit about me more than his wealth, and I'll forever be grateful for that. *Bet he didn't think he'd be dead this early, and I'd be the one left to carry on things for him...*

My mother is too caught up in her own life to care for me. She never bothered with me unless she needed something from me, or she needed me to do something for her. As soon as I get settled in, I need to find out what her agenda is because I know she's up to something.

If there's one thing Emilia Crowne is good at, it's

guarding her secrets well until she's ready to use them for her own gain.

She might be heartless, but she's bloody smart and conniving when she wants to be. I know that whatever she's up to, she's planning on winning. Too bad for her, I plan on winning too. As much as I want to think that she's over not getting the company, she isn't and whatever her plans are, they include me somehow.

"Get your stuff out of the car," she says impatiently, before walking off into the house. I realize I zoned out again. I have no clue why she's in a mood. It's not like the house is going anywhere if I don't go inside right away.

I quickly grab my bag just so she won't be a bitch anymore and head toward the front door. Once I'm inside, I drop my bag by the stairs and head toward the kitchen.

Oh great, she's in here too. She's on the phone already, talking to someone and making plans to attend a party. Is she serious right now? We literally just got here. Her husband just kicked the bucket, and she wants to be mingling with the high-society crowd already?

I'm literally gobsmacked at her right now and before we end up in another argument, I decide to let it go and walk out of the kitchen. I look around the space as I make my way back to the stairs, intent on heading up to my room.

Everything looks the same on the inside as it does on the outside. I wish it were the same for me. It's disconcerting, everything else has changed over the last six years.

My life, the people around me and I know it would be a dream to wish that none of those things changed, but that's what growth is supposed to do, right?

The girl standing here right now is different, even though I wish she were the same person who left here six years ago. In reality, too much has happened for her to still be the same.

This house has always been like one of those castles in fairy tales, that's frozen in time while the outside world moved on. Now this is just a house and not a home. Maybe it was always just a house and never a home, but I was too young and naïve to notice it for what it really was—a place with barely any warmth and half a family. We were never whole, and it's taken this moment in time to realize that.

I make it to the stairs and pick my bag up. I'm just about to head up when my mother gets off the phone and calls out for me to wait for a second. She takes her sweet time strolling out of the kitchen, and the first words out of her mouth are things I'm not interested in.

"We're going to the annual charity masquerade ball the town throws every year. People need to see that we're back and ready to take over the town once again."

"I'll just stay home. I don't feel like going to some ridiculous party when I'm still grieving my father. I don't need to take over anything. All I need to do is keep Dad's company running and make it better."

"This isn't up for discussion. You need to be there!"

"Why do I need to be there? I'm sure people will understand that I've just lost my father and am not in the mood for a party."

"It's in honor of the father you keep talking about and also a welcome back for us," she tells me, digging in the sword just a little. She knows how talking about my father hurts me, yet she does it every single chance she gets.

"I'm still not going. None of those people really know or care about my father! They just care about throwing another party just because they can. How can a masquerade party even be in honor of him?" I ask her, genuinely curious about what her answer will be. Clearly, she's going crazy.

"Listen here, Winter! I'm still your fucking mother so whatever I say goes and if I'm telling you that this is something in honor of your father and you need to go, then you'll fucking shut the hell up and go!"

"How nice, you're only my mother when it's convenient for you! Don't you think it's too early to be out socializing? Your husband just died! I don't think he'd be interested in a supposed party that wants to honor him! None of these people give a shit about him!" I'm yelling by the time I finish speaking and she just scoffs and looks at me like I'm an idiot.

"He's already dead, so what's the point of being home and sulking over something that I can't change. I will not spend the rest of my life pining over a man that's dead! And I think it's the perfect way to honor him." I'm literally left speechless for a minute before I find my voice and respond to her.

I get what she's saying; I don't want her to spend the rest of her life lonely or whatever, but come the fuck on, it's literally been less than three months since he died! Who the hell moves on that fast?

"You're such a bitch, do you know that? How can you be so flippant about the man who made sure you had the lifestyle you wanted and are still currently living? All these people will care about is getting information on who will run the company now and we both know who that is, don't we?" I ask with a smirk. Yeah, I should have seen it coming because she has it out for me.

Before I even know what's going on, she walks up to me and slaps me right across the face. It stings, but I don't even flinch. I don't want her to have the satisfaction of seeing me wince.

I guess I should have expected that since she's been mad from the beginning after finding out that I'll take over instead of her.

"Don't act like you know anything about our relationship! You're going and that's final. Just because you're the one controlling the money doesn't mean you don't have to listen to me anymore. I'm still your mother!" she screams at me.

"Then fucking act like my mother! Why can't you understand me not wanting to attend a party when I'm still grieving my father's death? Why do I have to go just to pretend that everything is fine while you get to pretend like you're some grieving widow when we both know that you don't give a shit!"

This time she grabs me by the hair and pulls it tight. "Listen here, you little cunt, if you know what's good for you then you'll fucking listen to me and stop arguing. I don't know how I got saddled with such an ungrateful brat as a kid. You wouldn't want the board to make some poor business decisions that would affect your precious company, now would you?" she asks.

"What the hell are you talking about?"

"I don't know what you did to make your father put everything in your name before he died, but I'm still on grand terms with the members of the board. If I truly wanted to make your life a living hell, I can," she sneers at me.

"You wouldn't because then you wouldn't get any money!"

"If you don't start showing me some respect, I won't hesitate to get them to vote on decisions that would be bad for the company. Do you think that they'd listen to some little slut with no experience compared to me, who has been with your father for years? I've helped him a lot since we've been married and trust me, I have other ways of getting money. You wouldn't want the company to be under investigation for embezzlement now would you, daughter of mine? Everything you and your father worked for, down the drain because the media frenzy would be on a story like that, like flies to honey," she says maliciously.

I hate to say it, but I think that I may have underestimated her hate for me and knowing her to an extent, she really would sabotage this company if I didn't listen to her.

"I didn't ask him to leave anything in my name. I didn't even know he had a will but I am his heir so it makes sense why he would leave his companies to me. Fine you win! I'll go to the stupid party with you."

"Glad you're seeing things my way. I'll make sure I get back what rightfully belongs to me," she says before she lets go of my hair and walks away, leaving me standing on the stairs staring after her.

I can't believe she would actually threaten the company just to get her way. What the hell does she even mean when she says she'll get what belongs to her? Somehow, I know that can't be anything good. Now I know for certain that I need to watch it with her.

She's just thinking about herself and how to win. She doesn't even care about the ramifications that would follow if she actually did what she just threatened and how many innocent people it would affect. Thousands if not more would probably lose their jobs because of her callousness.

No, I absolutely cannot let that happen under any circumstance. Guess this is why my father didn't want her to have his company. Did he know she would try to sabotage it? I seriously cannot believe what she just threatened me with. She really is a coldhearted bitch.

Now I'm even more firm in my decision that Dad did the right thing when he left his company to me. I'm the only one who really cares about what happens to it and the people. I might be nervous about taking over, but this little interaction has made me realize I can't let these people down.

For now, I'll just have to listen to her until I can figure out what she has planned. This also brings out the fact that she has things planned for me. I just hope I can survive whatever she throws at me.

I walk up the stairs and walk straight into my bedroom, dropping my bag on the floor before going to the bathroom. I look at my face in the mirror and see that it's only red. Thankfully, that probably won't leave a bruise.

This is new. I'm used to her verbal abuses ever since I was a child, but that was the first time she's ever gotten physical with me. Somehow, I know that if she doesn't continue to get her way, then it won't be the last time. I'll just have to make sure I'm ready for her next time because I will not let her take advantage of me.

Ugh, just thinking about her is making me angry. I wish she would have just respected my boundaries but *noooo,* she just has to get what she wants. All she cares about is money, power, and putting on the best show like she's on Broadway or something. This is another one of her power moves.

I don't know why I need to be involved. She's nothing but fake around these people who attend all these parties so I have no idea why she's hell-bent on even going. These parties are always the same, and it gets tiring after a while.

I don't care about how much money I have in my bank

account; the only thing I care about is the fact that she's threatening to purposely ruin the business my father spent his whole life building up, and that does not sit right with me at all.

He may have inherited it from his father, but it was nowhere near the status it's at now. He spent his entire life making it into something greater than it ever was before. Now it's my turn to take it to new heights.

Maybe he knew I'd do whatever it took to build it up instead of my mother, who just wants to tear it all down. I can't let her destroy our legacy. She's acting like a child and throwing a tantrum just because she didn't get her way.

I walk back out into my room. This used to be my childhood room and I cringe at the sight before me; it looks like Disney threw up in here. I definitely need to redecorate if I'm going to be living here. Something tells me she's not going to let me get my own place.

I walk over to the balcony door and open it, letting some fresh air flow through my room. My balcony faces the backyard so the first thing my eyes land on is the treehouse, and I'm instantly reminded of the last time I was in there six years ago and all the hurt and pain that followed.

Pushing those thoughts away, I walk back inside and lie on my bed before bringing up Netflix. I'm jet lagged, so I'm just going to spend the rest of the afternoon relaxing while also avoiding my mother.

SEVEN

Winter

THE WEEK WENT by faster than I expected it would. I spent all of that time getting my room ready and completely redecorated.

My bedroom now has dark walls with purple curtains that trail to the floor and an enormous king-sized bed replaces the queen I had in here as a teenager.

The rest of my suite is also decorated in dark colors, much to my mother's dismay, but who gives a shit? This is my space, but she couldn't leave it alone until she told me what she really thought of my room. *I can never do anything right to please her.*

She annoys me to no end, and it feels like it's always a battle whenever we interact with each other and let me just tell you now, it's draining as hell. It's like she picks these fights just to play with my sanity.

I can't even remember the last time we had a conversation without one of us jumping down the other's throat. We almost never see eye to eye and she always has to have the last word.

I wonder if I could pay her to be less annoying? Now that's an idea worth trying. I chuckle at the thought, but then realize that she'd just take my money and still be annoying just to piss me off.

I'm putting away the last of my clothes into my closet when she comes strolling into my room. She's standing with her back straight like she's ready for a fight. I hope she isn't because I'm tired of fighting with her. It's only been three days since we've been back in Ravenwood.

I tried to stay out of her way as much as possible this week, but somehow, we still clashed a few times since she slapped me across the face. Thankfully, just like I hoped, my face didn't bruise.

While hiding out from my mother this week, I ended up having a lot of free time on my hands for my thoughts to wander. As usual, they went to douchebag extraordinaire Mason and then straight onto thoughts of how I'm going to make this move back here work with everything I'll have on my plate. Just thinking about it is intimidating. It's a huge to-do list.

I also go over the fact that Dad said to trust no one in his note, and after my mother's threats earlier this week, I know I absolutely cannot trust her at all. Hell, I can't even trust any of the board members really. For all I know, maybe she is right and if it came down to it, they would trust her and follow along with whatever she was asking them to do.

They could be secretly working with her right now, and I'd have no clue. Do they even know that I'm taking over yet? Or are they all in the dark for the time being?

Now I really wished I would've asked to shadow my father much sooner, then I wouldn't be feeling lost right now and so out of my depth. The one thing I have to keep reminding myself of is the fact that I have to do this no matter what happens because this is our legacy. My father left it to me, and I don't want to disappoint him.

If I ever have children, this will also one day become

their legacy as well. I can't leave them something that's tarnished. I need to leave them something that's better than what it is right now.

"The stylists will be here around four this afternoon to fix your hair and makeup. They'll also be bringing some dresses for you to choose from. Lord knows you need all the help you can get," my mother says, pulling me out of my thoughts while she scans me from head to toe derisively. I forgot she was even in here. Of course she had to throw in a dig at me as well. It wouldn't be her if she didn't.

"Yeah, fine. I still don't see why you can't just go alone."

"Do I need to remind you of what happens if you disobey me?" she asks, as though I could ever forget what she's threatening me with. We've gone over this a million times already. That woman is the devil, determined to make my life as miserable as hers.

I mean, you'd have to be miserable in your own life to want to destroy someone else's right?

"No, Jesus! How many times are you going to bring up the fact that you want to destroy Dad's legacy just because he didn't leave you everything?"

"As many times as I need to. I need an incentive to keep you under my thumb, don't I?" she asks before walking out of my room. I sigh. Would it make me a bad person if I said that I just want to punch her lights out?

I fucking hate her so much! I don't know when I got to the point where I stopped wanting her approval, but once I realized I didn't want or need it anymore, my tolerance for her bullshit went straight to zero. Now I just want to kill her every time she annoys me. *Not really, but totally...*

I walk over to my bed and plop down on it while staring up at the ceiling. Ever since Dad died, she has become more overbearing than she was before. I guess I never really noticed how much she hated me before because my father was always the buffer between us. He usually kept her out of my way and now that he's no longer here to steer her away, I'm getting all her hate full force.

If you asked me why my mother hated me so much, I'd never be able to answer; it's a mystery even to me. She's like the ice queen herself. I can't even remember a time when we ever had an actual mother/daughter relationship.

We're pretty much strangers related by blood, living in the same house. I hardly know anything personal about her, and I'm absolutely certain that she knows nothing about me either.

What has my life turned into? And this isn't even going to be the worst of it. No one here in Ravenwood knows that I'm taking over yet, so I can only imagine the shit they're going to write once the news becomes public.

I might feel like I'm drowning now, but it'll be nothing compared to what's going to be coming in the next few weeks and even months.

I must have fallen asleep because the next thing I know, I'm being woken up by a knock on my suite door. I groan before getting up to open it. The stylists are here already. The woman who seems to be in charge introduces herself as Eve. I move to the side and gesture for them to come in.

I grab my phone and look at the time; it's already four. Shit, I slept for a long time. There are five of them in total. I don't know why I need this many people just to do hair and makeup for a party I don't even want to attend.

As they bring all their stuff into the suite's living room, one woman gives me an expectant look, which I took to mean that they were ready to get started. Since I haven't showered yet, I just tell her I'll grab a quick one before we begin.

She nods in understanding as I walk back into my room. I decide to wash my hair too because why the hell not. I'm picking the dress that my mother would hate the most because why not piss her off a little?

She might be making me stay here with her, but that doesn't mean I have to listen to her every command. Got to win the minor battles wherever you can.

Once I'm done with my shower, I quickly dry my skin and then put on a black lace bra and matching panties before putting on my robe and heading into the sitting room again. Everything is already set up and waiting for me.

One of the women motions for me to sit in the chair in the middle of the room and they instantly begin working on my hair and then my makeup, while another one works on my nails. This is why I hate going to these parties; you have to put in way too much effort.

We also can't forget that these parties just consist of a bunch of fake upper-class socialites who are always actively trying to one-up each other. Though, don't get me wrong, there are some genuine people who attend these things too.

If I had my way, I'd be in sweats, snuggled up in bed watching Netflix and stuffing my face with junk food or something.

Three hours later, I am waxed, and my hair, nails, and makeup are done. Why I needed the wax when my legs were already shaved beats me. When I asked, they said they were following my mother's orders. *Figures...*

Now it was finally time to pick a dress and shoes. I was actually excited for this because I will not lie, some of these dresses are beyond gorgeous and I have a shoe obsession that can't be helped. *If it were up to me, I'd have a house filled with just shoes.*

I shrug off my robe and stand there in my bra and panties while Eve shows me the dresses she brought with her. It is a black-and-white masquerade party, and every single year the ladies always wear white. No idea why, but like the rebel I am, I'm absolutely not wearing white tonight.

My mother can just suck it. It's a good thing I had the foresight to call the company and ask them to bring along some black gowns because knowing my mother, she probably told them to bring only white.

The gown I ended up choosing is a black full-length 3D floral gown with silk chiffon as the outer layer with an off-the-shoulder design. It's fitted at the waist with a flared skirt that ends at my ankles. There are 3D roses on the little sleeve and gold and red roses stitched onto the fabric from the knee all the way down the gown. I am absolutely in love with this gown and couldn't have been happier with my choice.

My mother will probably catch a hissy fit later, but I can't bring myself to care right now. I look amazing in this dress! *Not to toot my horn or anything.*

I grab a pair of black, red bottoms and after putting them on, I walk over to the full-length mirror in my bedroom and look at my reflection. The girl in the reflection looks nothing like me. She looks put together and sophisticated while I know I'm nothing like that in real life. *Looks really are deceiving.*

The girls did my eyes with a light smokey eye and my lips in blood-red. It accentuates the dress and I love the overall look. My dark waist-length hair is straight down my back. The next thing I need to complete my outfit is a mask.

I grab a black venetian mask made of red and gold rhinestones that matches the red and gold flowers on my dress. Perfect! It was one of those masks that only covered up to your nose, but it would have to do. On the right side of the mask were peacock feathers painted halfway to the center in red.

After grabbing everything I needed, I check the time and see that it is already seven thirty and time to go. I thank all the women and then walk out of my room to head downstairs and wait for mother dearest.

I walk into the sitting room to wait there instead of in the foyer. If I know one thing about her, it's that she takes ages to get ready, and she likes to make an entrance. I wait for half an hour before she comes waltzing into the room, telling me she's ready to go.

Just like I predicted, she's wearing a white dress. Her dress has a deep V in the front which ends halfway down her stomach and the skirt of the dress flares out revealing a long slit up to her thighs. She has on silver heels and a silver mask to match.

She looks beautiful, not going to lie. She is a stunning woman, but it's too bad her inside doesn't match the outside. Her dress is simple and honestly. I'm a little taken aback because she always dresses over the top.

Then she goes and ruins my appraisal of her by opening her mouth. "What the hell are you wearing?" she practically growls at me.

I just give her the sweetest smile that I can muster before responding to her. "It's not like you're blind, are you? It is after all a black-and-white ball, is it not? And since you insisted I needed to go, then I get to choose my outfit. I'm not some sheep like everyone else in this town, who only strive to fit in instead of embracing who they were really meant to be." If looks could kill...

"Whatever, you fucking bitch! Let's just go, we're

already late!" she says in a tone that makes it sound like it's my fault that we're late. I could swear I hear her muttering that *eventually I'll get what's coming to me* as she walks past me and out the door.

"And whose fault is that?" I ask, referring to her last outburst.

She stops in her tracks before blowing up at me. "I've had enough with your fucking attitude and smartass comments! You really don't want to piss me off too much because then you'll see firsthand what I'm really capable of!" she says angrily.

"Sir, yes, sir!" I even give her a salute to which she walks back closer to me before whispering in my ear so no one else can hear since our driver is already out front.

"You think you've got it all figured out, don't you? But you have no idea what's coming to you. Let me just tell you now, I'll be kicking it back while enjoying every moment of watching you fall. You really don't have a clue what you're in for," she says before stalking off to the car.

Okaaay... maybe I pushed her a little too far, or she's just really unstable. At this point, I'm not sure, it could be either one. But her ominous threat has definitely raised some questions. What the hell does she know that I don't?

"Hey, Martin," I greet our driver when I get to the car before I slide in and onto my seat. He closes the door before getting into the driver's seat, and then we're off. I didn't even think to ask her where this party was being held, and even if I knew, it's not like I can back out of it now.

I look out the window, not actually paying attention to where we're going. For the millionth time, my mind goes back to all the things I can't change and all the things I plan to.

I'm still trying to figure out what Dad meant in his note,

but I still have no clue. He should have been more specific, for fuck's sake!

"Make sure you're available tonight when I need you. There are people you need to meet," she says while holding her compact mirror in front of her face.

"Isn't it enough that you got me to come along? Why do I need to meet people?"

She looks at me like I'm an idiot before she continues, "While everyone may not know you're the new CEO of Crowne Enterprises yet, you still need to meet them. You'll be doing business with most of them in the coming months. But if you don't think you're cut out for the job, then I can always take your place."

"I wonder why they don't know I'm the CEO yet," I ask, smirking at her. She gives me a deadly stare. We both know that she was the one who wanted to keep it under wraps because she should have been the one holding the position instead of me. Why my dad chose me is still a mystery to both of us.

"Don't worry, that can change in an instant, you just never know what can happen in the future..." The way she says that instantly has goosebumps breaking out over my skin. *She wouldn't like kill me in my sleep or something, right?*

"Fine, I'll schmooze whoever you need me to tonight," I say just to end the conversation.

I seriously hope my friends are here tonight. I haven't had a chance to see Riley, Avery or Luna since I got here but I have talked to them. They assured me they would be here tonight.

I hope I see them right away because I don't want to spend all my time being bored to death, alone in a place where I don't know anyone.

"Tonight is going to be so much fun!" my mother says excitedly. I wonder why she's so happy suddenly.

"Why are you so happy all of a sudden?" I decide to bite the bullet and ask her, but she just smirks at me.

"All in good time, Daughter. Don't mention to anyone tonight about you being the CEO yet, they'll all find out soon enough." she says with outright hate in her voice.

"Wasn't planning on it," I say with a bored tone in my voice.

All she's looking at is the money and not the fact that running a billion-dollar company takes time and effort plus she has employees to look after. I also know that she's pissed at the fact that my dad left her what she considers a paltry allowance.

"Have fun tonight, darling," she says this time, giving me a genuine smile that I've never seen on her before. Again, not going to lie, she looks absolutely beautiful with an actual smile on her face. Not for the first time in my life, I wonder what it would have been like to see her smiling at me like that and actually being a mother to me.

Our conversation comes to a halt when we come to a stop, so I don't get to ask her again, why she's happy. She puts her mask on and slides out of her seat when Martin opens the door for us.

I just sigh and put my mask over my face before stepping out of the car to follow behind her.

EIGHT

Winter

Once we're both out of the car, I take a step forward before looking up at the mansion where the party is being held and stop dead in my tracks.

Motherfucker!

The party is being held at the one place that I never wanted to step foot in ever again. Now the reason she was so happy suddenly makes sense. *Fucking witch!*

From the smirk that's currently splayed across her face right now, she knew exactly where this stupid party was being held tonight.

Mason-fucking-King's house.

Does she know we were together once, and that I was in love with the guy? We had always been careful to keep it from our parents, though after everything went down, my father was the only one who knew.

Did my father tell her what happened when I came back here that one time after we moved? I don't think my father would have betrayed me like that, so that brings me to wonder whether she knows about us.

Also, if he didn't tell her, how did she know? Obviously she knows something and right now, me being here is affecting me. No wonder she was smiling at me right as we got here. Ugh!

"What's the matter, honey?" she asks in mock concern while trying to hide her smirk.

"Why did you bring me here? You insisted I needed to come to this party, all the while knowing that I would never want to be here again."

I've got to hand it to her, she knows how to get information. There's no way she doesn't know there was an us, judging from the way she's acting right now. She really knows how to hit you where it hurts the most.

"I have no idea what you're talking about," she says, acting innocent.

"Cut the shit, Mother! Acting like you're innocent doesn't suit you," I spit out at her.

"Like I said, you needed to be here because you have people to meet. It's not my fault that this party is being held at your ex-boyfriend's place," she says, shrugging. And there it fucking is.

"How do you know about Mason?" I ask.

"Oh, I know a lot of things, but don't you worry about it. Now suck it up and get in there. You have a job to do. It's not my fault that your boyfriend left your skanky ass!"

This is the second time she's alluded to me being a slut or a skank, and it's really pissing me the hell off. I have no clue what she's talking about. Before I had sex with Mason-douchebag-King I was a virgin, and while we were together, he was the only one I slept with. After him, I had sex with a few one-night stands, but even then, it wasn't a lot. Hmm, I wonder if that is why she's calling me a slut. Whatever, we weren't together so I'm just going to forget about her dumbass comments.

I won't let anyone slut shame me for trying to move on with my life, least of all my mother. It took an entire year after he destroyed me to even attempt being with someone else. So yeah, no one gets to make me feel like shit for that.

With the way she's looking at me, I'm now realizing that she brought me here intending to hurt me. I could've met these people at any time, but she chose to bring me here tonight to bask in my pain.

I shake my head at her and turn around intending to leave, but her voice stops me in my tracks.

"If you leave now, I'll send an anonymous tip to all the media outlets here saying that Crowne Enterprises is involved with embezzlement."

"That's not true and you know it!" I yell at her, getting tired of all the fucking threats she keeps throwing my way. Thank God we're nowhere near anyone. As always, she's used to waltzing into these things late. I have to say that I've never been more glad for that than right now.

"Do you think anyone would care whether it's true? Once the media gets a tip like that, it will blow up and then you'll have the feds to deal with before you even start working at Crowne. I have documents that would back up my statement. With your father gone and you just about to take over, who's going to believe a word you say? You think people will believe a twenty-two-year-old who doesn't know much about her 'job' yet? And the better question is, are you willing to risk it?"

I just stare at her with hate because even though I hate what she's saying, it's probably true. No one is going to investigate it before running such a story. "You're lying! Whatever document you have is obviously fake!"

"Obviously, but all I have to say is that I'm an employee and give them those documents. They'll most likely believe me without taking the time to actually investigate first." She smirks.

A stunt like that would cause the company to lose millions of dollars in revenue and people could lose their jobs. Not to mention the fact that it would tarnish my father's reputation and everything he worked for.

With no other option for now, I turn back around and walk toward the front door of the mansion. I'd rather endure this party than have to deal with a media shitstorm and give her the satisfaction of seeing the company be dragged through the mud.

"Glad you could see things my way," she says behind me.

"What the fuck ever," I mutter under my breath.

When I see my best friends, I'm going to fucking kill them too for not giving me the heads-up in the first place of where this fucking party was being held tonight.

I don't really drink that much, but I'm going to need all the alcohol I can get just to make it through the evening. I can't believe I have to be in the place I hate more than anything in the world tonight. Like being in Ravenwood wasn't bad enough already.

Mom - 1, Winter - 0.

Once we get to the front doors, a staff member greets us and leads us toward what I'm assuming is their ballroom. I've only been inside this house once, and that one time was enough to make me not want to see it again.

All thoughts of Mason stop when we walk into the ballroom because wow! This place is gorgeous. The room itself is huge, and it's filled with enormous floor-to-ceiling windows to the right side of the room.

There are giant chandeliers hanging overhead through the length of the room and the ceiling is carved in various patterns, like how the Greeks do it.

Not going to lie, this place is breathtaking and expensive, though I guess I wouldn't expect anything less from Mason's dad. From what I've heard, he likes to show off his wealth.

They set the middle of the room up as the dance floor and on both sides are tables and chairs for the guests. The black-and-white decor matches the theme of this party and is absolutely beautiful. I'm left staring at it for a few seconds more before my mother jabs her elbows into my side, motioning for me to follow her.

Just as I predicted, most of the women are wearing white with just a few exceptions like myself, wearing black gowns. This place is already packed and thank God for the masks, they maintain a bit of privacy. But judging by the looks we're getting, I'm pretty sure everyone already knows who we are.

So much for keeping a low profile. I sigh. It's like we're the newest attraction at the zoo or something.

My mother stops to talk to everyone she passes as we're making our way to our table. How the hell does she know this many people? I only know like eight people and those are my best friends and the guys, aka Mason's best friends. Once upon a time, we were all friends.

Thinking about the guys, I wonder if we're still friends. I mean, just because Mason and I don't talk anymore doesn't mean we're still not friends, right? *Oh, who the fuck are you kidding with that delusion, Winter? The guys will obviously follow his lead.*

Well, that sucks because I know I'm right. Just like the girls will take my side, the guys will take his.

I don't *people* too well, and I can feel my anxiety trying to break the surface because of all the people that are here already.

Their stares are making me itchy all over, and I have to

resist the urge to actually scratch my skin off. It's times like these where I wish my father were still around. Then I wouldn't have to go to these things.

If he were alive and knowing exactly who lives here, he never would have made me come. He wouldn't get any satisfaction from my pain like my mother clearly does.

The thought of my father not being here with me anymore sends a pang straight to my heart, as it does every time I think about him. I wonder if the pain of losing a parent will ever lessen, though with the way my heart hurts; I don't think it ever will.

When I returned to London after coming here, I had an epic breakdown and he was the one who took care of me for weeks when I didn't want to go anywhere further than my bathroom and on the days I couldn't make it out of bed. Eventually, he said enough was enough, and he reminded me of my worth.

That was a huge pill to swallow, especially when I look back and remember how bad things had gotten. Depression and anxiety ruled my life, and it made me turn into someone I couldn't even recognize. I was utterly broken and useless.

Yeah, Mason-fucking douchebag-King can go fuck himself with a spiked dildo.

I inwardly sigh and take a deep breath. *I can do this!* I tell myself. Maybe God will be kind to me, and I won't see him at all tonight. There are like hundreds of people here and most of them have masks on, so I probably won't notice if he's around.

Once we get to the table we're supposed to be sitting at, she drops her clutch before walking off to go mingle while I just take a seat and hope no one notices me.

I have no clue why we're at the front of the bloody

room. I monitor her for a while; watching as she goes around the entire room and talks to everyone she comes into contact with.

At one point, I even see her fake crying. Someone must have asked about my father. Just watching her act like a grieving widow makes me want to smack her across the face. She doesn't give a fuck about him. Anyone who actually believes that she cares about her dead husband is an idiot. Someone needs to give this woman a fucking Oscar for her acting skills.

I'm pulled out of my thoughts when the older woman sitting next to me grabs my attention by talking to me.

"Oh my God, Winter, honey, is that you?" she asks.

"Umm, yes, hi," I say as I take off my mask. Half the people here already have their masks off, anyway. I don't know why they even call it a masquerade ball when people always take off their masks as soon as they get here. They all want to be noticed.

I have no idea who this lady is and I kind of feel bad not knowing since she clearly knows who I am. But then I have to remind myself that I've been away for years and I don't owe anyone here anything, but that doesn't mean I'm a bitch about it.

"You probably don't even know who I am. My husband used to do business with your father and I just wanted to let you know how sorry I am about him. It was so shocking and such a tragedy," she says. *Indeed, it is.*

"Ahh, thank you for your kind words," I tell her as I close my eyes at her words. Though she probably meant well, it causes my insides to burn. It brings back all the memories of my earlier thoughts that I tried to keep buried under all the layers in my brain that say *do not touch*.

My throat closes up as the pain comes back full force. I

barely rasp out a thank you to her. To get my mind off the thoughts of my father, I grab my phone out of my clutch and pull up the group chat with my best friends to text them.

ME: *Where the hell are you, bitches? I want to leave this party already!*

Riley: Beckett is acting like a fucking girl, taking forever to get dressed! I swear this asshole is worse than my mom and me!

Luna: Just left my house, will be there soon!

Avery: Just left mine too. Be there soon! My parents were taking forever!

Me: @Riley hahaha I can't wait to see those idiots!

Me: Also, I have a bone to fucking pick with you bitches! Why the fuck did no one tell me this party was being held at Mason's house?! I hate you bitches for this!

Riley: What? I thought you knew!

Avery: Sorry, babe! Totally slipped my mind!

Luna: Oops! Sorry!

Me: @Riley, you did not just say that you thought I knew because WTF? Do you guys seriously think I would've come if I had known?

Riley: Shit! Sorry, babe! That totally didn't even cross my mind!

Luna: *facepalm* I wasn't thinking!

Avery: Shit! Sorry, babe!

Me: Just get your asses here, ASAP!

THEY ALL KNOW we're no longer together, so yeah, I hate him more than any other person who exists in this world. I even hate him more than I do my mother and she's high on that list, but he's public enemy number one.

I've felt nothing but the stares and whispers all night long and everyone here is so predictable it's almost laughable.

All they do is judge. They think they know you from the bits and pieces they gather from the media.

I just know that being back here in Ravenwood will not be easy. This time there's an unknown world that's been opened to me.

I want to hate my dad for making me come back here but when I think about it logically this is the best place to be to run things. This is where it all started. *Sometimes you just need to sacrifice yourself for the greater good.*

I hope that I can be everything he envisioned me to be. I hope I don't cave under the pressure because if nothing else kills me, my anxiety probably will.

I'll have to act like I have thick skin because I know people will rip me to shreds because of my age and the fact that I'm a woman. *Pure shit, I know!* I basically have no experience, but it doesn't matter because it's my company and not theirs.

I know people will react to things that don't concern them. They always asked my father about his heir. Like, did they not see me there as his only child? Fucking reporters always had the audacity to ask him what it meant for the future of Crowne Enterprises since he didn't have a 'male' heir. *Cue the eye roll.*

To his credit, he always backed me up and let them know he has an heir, and it was me. But never in my wildest dream did I ever think when he said I was his heir it meant that he would leave everything to me. I thought I'd probably work there or some shit.

Half an hour later, I need to pee, and I decide to go in search of the bathroom that's on the first floor. I do not under any circumstance want to go upstairs just in case Mason is up there.

I'm glad that I haven't seen him tonight and that in itself is a freaking miracle, like my dad is watching out for me wherever he is.

After walking through the halls, I find the bathroom and quickly take care of business before washing my hands and heading back to the party. Let me just tell you, going to the bathroom while wearing one of these gowns is like a whole-ass job by itself.

I'm passing along the corridor on my way back to the ballroom when I hear voices coming from one of the rooms. I walk up closer and see that the door is ajar.

The only reason the sounds caught my attention is because I'd know my mother's voice anywhere. It's so distinct and annoying that you can't miss it, ever.

I creep closer to the barely open door and try to listen in. A few seconds later, when I'm sure that no one heard me, I move forward a little more to peek inside. She's sitting on top of a desk and I see a suit-clad arm around her waist. I can't make out who it is. She's blocking him and he's still sitting in a chair.

"Don't worry, it's only less than a month before we announce it to the public," I hear the man tell her.

"I hate waiting. We've waited years for this, and I hate the fact that we still need to wait," she says with a whine in her voice that is so uncharacteristically her, I pause for a second.

I need to find out who the hell this man is. What the fuck? I'm so confused. She said she was waiting years for this—what the hell does that mean? What has she been waiting years for? Is this the man she was probably having an affair with?

"Don't worry, darling, soon everything we have planned will start falling into place and we'll get everything that rightfully belongs to us," he tells her.

What is rightfully theirs? I don't like the sound of that.

I hear the unmistakable sound of kissing and when I look into the room again; she climbs onto his lap and straddles him. I still can't see who it is, but I'm not sticking around if they're about to have sex right now. That is just a big no-no and something I definitely don't want to see my mother doing.

As quietly as I can, I rush down the hallway and look for the nearest exit. I'm going to be sick. How could she do this to my father?

Once I get back to the ballroom, I walk all the way to the back of the room where I notice doors that lead outside. Without thinking, I head straight for the open doors and walk out onto the dimly lit balcony.

NINE

Winter

As soon as I step outside, I let the chilly air sweep across my overheated skin, and let out the breath I didn't realize I was holding in until now.

Tonight definitely took an unexpected turn, and I'm not sure what to do with the information I just uncovered. All I know is that I need to find out what she was talking about somehow. I also need to find out who the mystery man is.

Now I know that's the reason she isn't too torn up over my father's death. She already had someone new—or rather old if her comment of years is anything to go by—warming her bed.

It's only been about an hour and a half since we've been here, and it already feels like tonight is too much. Every person I've met tonight had some version of their bullshit sympathy to give ranging from 'I'm so sorry for your loss' to 'your father was a good man,' acting like they knew him and I didn't. Of course I know he was a good man.

After the fifth 'what's the plans for Crowne Enterprises now,' I was ready to punch someone's lights out. Like I said, bullshit sympathy. What they really cared about was getting information. *It's cute that people think I'd actually give them information about the company.*

Right now, people only want to know what's going on with the company because they want to know who they need to form a relationship with. Wouldn't want to schmooze up to the wrong person now, would they?

Everyone is basically looking out for their own interests and I guess I can't fault them for that, but the fake concern gets on my nerves. I wish people would just ask their goddamn questions instead of pretending to care when they don't. Be real and don't hide behind that fake caring bullshit.

Never thought I'd say this, but I'm glad that my mother made us keep my upcoming position under wraps. I have a feeling that if people already knew, they would have been all over me tonight instead of focusing on her. *Small mercies, I guess.*

I don't think I've ever been more thankful for her tonight, but I'm under no illusion that she did it for my best interest. I know she has her own reasons for doing whatever it is she's doing, and none of it benefits me. When it comes down to it, all she cares about is herself.

I grab my phone out of my clutch and check to see if I have any texts from the girls yet and after seeing nothing, I decide to look through the online rags even though I know I probably shouldn't. But curiosity and all that...

What do you know, there're already tons of articles about us on these sites. *"The Crownes Are Back in Ravenwood." "Aiden Crowne's Death, Such a Tragedy." "With Aiden Crowne Dead, Who Will Inherit the Multibillion-Dollar Company?" "Winter Crowne Is Back and Looks Better Than Ever,"* And my least favorite, *"Should We Get Popcorn and See What Happens with the Crowne and King's Family Feud? Is There Still One?"*

Since we came back earlier this week, I've made it a point to not look at any of the gossip rags, but right now I can't help it. It's all that's been talked about all week. Who knew that just moving would cause this much gossip!

The urge to flee back to London is strong. I'm already tired of this place, but I know I can't just run away from my issues. I need to just face them head-on. *Easier said than done when your own mind is against you on most days...*

Being here tonight has really messed with my head because I keep expecting Mason to pop out from some corner. Even though nothing has happened, I just know I'm not out of the woods yet. Add in the mystery of what is going on with my mother and my anxiety is just ready to jump to all kinds of conclusions whether they make sense or not.

All the questions people asked tonight have cracked my insecurities wide open again, bit by bit. I'll never let them know though, even if I'm terrified their observations are correct and I'm in way over my head.

People never realize that their simple comments can impact a person's mind and take on a whole life of its own inside their head, especially when the same things they point out have already been on their minds bothering them. Asking insensitive questions hurt even if you don't mean for it to.

The one thing I need to remember is I can't be vulnerable in front of anyone here. I don't want anyone else to have power over me. If my own mother can use my weaknesses against me, then I don't doubt other people will do much worse.

Ever since my dad died, I've had to pretend to be stronger than I really am. I have no one else who will pick me up if I fall or if it gets to be too much for me. I have the girls, but it's not the same. They're not the ones who will have to be in the public eye and there's only so much they can do as my friends.

Monday will be my first day going into the offices, and after speaking to Chase, we've already scheduled the press conference to let everyone know the plans for Crowne. I do not know what the public reaction will be, but I'm hoping it's a positive one. I'll definitely be making waves in the coming days.

I just need to get my head in the right headspace by the time Monday comes around and kick ass. The ball will officially start rolling then and I'll have to act the part and give the best performance of my life yet. *I should have asked my mother for lessons since she's apparently a pro at performing.*

I mean, Dad had to have had faith that I could do this; he wouldn't have left everything to me otherwise, right? I ask myself for the millionth time since learning of my new path in life. A path I didn't necessarily want but have to walk on because it's what's expected of me now.

Dad made it a point to tell me that by just being a Crowne there would be people who will want to knock the proverbial crown off my head because they think I'm not worthy of wearing one, but I should never show them any weakness or let them know they hurt me even when I'm down and can barely keep it together.

No one can truly knock my crown off unless I let them. If they tilt it a little from all the knocks that this life will give me, that's totally fine. Slanted crowns are still crowns and every queen will have to face adversaries throughout her reign as queen and I'll be no different.

Not going to lie, that was the day I finally snapped out of whatever was going on with me after the Mason phase, but it wasn't without incident because by that time, my anxiety and depression were so bad I had to be put on medications permanently.

I take in another deep breath and try to push away all the thoughts taking up residence in my head. I just need at least one more night to not worry about what the future holds. Come Monday, I'll have to worry about everything else, but for tonight I'm just going to forget about the things plaguing my mind.

I place my phone and clutch down on the rail and look over at the expanse that is the backyard and instantly my breath catches because it's beautiful. I wasn't paying attention to it before, but now as I look at it; I feel a sense of calm wash over me with how peaceful it looks.

Deciding now is as good a time as any for a walk, I look around to see how to get down to the garden. I spot a set of stairs to my left and walk over to it before heading down. This brings me straight onto a stone path with lamps strategically placed a few feet apart lighting up the walkway.

I keep walking until the path opens into a fork in three different directions. I keep going straight because that's the one that leads to what looks like a maze. I haven't seen one of those in years and I decide to explore.

It doesn't look like anyone else is down here, so the walk might help to clear my head further. I stroll toward the maze and when I'm closer; I see the hedges that make up the maze are higher than it looked from the house and there are rose bushes at the top of them.

The smell of roses instantly relaxes me as I take in a deep breath while walking to the center of the maze. Directly in the middle there's a bench and I walk over to it to take a seat. I lean back and look up at the sky. It's filled with stars tonight and gives me a sense of melancholy.

The last time I stargazed was with Mason. It was our thing, and I haven't been able to do something as simple as this in ages.

Life got in the way and then it got too much to deal with. Thinking back on things now, I wish I would have done everything differently. I wish I didn't let what he did affect me so much, and I wish I wasn't so weak as to let it become so bad it messed with my health. *You live and you learn, I guess.*

I decide to sit here for a while until I feel like I'm ready to go back inside. I've always been comfortable alone, so this suits me well. Hopefully my mother doesn't look for me while I'm out here. That will be another battle. Lord knows she loves to throw a fit for the slightest thing.

I can barely hear the music, so it makes being out here more peaceful. There isn't a lamp where I'm sitting, and I wonder if that was intentional. The other lamps from nearby cast a soft glow, so I'm not totally in the dark.

Sometimes I wonder what it would have been like to grow up in a different life, one where I didn't have to worry about the paparazzi or all the expectations of being an heiress. No one ever thinks about all the struggles you go through and having this name does not come without its challenges. I'd give it all up to have my father back.

I'm scared shitless of the fact I'll never be able to measure up to him. He was the best at what he did, and the pain of losing him hurts more when I think about the things he'll never be able to accomplish.

A few months before his accident there was a disconnect between us. I don't know what it was, but he was always preoccupied and acting weird.

I'm not sure if it had anything to do with the company or if he was just going through something. Now I'll never know. If it was something regarding the company, I guess I'll find out on Monday.

I'm so engrossed in my thoughts that I don't hear the footsteps coming my way until it's too late. Five guys step through the entrance to where I'm sitting and only one of them keeps advancing, moving closer to me.

The other four hang back, forming a semicircle in front of the entrance, which means they're blocking me if I were to try to escape. The one moving closer walks until he's standing directly in front of me. He's so close I can feel the tips of his shoes touching mine.

"Umm, do you need something?" I ask with clear irritation in my voice. Clearly, this one needs some lessons on not encroaching on people's personal space.

"I haven't decided yet. I just wanted to see if the rumors were true. You know, the ones of the little slut being back here in Ravenwood when she isn't supposed to be," he says with what sounds like hate in his voice.

"Hmm, seems like Ravenwood is still raising privileged assholes," I quip.

Clearly, I'm missing something in my own life because this is the second time someone has called me a slut. It's pissing me the hell off because I didn't know it was a crime to sleep with someone when you're single.

"You don't even know me to make that type of assumption, dumbass! And I'm exactly where I'm supposed to be."

"Mmm, looks like little Winter isn't the demure little princess she used to pretend to be, huh, boys?" he says loud enough for the other guys to hear and they all reply agreeing with this douchebag.

I can't see any of their faces because they all have on

their masks, and they're wearing black suits that hug their bodies to perfection. Their masks are all the same except for the guy in front of me. His has a slight variation.

They're all wearing a black mask that has cracks along the eyes and the cheeks and there's a silver crown on it though the douchebag in front of me has on the silver version of the mask with the same cracks but his has a gold crown on it.

I've seen these before, and on closer inspection, I realize they're wearing the Abyss King's venetian masks. Hmm, how fitting... not! Do they consider themselves kings or something? I just roll my eyes at the thought.

"It's called growing up. Maybe you need some lessons?" I ask sweetly. "Like I asked before, did you need something?"

He moves so fast I'm not even sure what's happening until he grabs me by the throat and lifts my head up to look at him while he angles his head down to look at me.

"Just thought I'd come over to give you a friendly warning," he says in a deep masculine voice that sounds so threatening I wonder if he spends his days giving threats. It sounds like it comes naturally to this jerk.

His voice is muffled with his mask on, so I can't tell if I know him from his voice. I mean, you'd have to know someone before you grab them by the throat and try to threaten them, right? I look up at him with a bored expression on my face.

"Thanks, but no thanks! I'm good." My smartass comment makes the hand on my neck squeeze hard. It's not enough to cut off my air supply but it is enough to let me know it's there. He probably wouldn't hesitate to choke the life out of me if he wanted to.

"I can't wait to snap this pretty little neck," he says,

leaning down to whisper in my ear, which sends a shiver down my spine and causes the asshole to chuckle. He did not miss that at all and now I'm just irritated.

"Fine, I'll bite... warning about what?" I ask. Maybe if I play along, he'll leave me the hell alone faster.

"Ah, now we're getting somewhere." If I roll my eyes any harder, they will probably roll out of my head.

"Do you get off on being an asshole or is this just a personality trait?" I ask. I am so over this conversation and we've only said a few words to each other. I hear the guys chuckle from behind us, which just makes me madder. I really want to punch them in their stupid faces.

Why the hell are they even targeting me like this? I've literally only been here for three days, and I spent all that time at home decorating my room.

"Do all of you idiots just go around cornering girls when they're alone?" I ask loud enough so they all know I'm speaking to them. "If this is what you usually do, then why not show your ugly mugs instead of hiding behind those masks?" I ask in a huff.

Of course I get no answers from the others and now I wish I were inside instead of out here with these idiots. I'm not sure what their angle is, but they wouldn't do anything stupid at a party with this many people, right?

Doucheface is the one who answers. Apparently, he's the leader of this little group of misfits.

"You knew one of us. Pretty well, I'd say. Someone here had their cock buried deep inside your pussy already, but that was before he knew what a bitch you really are. But don't worry, you'll get reacquainted with us soon," he says. A gasp leaves me. There is no doubt in my mind who this is.

"Mas—" I don't get to say another word because the

hand that's still wrapped around my neck squeezes and cuts off what I was about to say.

"Don't! You don't get to say my name after everything that you've done to us! Remember what I said to you last time you were here? In case you don't remember, I said if you ever stepped foot here again, I'd make you pay. Looks like you're not very good at listening," he says with anger in his voice. That royally pisses me off. How dare he pin the blame on me when he was the one who fucked us up.

"After everything I've done? Are you fucking kidding me, Mason? I wasn't the one who threw away what we had. I also wasn't the one who was fucking someone else in their bed! That was all you, asshole!" I scream out at him.

"Ha! That's rich! Yeah, I was the one fucking someone in my bed, baby, but that was after I saw what a cheating cunt you were! Though I guess I should've known you were easy after you gave it up to me five seconds after I said I liked you," he says. His words are like a slap to the face.

He doesn't have to yell or scream because the weight of his words punches me straight in the gut and the force of them lets me know just how much he really hates me.

When I came back to Ravenwood, I didn't think I'd see him... actually, I was hoping I wouldn't. Then I thought even if I saw him around, we'd pretend like the other didn't exist. I was not expecting to be met with this kind of deep-seated hatred.

I wasn't even expecting him to seek me out, but as usual, Mason doesn't do things the way you'd expect. He always has to do things the opposite of what you were thinking.

"I will not let you blame me for something that you did!" I say through clenched teeth.

"What did I tell you, boys?" he tosses over his shoulder,

directing his question to the guys. "Didn't I say that she'd act like she didn't know what I was talking about?"

Now I'm quite sure that the guys standing there could be none other than Grayson, Royce, Nate and Beck. I mean, where Mase goes the others follow. It's been like that since we were teenagers, and it looks like that hasn't changed.

"You know what? You're a fucking psycho who is clearly off his meds because this conversation we're having right now is stupid. Just get out of my face since you already have your ridiculous opinions of me." I knew I should have stayed my ass home tonight or left when I realized where this dumbfuck of a party was being held.

"You're seriously going to act like you don't know what I'm talking about? I wasn't the one who destroyed us! You are!" He practically yells this time.

"I don't have to act because I honestly don't know what the fuck you're talking about. I've been nothing but faithful to you our entire relationship!"

"Bitches are always lying when they get caught," he says.

"You've got some freaking nerve, especially when you had some skank in your bed. Stop acting like it was my fault things went to shit between us, you fucking grade A douchebag!" Before he can respond, I cut him off.

"Anyway, it doesn't fucking matter anymore because I'm over it just like I'm over you. The guys I've fucked after you made sure that you were no longer a thought in my head," I say with a smirk to piss him off. I will never let him know how much his betrayal broke me.

I think my taunt worked to piss him off because the hand still around my neck squeezes hard this time until it cuts off my air supply.

"If you know what's fucking good for you, Winter, then

you'll go back to London or move to some other state because I can guarantee you, if you stay, I'll make it my fucking mission to destroy you!" he spits venomously at me.

I must be fucked in the head because damn he sounds hot when he's pissed and spewing threats. It's at this moment I realize that Mason absolutely hates me. I'm talking about real unadulterated hate.

I'm not sure how to process that information. It's not like I expected us to be friends or anything after everything that's happened between us, but I also didn't expect this level of hate being directed at me.

Even though my body is trembling beneath me, I don't let it show because he's the one person I won't be weak in front of. I have a feeling that he'd use any type of weakness I show against me, and I can't let that happen.

He lets go of my neck and a cough bursts free. I answer with all the courage I can muster. "Well, I hate to burst your self-absorbed bubble but I'm not going anywhere, I'm here to stay so you'll just have to deal with it, asshole!"

"Your funeral, bitch!" he says before he storms off back in the house's direction.

I look up at the guys. "It's nice to see that I still have friends here!" I spit out at them as they follow after Mason.

"We're not the ones who fucked up and hurt the person they were supposed to love," one, who by the sound of their voice sounds a lot like Grayson, says.

"Yeah, well, I wasn't either," I say, as he walks away following after the others.

As soon as they're all gone, a sob escapes me. I have no idea what just happened. I have a feeling that his threats weren't light, either. He really will make my life a living hell.

But I don't care because I'm not here for him.

The kind boy I knew as a teenager is not the same anymore and in his place is a man filled with so much hate. I have no idea where any of it came from. Hate for what, though? Hate for me, apparently.

TEN

Mason

"If you know what's fucking good for you, Winter, then you'll go back to London or move to some other state. I can guarantee you, if you stay, then I'll make it my fucking mission to destroy you!" I spit venomously at her.

I fucking hate this bitch and even though I know what she's done, it still pisses me off to hear her talk about other men. It makes my hate for her grow.

I swear to God, if she doesn't leave Ravenwood, I won't be held responsible for my actions.

My head and my heart both agree that we hate her, but my fucking dick hasn't gotten the memo yet, apparently.

Just seeing her tonight has had me on edge the entire time she was here.

I made it a point to not let her see me until I was ready to make my presence known. And trust me, I've had eyes on her the entire night.

All night it looked as though she was in her own head and pain was radiating off her the entire night. I know it must be because she lost her father and the dozens of questions she's probably had to answer tonight.

I'm not even going to deny the fact that I loved watching the pain etched across her face all night.

Tonight is the least of her worries because I'll make it

hurt so good for her. She betrayed me, and I still haven't dealt with the pain she put me through.

It looks like things are about to change and I'll get to exact my revenge on her. Winter Crowne is the only person in this world I hate the most and it's about time she felt the full force of my hate.

I've waited two years for this and now that she isn't halfway across the world, I can't wait to play with her.

I'll make sure she feels all the pain I've felt since the day I saw her fucking some douchebag in a hotel room.

Over the past two years, I've tried to get over it and call it unresolved issues or whatever, but I haven't been able to. Maybe it's the fact that she was my first love that has me wrestling with my emotions constantly.

I haven't felt for anyone else what I felt for her in the two years we've been separated, and she'll pay for betraying me.

No one betrays me and gets away with it. She'll be another example on the list of the many I've already dealt with. I feel a twinge of excitement— that I haven't felt in a long time—at the prospect of hurting her. I need to start on my revenge agenda as soon as I can.

I smirk at the way her breath hitches when I tighten my hand on her neck. She's fucking loving this, but I bet she wouldn't if she could see the expression on my face right now.

I also see the way she's trying to act strong in front of me, but I know her, and she can't hide the fact that she's a nervous wreck right now.

That's one advantage of knowing someone completely. You notice all their insecurities and quirks as well as all of their weaknesses.

And trust me, I know all of her weaknesses and I can't

wait to use them against her. I have no sympathy for this bitch and seeing her pay will help me sleep better at night.

I give her neck one last squeeze before letting go of her. When I do, she lets out a series of coughs before answering me.

"Well, I hate to burst your self-absorbed bubble but I'm not going anywhere. I'm here to stay so you'll just have to deal with it, asshole!"

Mmm, looks like she came back with an attitude and a mouth on her. She might have cracks right now, but I won't stop until I'm done with her. Once she's completely broken, only then will I leave her alone.

"Your funeral, bitch!" I say as I storm my way back in the house's direction.

"It's nice to see that I still have friends here!" I hear her say to the guys as I'm walking away.

I don't wait to hear if any of them will reply to her because I know they'll be following me. None of the guys will side with her. They're my best friends and they all know what she did.

When I got back home from London after that trip with my father, it was to find out that my mother had died while we were away. She had been sick for a few months with cancer, but she was fighting it as far as I knew. So to come back to find her dead was a shock to my system, one that I'm still not over yet.

I buried myself in alcohol and pussy. I blamed myself for her death. If we weren't on that goddamn trip and if I wasn't trying to chase pussy, then I could have been here for her.

I was also pissed at myself because I wasn't here for my brother and he had to deal with it for a few hours before we got home.

He's fine, but as the oldest, it's my job to always take care of him. Gray is sensitive, and he takes things like that hard.

Somehow, he was the one who remained strong, and I was the one crumbling. After weeks of swimming in alcohol and pussy, the guys finally decided that enough was enough and staged a fucking intervention for me.

That was when I came clean about all the shit that went down in London with Winter, and it was when I remembered the promise I made myself. I'd destroy her if she ever came back to Ravenwood. It looks like my prayers have been answered because here she is, back like nothing ever happened.

As soon as I make it out of the maze, I hear footsteps behind me and know that the guys are already following. We've all been best friends since we were in diapers, so I know I can always count on them for anything that matters.

We make our way up the balcony steps and once I get to the top; I see Amber outside waiting for me.

"Where have you been, baby?"

"I had some business with the guys," I say. I turn around to the guys and tell them to head into the den, and I'll meet them there in a second. They all head off, leaving me and Amber alone for a second.

"You're the one who asked me to come to this party," Amber says in a pissed-off voice that grates on my nerves.

"I know but I had important shit to deal with and that will always come before you. You know how busy I am."

"Who the hell is that?" she asks a second later, interrupting our previous conversation.

I turn around just in time to see Winter wipe at her eyes

as she's coming out of the maze before heading to the side of the house.

"No one," I reply before motioning to Amber for us to go back inside.

"I'll see you in a few minutes. I need to talk to the guys again," I tell her.

"Ugh, didn't you already talk to them? You're supposed to be with me tonight, not anyone else! How do you think it makes me look when my boyfriend is all over the place without me by his side?"

"I don't care what it looks like because you are not my girlfriend. We've established the fact that I don't do girl-friends. You're the one who still wants to stay and be my fuckbuddy," I say, arching a brow at her.

"Whatever, find me when you're done," she says, walking off to find her friends while I make my way to the den.

You might think I'm an asshole... well, I am, but they all know the score before they jump into my bed. The only reason I've kept her around for so long is because it's easy, and I don't want to be with anyone who thinks they'll be the one to change my bachelor status.

"What are you planning on doing with her?" Gray asks as soon as I enter the room. I know who he's asking about without him having to say her name.

"Have some fun with her and break her, of course."

"And you're sure this is what you want? What if she wasn't actually cheating on you?"

"Really, Gray? You're telling me my own eyes saw differ-ently?" I deadpan.

"I just want to make sure you don't do anything that you'll regret later in life," he says.

My reply is interrupted when we hear a commotion

outside and I walk to the door, opening it slightly just as the unmistakable voice of Winter reaches my ears.

"Yeah, okay, trust me, I wouldn't want to be anywhere next to him at all, 'cause I might catch a disease or something from just being next to him or any of the guys really... but you do you, sweety," she says in a voice dipped in sugar.

"What the hell are you even implying? Mason is clean!" I hear the second unmistakable voice that is Amber's.

From here it sounds like Winter is snickering, and I pull the door fully open this time before stepping out into the hallway with the guys all following. When she sees us, she lets out a groan.

"Aww, were you talking about us, Winter?" Nate asks.

She doesn't answer, but I see her taking us in. She's now seeing us without our masks on.

When she finally gets to me, her expression changes. I know she can see just how pissed I am.

"Way to pick 'em King," she says as she tries to walk past me. Not one for leaving things unfinished, I grab her by the arm, stopping her movements.

"I'm not playing games, Winter. Leave before things get worse for you."

"Mason, baby!" Amber cuts in, probably wondering what I'm doing with Winter, but I don't give a shit. My attention is focused on the girl in front of me.

"So you've said... better go give your cum bucket some attention," she says before she yanks her arm out of my grasp and walks away.

I let her go. I know I'll have more time to deal with her in the coming days.

"Don't say that I didn't warn you. I'll make sure I destroy everything you love and hold dear to you," I call out to her. I know she hears me with the way her body stiffens for a second.

"Give it your best shot, *baby*" she calls out over her shoulders before she disappears.

"Geez, I don't know if that was actually hate or just some really hot sexual tension," Royce pipes in as soon as she is gone.

"Yeah, my dick got hard just watching that interaction," Beck says. I flip them both off.

"Assholes," I mutter under my breath while they all just chuckle.

Amber chooses that moment to sidle up to me.

"Let's go back to the party," she says. I decide it's for the best, and we all make our way back into the ballroom.

ELEVEN

Winter

A FEW MINUTES LATER, I wipe my eyes. This is the last time I'm going to cry over that asshole. He doesn't deserve any more of my tears.

I get up, deciding to go back inside to use the bathroom and clean my face up. I probably have racoon eyes by now.

I walk around the house until I make it to the front and walk through the front doors. There's no way I was walking through the ballroom with tear stains on my face for the masses to talk about. Plus, it's easier to walk over to the bathroom from here without being seen.

I quickly step into the bathroom and thankfully my makeup is still in place. Damn, I need to ask the ladies what they used because the tears did nothing to this makeup.

I look at myself in the mirror and sigh as my mind goes back to what just took place in the garden. Mason's jab about something I did and then him turning it around so that it sounded like it was my fault he cheated is grating on my nerves. He cheated because he wanted to, not because of something I did.

Well, Mason-fucking-King can suck it because I'm not going anywhere. He'll just have to deal with seeing me around this place. I won't let his threats scare me because what's the worst that he can do?

Even with those thoughts, I'm not one hundred percent sure. I don't know Mason as the man he's become, and that's a bit concerning. I don't know what he's capable of, but then again he doesn't know what I'm capable of either.

The guys clearly have his back too, so I can't expect any help from them. Well, what do you know? Things just got a lot more complicated around here for me.

I feel lightheaded for a second and instantly get annoyed with myself. Now is not the time for a panic attack or my nerves to bother me. I already have enough to deal with. I need to go back to the table, grab my clutch, and get my ass home to take my medications.

It really is a good thing I didn't bother to get wasted tonight because who knows what would have happened in that confrontation if I was drunk. Plus now that I actually need my meds, it's a good thing.

Life is about to change drastically again. I know it. In the coming days I'll have Mason and his vendetta against me to deal with, my mother and whoever her mystery man is to deal with, and then the company and the people to deal with. *Ugh, kill me now!*

I wash my hands and open the door to walk out and head back into the ballroom to get my clutch. I don't make it more than two steps before I bump into someone.

"Shit! Excuse me. I'm so sorry, I wasn't looking at where I was going," I say to the blonde bombshell standing in front of me.

"Next time watch it, bitch!" She sneers at me in response.

I'm taken aback for a moment because I have no clue who this girl is for her to be so hostile toward me. Great! My first day interacting with people and it's already with a psycho and now a bitch.

"Excuse me?"

"You're excused, bitch! Let me just make something clear to you now. Mason is mine, so you'd do well to stay away from him!" she spits out. Damn, so much hate inside of her too. They definitely look like they deserve each other.

"That's totally fine! It's not like I want that asshole and from the looks of things, you two definitely look like you deserve each other," I say to her.

"Of course, we do! But don't think I didn't see him coming out of the garden and then you coming out a few minutes later after all the guys. Just stay away from my man! You've been here for less than a week and you're already whoring yourself out to the guys," she says venomously.

Wow! She clearly did not catch that dig at her just now. Damn, is that jealousy I detect in her voice? She clearly does not know what's going on.

"Yeah, okay, trust me, I wouldn't want to be anywhere next to him at all, 'cause I might catch a disease or something from just being near him or any of the guys really... but you do, you, sweety," I say in a voice dipped in sugar.

"What the hell are you even implying? Mason is clean!"

I can't help the snicker that escapes me because she really is dumb. I move to walk away at the same time one of the doors from up ahead opens and Mason walks out of the room followed by the four stooges. I let out a groan. I've already had my quota of assholes for tonight.

"Aww, were you talking about us, Winter?" Nates asks. They've all taken off their masks now. They look the same as they did all those years ago, but these are men now and I'm so out of my depth with them.

Judging from the furious expression on Mason's face, he

heard everything I just said and even though I tried to hold it back, a laugh still escapes me.

"Way to pick 'em, King," I say, laughing as I walk past him. He grabs my arm halting my movements further.

"I'm not playing games, Winter. Leave before things get worse for you."

"Mason, baby!" I hear his supposed whatever she is whining from behind where I left her.

"So you've said. Better go give your cum bucket some attention," I say, yanking my arm out of his grasp and walking away.

"Don't say that I didn't warn you. I'll make sure that I destroy everything you love and hold dear to you," I hear him call out after me.

I turn back around and walk back toward him. "Give it your best shot *baby*," I mock.

With that, I walk away for real this time. Deciding it's time to leave this stupid party and this stupid house, I walk into the ballroom intending to grab my stuff and leave with or without my mother.

There wasn't even anything going on that honored my father, or if there was, I missed it. That's highly unlikely, which means my mother brought me here to intentionally hurt me. *What a bitch!*

As soon as I reach the doors, I see my best friends and walk up to them.

"Where have you been? We've been looking everywhere for you!" Riley says as soon as I get close to them.

"I'm sorry, but I'm about to leave. I have a headache right now."

"What happened?" Luna asks as I heave out a sigh. I was supposed to hang out with the girls tonight, but now I'm not even in the mood to stay here.

"Mason happened."

"What did douchebag do?" Avery asks.

"I don't want to talk about it right now. I need to leave but I'll fill you guys in tomorrow, okay?" They all agree and I move to go to the table and grab my clutch. I open it to get my phone, but when I look inside, it's not there. I think back and then realize that I left it on the balcony.

"I need to get my phone first, I think I left it outside on the balcony."

"Come over tomorrow and we'll have a girls' day," Riley says as I walk away telling them I'll be there.

"Winter, darling! Hold on for a second, I have someone for you to meet." I hear the unmistakable sound of my mother when I'm about halfway across the room. I rub my fingers across my temple, hoping it will take the pain away. *What now?*

I'm standing off to the side of the room when I see her walking up to me. The first thing I notice is the man standing next to her, he has his arm on the small of her back as they walk closer.

He looks familiar, but I can't quite place him. They definitely look like they're familiar with each other and I don't know how to feel right now. Is this the mystery man she was with earlier tonight?

They both have discarded their masks as well. When I look up at him, I can tell that he's older than her, but not by much. Well, at least she's not a cougar... or she could be? I have no idea because I have no clue what she does in her spare time.

I plaster a neutral expression on my face as he looks me up and down with a glint in his eye that instantly has me feeling uncomfortable. If I had to guess what that glint meant, I'd say it looks like hate, but that's ridiculous because this man doesn't know a thing about me to have any kind of feelings toward me.

What is with the people in this town? Except for my best friends, basically everyone I've come into contact with tonight has shown some kind of hatred toward me, and I'm getting tired of it already.

"Winter, I'm sure you remember Mr. King, don't you?" she asks with a smirk. Well, that explains why he looks like he hates me. Maybe he knew about Mason and I and he hates me because of whatever fabricated lie Mason told him about me.

I don't even know why the two of them look like best friends right now. I thought we were supposed to hate each other, yada yada yada... though the Kings have the hate part down to a T. I'm so confused right now and the two of them are throwing me for a loop.

"Um yeah, hello, Mr. King, it's nice to finally meet you?" That sounded like a question even to my own ears, but I squash down the nerves. I'll be polite until I know what the hell is going on. Might as well try my hand at being fake like my mother.

Even though Mason and I were a thing for almost four years, I've never actually met his father before. I never even saw him at the parties we went to when we were younger because we were always hiding away. This is the first time I'm seeing the man in the flesh.

Mr. King however does not care about acting nice or whether I see what he's really thinking or not. His expression right now and the way he's looking at me sends unwanted shivers coursing down my spine. I have a feeling that just like his son, he's not a fan of mine. Not that I'm a fan of his at the moment, but appearances, right?

The saying *always trust your gut* is running across my brain right now. He has bad news written all over him.

"I wish I could say the same," he says with a smile on his face like he didn't just insult me. My mother just smiles like she won the lottery or something. I should care about what he just said, but I can't find it in me at this moment. I have a whole heap of other things to worry about right now.

"Ha, I should have expected a response like that since you're hanging out with my mother. After all, I can't say her company wouldn't make anyone's personality a nasty one," I say smiling sweetly at both of them. His expression has changed to one of open hostility.

"It's such a tragedy what happened to your father, isn't it?" he asks with a slight smirk in his tone which causes me to narrow my eyes and advance on him.

"Listen here, asshole! Don't you dare talk—" I'm cut off when I feel an arm wrap around my shoulder. When I look up, I see that it's Grayson.

"I'll just get this one out of the way," he says to his father before pulling me along with him onto the dance floor.

"What the hell was that, asshole? I don't need your help! I had it handled," I say with fury in my voice. How dare this asshole act like a friend right now when he was supporting his brother's actions earlier.

"Stay away from my father. He's bad news and you have no idea what he's capable of. If I were you, I probably wouldn't make any threats toward him," he says while dancing with me.

"I don't care. No one gets to talk about my father like that!" I say to him in a pissed off voice. I'm even more annoyed than before.

"I don't know what Mason has planned for you, but be careful Winter," he says so sincerely that I believe him.

"I'm a big girl, I can take care of myself," I tell him.

"Why'd you do it? I thought you two were like soul-mates. Why would you hurt him like that?"

"Do what? I don't know what you heard, but I didn't do anything! Why does everyone keep accusing me of being the one to hurt Mase when it was the other way around!"

"We had proof, babe."

"Proof of what? You know what? Fuck you too, Gray! I thought if there was anyone who believed me then it would be you. You knew how much I loved that asshole!"

"He was there, Win. He saw what you did firsthand." Every time I try to think about what it is Mason could have seen I come up blank. I don't know if it had something to do with that party where I was drugged. My mind is still a blank even after all this time.

Though he wasn't in London at the time so I'm still unsure of what he saw and when he saw it.

"No! You don't get to call me that after not sticking up for me. I thought we were friends Gray, but it seems like all of that was just a lie. What did he see? Because he's been alluding to the fact that I cheated on him when you fucking know I never would have done something like that. If he didn't want to be with me anymore then he could have not been a coward and been straight up with me."

I wrench myself out of his arms. I just can't deal with this and him anymore. My quota for people tonight has officially been reached. As soon as I turn around to get away from him, my face collides into a hard chest. I let out a long groan.

I don't even have to look to know who it is. He smells

the same, like sex, destruction and poor decisions. Mason grabs my hand and pulls me in closer to him while he dances with me. I hate how my body responds to his proximity. I know I should hate him after what he did to me, but right now I just push the thought away and concentrate on how his hands feel on me. *Stupid, I know! You don't have to tell me. I'll be the first one to admit that shit.*

"Are you going to leave?" he whispers in my ear.

"I can't and even if I could, I wouldn't leave just because you said so," I retort.

"Suit yourself." As he speaks, his hand tightens around my waist to the point of pain. I see his girlfriend looking at us from the side of the room. If looks could kill, I'd be dead on the spot by now. He spins us around.

"What the hell happened to you?" I ask, genuinely wanting to know after he spins us back in place.

"You happened," he whispers, bringing his hand up to my throat. To anyone looking at us, it might look like a simple caress but it's not. He's squeezing and slowly cutting off my air supply. "If you weren't such a whore, then I wouldn't be like this."

"I don't know what you're talking about! I have been faithful to you for the entire time that we were together, so don't bring your bullshit to me. You were the one who couldn't keep it in your fucking pants! And last time I checked, fucking other people when you're single doesn't classify you as a whore," I seethe at him.

"How many assholes have you fucked, Winter?" he asks through clenched teeth. He might act like he doesn't care, but I can tell he's pissed.

"Wouldn't you like to know? Did you think after you were in bed with someone else, I'd be waiting around for you? You hate me, right? Why does it matter how many people I've let fuck me and fill me with pleasure?" I ask.

"You really are a fucking whore," he spits out. I just shrug, not confirming nor denying because whatever he thinks doesn't matter, anyway.

"Takes one to know one, asshole! I don't care what lies you have to tell yourself just so you won't feel guilty for being a two-timing prick!" I scream so loud it takes a second to realize that everyone has stopped what they were doing and their attention is focused solely on us.

Fuck!

I let my anger get the better of me and lashed out. Now everyone is getting a front-row seat to this train wreck and judging from the smile on his face, this is exactly what he wanted. I can already hear the cameras clicking. That's when I realize that I need to get out of here as soon as possible.

"I don't even care anymore. Believe what you want because I'm done trying to prove myself to someone who doesn't give a fuck!" I spit at him before storming off.

Everyone continues staring as I walk out of the ballroom and make my way outside. As soon as I reach the front, I see Martin standing off to the side. When he sees me rushing toward him, he walks over to the car. Once I get inside the car, I tell him to take me home.

I'm tired of tonight and I'm tired of this place already. As soon as I get home, I walk into what was once my dad's office and grab a bottle of his whiskey before drinking it straight from the bottle. I need something strong right now.

I can't believe that Mason's still going on about me cheating on him when I never would have. I had stupidly thought that he was the one.

I've downed four shots of whiskey by the time I hear my

mother storming into the house and yelling my name. Fuck! She sounds pissed. How the hell did she get home so fast? I thought for sure she'd spend a few more hours at the party. I get up out of the chair, intent on going up to my room when she storms into the office.

"How fucking dare you embarrass me tonight!" she screams at me.

"I did nothing. That asshole started it!" I answer her in a cool voice, or at least I try to, but even I can hear that my words are slurred a little.

"You disrespected Alister and his sons in their own home. Can you imagine how that makes me look in front of everyone?" she screams at me.

"Relax, you'll be fine. You could probably stand to lose a few friends," I tell her. She slaps me in the face. I stagger backward and bump into the desk while she advances on me.

"How many times do I need to remind you I can fuck up your life if you don't start fucking listening to me!" she screams. Geez, I don't know why she has to keep screaming, that shit is annoying as hell.

"He was the one pushing my buttons all night! What the hell was I supposed to do?" I scream at her, exasperated at always being blamed for shit.

"You're supposed to act like you have some fucking class, you bitch! I swear to God, if you continue testing me, I will make your life a living hell!"

I chuckle because Lord knows it already feels like I'm living in hell every fucking day of my life since my dad died and left me here to deal with her shit.

"You should not be talking about class right now when you were the one cheating on her husband!" Her eyes narrow on me. "Oh yeah, I know all about that. Trust me, it's already a living hell with you existing as a selfish person who only cares about herself!" I spit out at her.

When she moves closer to slap me again, I'm ready for her. It must be the liquid courage that has me fighting back. She's never raised her hand on me before except for the day we got back here, and I've never done the same. I have a feeling that if I let her, she'll want to continue, and that shit will not fly especially when I have the world at my fingertips. I don't need her but she needs me. I catch her hand and hold it in my own.

"Don't get any ideas. I will not let you take out whatever misguided anger you have on me! Don't you ever touch me again because it will not end well for you. You think you're the only one who can dish out threats?"

"Oh, you're going to be in for it soon enough!" she yells.

"Bring it! I don't need you, however you need me. If you keep annoying the fuck out of me, I'll find a way around giving you any money! Let's face it, your threats about destroying the company are only threats. If you do anything, then you won't be getting free money anymore!"

"I fucking hate you, you ungrateful bitch!"

"Yeah, well, the feeling is mutual, Mother Dearest. I'm not ungrateful, you've just never been the one to give me anything to be grateful for. I might live here with you because you're blackmailing me into staying, but don't test me! I have the best lawyers in the country at my fingertips and I won't hesitate to use them!" I tell her before storming out of the office and leaving her there.

I realize that if I want to make it as the CEO then I need to act like one and not let her walk all over me. It felt absolutely amazing standing up for myself. I'll keep living with her for now to keep the peace, but that doesn't mean I'll let her use me as her punching bag.

I have more to worry about than her. One way or another, I need to let her know that I'm not playing when it comes to how serious I am about keeping my father's legacy alive.

I slowly make my way up to my room and into the bathroom. As soon as I walk into the bathroom, I take off my dress. Once it's off, I go to stand in front of the mirror and look at my face.

I stand there for a while, staring at my reflection as tears stream down my face. Tonight has just been too much, and it was only my first day in public. I fucking hate her so much and wish that she was the one who died instead of my father. At least my father cared, where she's nasty toward me.

I'm only crying because I'm not normally a confrontational person. I wish it didn't have to come to this, but it seems like she doesn't care if we end up destroying each other as long as she gets what she wants.

For the millionth time I wish she were a caring mother who supported me and wanted to see me succeed in taking this company to greater heights instead of trying to drag me down and seeing me fail.

I continue staring at my reflection until I hate what I see. When it gets too much, I walk into the shower and quickly rinse off my skin.

Once I'm done, I walk back into my room and pull on my pjs before crawling into bed. I just want to sleep and forget this entire day existed. It's not long before I fall into a restless sleep.

THE NEXT MORNING is when the actual nightmare begins. When I wake up and head downstairs, I'm glad to find that my mom isn't here.

I'm glad I don't have to face her this early in the day. I hope she stays where she is all day. When I walk into the kitchen, I see that there is an envelope with my name scrawled across it with serial killer letters and I'm a little freaked out.

I'm seriously going to punch that douchebag in the nuts if this is his idea of another one of his jokes.

I grab the envelope and open it, throwing the contents on the counter and freeze.

I lift the pictures one by one. The more I flip through them, the worse it gets. There are pictures of me at the party dancing with Grayson, sitting at my table last night, followed by ones with us all in the garden. Shots of Mason with his hands wrapped around my neck, though those pictures have an X across his face.

The next one is of me dancing with Grayson, followed by Mason. Those pictures place close emphasis on Mason's hand on my body.

The most unsettling of them all are the ones of me changing in my room last night after I got home. Holy shit!

After the last picture there is a note...

Why are you letting him touch you like that when it's no secret he hates you?

You're mine to play with, baby.

And the best part of this is, you'll never see me coming until it's too late.

I'm looking forward to playing with you, baby.

If I see you with him again, somebody is going to pay...

. . .

AFTER SEEING the note and pictures, fear and anxiety washes over me making it too much to deal with at the moment. I give Riley a call and let her know that I'm canceling, and I'll go over to her house tomorrow instead. Surprisingly, she agrees which I'm thankful for.

TWELVE

Mason

WE'RE SITTING at our table when I notice my dad and Winter's mother stopping her before they go into conversation.

She looks like she'd rather be anywhere else while my father is looking at her with pure hatred.

He hated her father and I'm not sure if he hates her by default or what, but some emotion is definitely there.

My father has been weird ever since Mom died. I've never dug too deep into his behavior before.

He looks awfully close to Winter's mother, too close for my liking. That doesn't even make sense. Why would he be chummy with her mother but hate her?

Since Mom's death, my brother and I drifted further away from my father. We're not as close as we were before. He still takes care of us, but that is it. We don't do the heart-to-heart, not that we ever did, but you get the point.

I don't know what's going on but suddenly things look heated between the three of them. My father is not one to mess with and he's a scary motherfucker when he wants to be and judging from his expression, he is about two seconds away from putting her in her place.

Leave it Grayson to play the hero. If she runs her mouth too much there's no telling what could happen. He pulls her onto the dance floor and now they look like they're having a heated conversation. As the minutes go by, I can tell from her expression that she's getting angrier by the second and I'm loving every moment of it.

Deciding that it's my turn to toy with her a little, I get up and walk over to them. My brother notices me coming and gives me a slight shake of his head before smirking, all the while carrying on his conversation with her.

I'm standing behind her when she wrenches herself out of Grayson's arms, spinning around to leave, but she crashes right into my chest.

When she started talking to my father and her mother, I noticed the few photographers we let in tonight we're taking pictures of them.

I'm sure they're all wondering why the three of them were having a conversation. No one knows what is happening with Crowne Enterprises yet, though I'm sure my father already does.

I can use this to my advantage. I know Winter hates me as much as I hate her, so it won't be too difficult to get a rise out of her, especially with the paparazzi around to take pictures.

I pull her closer to me and wrap my arms around her waist tightly so she can't get away.

"Are you going to leave?" I whisper into her ear, and she stiffens in my arms.

"I can't and even if I could, I wouldn't leave just because you said so," she says with a defiant tone in her voice.

"Suit yourself. I can't wait to destroy you, and I'll start by destroying everything you love," I say as I tighten my hand around her waist.

She looks at something behind me and her face screws up. When I spin her around, I see what she was looking at. I see Amber looking at us with a deadly expression on her face.

I don't care about her and never have, and I've made that abundantly clear too many times to count. So, she can be mad all she wants. She's just someone who warms my bed on the nights when I don't want to go out.

"What the hell happened to you?" she asks when I spin her back into the position we were in before.

"You happened!" I say as I lean down to whisper in her ear while bringing my hand up to her throat. To outsiders, this would probably look like a caress, but she knows exactly what this is. I squeeze until I know I'm cutting off her air supply. "If you weren't such a whore, then I wouldn't have turned into this," I spit at her.

It's true because if it weren't for her actions then I wouldn't have turned into such an unfeeling bastard whose only intention is to destroy her.

I look up behind her and see the paparazzi are paying more and more attention to us because according to history, we're supposed to hate each other.

God do we ever, but it's for different reasons than what they think. They think it's because of our companies and the long-standing rivalry. If only they knew. My last statement seems to be the one to have gotten to her, and she basically blows a gasket.

"I have no idea what you're talking about! I have been faithful to you for the entire time that we were together, so don't bring your bullshit to me. You were the one who couldn't keep it in your fucking pants! Last time I checked, fucking other people when you're single doesn't classify you as a whore," she practically seethes at me.

"How many assholes have you fucked, Winter?" I ask through clenched teeth. I don't even know why the fuck I'm pissed when I shouldn't care. I despise this woman, so who and how many assholes she's fucked shouldn't bother me one bit.

"Wouldn't you like to know? Did you think after you were in bed with someone else, I'd be waiting around for you? You hate me, right? Why does it matter how many people I've let fuck me and fill me with pleasure?" she spits at me.

"You really are a fucking whore." I say this last part loud enough that I'm sure people heard.

"Takes one to know one, asshole! I don't care anymore what lies you have to tell yourself just so you won't feel guilty for being a two-timing prick!" She screams so loud it's like all she's seeing is the rage I'm invoking in her.

I smirk at her because this is exactly where I want her. It takes a second for her to realize that everyone has stopped what they are doing and all their attention is focused on us. Her eyes widen, finally realizing what she's just done.

"I don't even care anymore. Believe what you want because I'm done trying to prove myself to someone who doesn't even give a fuck!" she spits at me, making sure she has the last word.

She might think she won this battle between us, but I'm intent on winning the war. That's what it is after all, a war between us and there can only be one victor.

I'm just getting started with her and she'll wish she never crossed this devil. I will do everything in my power to make her life a living hell and I'll be as brutal as I can since she deserves nothing less.

After she leaves, I motion for the photographer to follow me and we head into the den again.

"Did you get some good shots?"

"Sure did," the slimeball replies.

"Good, make sure you run it tomorrow."

"Absolutely, Mr. King," he says, and I give him his payment.

I knew provoking Winter all night that she'd eventually blow. What can I say, I know my girl. Well, not my girl because what the fuck? She's not mine anymore and I hate her.

Setting her up tonight was fun. She'll definitely be front page news tomorrow.

THIRTEEN

Winter

It's late when I wake up on Sunday morning and discover I have a bit of a hangover from drinking all that whiskey last night.

I spent all day yesterday in a daze after getting those pictures and by the time last night rolled around, I needed a stiff drink to get my mind to stop focusing on that. It has to be another one of Mason's pranks to get me to leave Ravenwood.

But what if it isn't? What if this is an actual threat? What do I do then? Gahh, I'm making myself worry again for what I'm sure is nothing.

I groan, feeling like shit because I'm never this stupid with my health but last night was the exception, apparently. I'm never mixing alcohol with my medications ever again if this is the feeling I get after. The feeling is like death warmed over.

As soon as I'm fully awake, I head straight for the shower to brush my teeth and get dressed to head over to Riley's.

If I didn't think she'd kill me for not showing up again, then I wouldn't because I feel so tired and out of it. I can't tell anyone what is happening yet because hopefully it's nothing. It could be my mom or Mason who sent those, playing games.

So, I won't freak my friends out until I have proof.

I know everything that happened Friday night was just a taste of what's coming because Mason does nothing half-assed. He is as meticulous as ever and I'm not sure that bodes well for me.

Once I'm done showering and getting dressed, I walk over to where my clutch from last night is on the night-stand to look for my phone.

When I don't find my phone, I realize that I never had the chance to go look for it Friday night like I planned. I was interrupted by my mom and Mr. King, Grayson, and then Mason.

Yesterday I was too freaked out to even bother with my phone or anything else. I spent the entire day in bed feeling too drained.

It's a good thing I didn't keep any important informa-tion on my phone. It's just my social media accounts, though I guess if someone got a hold of my phone, they could probably do some damage with that if they wanted to.

I doubt I'm going to ever see it again, so I'll just have to get a new one tomorrow. I'll have to let Chase get me one.

Once I'm done, I walk out of my room and head down-stairs to grab a quick bite to eat before I head over to Riley's. I'm surprised to find the house quiet. My mother is prob-ably not home right now. I wonder where the hell she goes every day. She's probably with her new man, which reminds me, I still need to find out who that is.

I swear if she weren't my mother, I'd deck her ass. I'm not usually one for confrontations but she's pushing her luck. I get she's angry, but I can't wrap my head around why. If I were in her position, I'd be happy my child claimed what is rightfully their birthright, not be angry about it.

"Good afternoon, may I get you something to eat, Miss?" one of the kitchen staff asks as soon as I step into the kitchen.

"Umm, good afternoon, just a coffee and a muffin please," I say as I take a seat by the kitchen island to wait.

My thoughts go to my mother again and I wish I could one hundred percent call her on her bluff, but she's an unpredictable psycho. She would do what she's threatening to do by going to the media and giving them incorrect information that would cause a shitstorm.

I don't even know why I'm still putting up with her and her ridiculous demands, especially living here with her when I could very well get my own place. Maybe I have some underlying mommy issues I'm not aware of.

Even though an actual investigation would show that she's wrong about any embezzlement claims, the damage would still be done, and it would cause problems I don't need right now.

We all know that those sites never check their facts before they publish their articles. All they really care about is their clicks and any headline with the words embezzlement and Crowne Enterprises would definitely be clickbait.

I need to remember why I'm doing this and putting up with her. It's all because my father believed in me and I want to make him proud.

"Here's your food, Miss," the woman says.

"Thank you, and please call me Winter," I tell her. She nods her head before she walks off to do whatever it is she needs to do.

My thoughts go back to my father and the words he

often told me to remember. *A Crowne never bows and never breaks just because her crown is tilted.*

My thoughts then go back to Mason. It appears since I've stepped foot back into the United States, two people and the upcoming events have been on repeat in my head, on a loop that I can't seem to stop.

It usually goes from my mother to Mason and then to how the hell I'm going to contribute toward the company.

I know nothing... I don't even have my MBA yet, so what the hell am I doing? Friday night none of them even thought to ask me questions regarding the future of the company. They all focused on my mother and she ate that up while smirking at me the entire time as if to say *yeah, none of these people will ever take you seriously.*

I'm glad that no one bothered me too much because I was already feeling out of sorts. I'll just have to make them take me seriously once I'm working there.

Thinking about Friday night again brings on more thoughts of Mason. Not going to lie, his appearance shook me up even more than I already was, especially with his hate-filled stares and words. I could feel the unsuppressed rage coming off him in waves.

I have a feeling that wasn't the last I've seen of him and I'm not sure what he's planning or what his game really is, but I have a feeling it won't be good. Something tells me that man does not make threats lightly.

I hope that I'm strong enough to weather his storm. I have a feeling that we're going to crash until we burn and only one of us will come out of whatever this is unscathed. I just hope that I'm the one who survives. I'm not going down without a fight.

I may have loved the guy before, but that doesn't mean I'll let him do whatever he wants to me without fighting back. It sounds like he wants a war. If that's what he wants, then I'll make sure I give it to him.

Once I'm done eating my muffin and drinking my coffee, I walk out of the kitchen and out the doors, getting into my car to drive over to Riley's. It's about a fifteen-minute drive. As I park in her driveway, I let out a groan when I see there's already a few cars parked in front of the house.

Great! It looks like we're having a get-together just like old times—one I don't want might I add. I let out a snort because this will in no way be like old times since we're all on opposing sides of the fence.

Nothing about said cars lets me know which one belongs to who. All of them are flashy and expensive, though I wouldn't expect anything less from the guys. I might not know them that well anymore, but some things never change. The fact is, they're all rich assholes who love to show off, and it's always been that way for them. That thought causes a smile to spread across my face. It brings back some wonderful memories.

Back in high school we were known as the Ravenwood elites because of our status and the fact that we were always together. We never let anyone else into our group. The guys basically ruled the school because they were hot and always got into shit.

No one messed with them, and we were there along for the ride. Many of the girls in school were jealous because we got to hang with the guys and yeah, that was a wild time in my life. People can get creative when they're jealous.

I'd bet my life it hasn't changed much for the guys over the years, and they are probably still seen as the elites. They're all hot now—hotter than they were in high school

—and I'm sure they still get lots of attention wherever they go.

I just wish things could have remained the same between us. Wishful thinking after everything that went down, but a girl can dream.

I'm hoping none of the cars belong to douchebag. I don't want to be in another battle with him since the last one between us still has me tied up in knots.

I'm already tired of always having to keep my guard up around people. I don't need to see his ugly mug today, especially when I'm still not feeling my best.

With him, I'll constantly have to keep on my toes and already having to do it with my mother is exhausting. Adding more people to the mix is just a disaster waiting to happen. Mason is the type of person to strike and use your weaknesses against you when you least expect it.

I know he won't stop until he destroys me for whatever it is he thinks I did. The joke is on him, I'll always fight back. I will not let him blame me for something he did.

I get out of my car and walk up to the front door. I ring the bell and stand there, waiting for someone to come open it. I take in my surroundings; I haven't been here in ages and it brings back so many memories. Memories of when I was having the time of my life, not knowing that the future would bring nothing but disaster for us.

A few minutes later a shirtless Beck opens the door and man is he ripped. If I hadn't dated Mason before I'd totally shoot my shot. Who am I kidding? I've never gotten that vibe with him and also my best friend is still crushing on him. I'd never go there.

Looking at him as he's looking at me, it's at that moment it really hits me that things have changed between all of us and it's because of the divide between Mason and me.

I don't know who my friends are as people anymore, especially the guys. They've clearly taken Mason's side and none of them ever asked me what happened between us. That can only mean one thing, they believe whatever he said happened.

"You like what you see, Win? Now that you're single, maybe we can have a go at it?" I know he's joking. He would never betray Mase like that.

"Eww, in your dreams, asshole! I wouldn't have a go at it even if you were the last dick on this earth and I was dying for some cum," I say smiling at him.

"You wound me, babe!" he says with an exaggerated pout and a hand across his chest like I truly injured him.

"You'll get over it! Where's Riles?" I ask as he moves aside to let me in.

"In her room with the other two annoying brats," he says while I just roll my eyes at him. He's been calling us brats for as long as I can remember, and it kind of stuck.

I make my way to the stairs to head up to Riley's room and I can hear the voices in the living room. One in particular washes over me. Fuck my life! Why the hell did he have to be here today of all days? I'd bet my left tit he knew we were going to be here today, and that's why he came, just so he could piss me off.

Once I reach the top of the stairs, I make a right where Riley's bedroom is. When I push the doors open, I see that the three of them sprawled across her bed.

"What the hell bitch? We've been waiting for ages and have been calling you for just as long!" Riley yells as soon as she sees me in the doorway.

"I'm sorry! I don't know where my phone is. I never found it Friday night," I tell them as a way of explanation.

"Get your ass over here!" Avery states, and I head over to the bed and drop onto it. We rearrange ourselves so that we're all comfortable and seeing each other's faces.

"Want to tell us what the hell is happening with you and Mason? Friday night was kind of intense," Luna says, starting what is definitely going to be a long gossip session.

"I honestly have no idea. He said some things that may or may not refer to me cheating on him, but I'm not one hundred percent sure of that. As if I would ever. You guys know right after I got out of the hospital, I flew straight here to see the asshole and he was already in bed with some skank."

"Yeah, but none of that explains what the hell happened the other night. I don't think I've ever seen Mason look at someone with that much hate in his eyes," Avery says next.

"He and the guys cornered me in the maze while I was in the garden. I'm assuming that was when you girls were looking for me. He wants me to leave Ravenwood, but you guys know I can't leave because of everything my dad wants me to do here. He also said if I didn't leave, he'd destroy me."

"What the fuck?" Luna yells. "And you waited until now to tell us?"

"Can't find my phone, remember! And yay! That's one thing I have to look forward to with my move back here," I say, trying to lighten the mood, but none of them are impressed.

"Do you think he'd honestly do anything to hurt you?" Avery asks.

"Honestly, I have no idea. It pains me to say this, but I

don't know who Mason is anymore. For all I know, he could be bluffing, or he could be dead serious."

"Did you at least punch him in the nuts when you were here last time?" Luna questions next.

"Ha, I wish! But no, we were too busy yelling at each other. Oh, and come to think of it, that was the first time he ever said if I came back here, he'd destroy me."

After that day, I never tried to contact him and he never tried either. We became two strangers. I pretended like I didn't know he existed, and he probably did the same. I still can't believe I was such an idiot to think that we would have a relationship that lasted.

"I'm so sorry, babe. I really thought that you two were like soulmates or something," Luna says from across the bed.

"It's fine... It's been two years already, so I'm over it," I tell them. My words sound like a lie, even to my own ears. I honestly wish that they were true because then life would be so much easier.

We spend the next two hours catching each other up on our lives and what's been happening with everyone. I also tell them about my upcoming dilemma on Monday and how my mom has basically been a nightmare since my dad's lawyer read the will to us.

The girls fill me in on everything that has been happening in their lives as well, and by the time we've bared our souls to each other, I feel much lighter than I've felt in a while. I love it—no matter how much time we spend apart—once we're together, it's like there was never any distance between us.

Having friends you can actually trust, who are always there for you, is an amazing feeling, and I'm thankful for them. Lord knows they've kept me from going off the ledge many times.

After we're done gossiping, we decide to sit by the pool since it's a nice day. We change into bathing suits that Riley always keeps here for us because you never know when you'll have an impromptu pool day when you're at her house.

After our bikinis are on, we grab some coverups before heading downstairs. We head into the kitchen to grab some snacks and make drinks for outside.

The peace doesn't last for long. One minute we're alone and the next all the guys are suddenly in the kitchen with us, including *him*. Ugh!

I don't pay them any mind while I continue making my drink. One minute, I'm mixing drinks, and the next, I'm airborne before landing over someone's shoulder.

"Graysonnnnn!" I scream out once I realize that he's the one who grabbed me. "Let me down, you big oaf!"

"Not until you tell me if we're good or not," he says in response, giving me a slap on the ass. I try to look up and then struggle more when I see that we're already outside and he's moving toward the pool.

"No! We're not!" I yell out. When I see that he's moving to drop me down into the pool, I screech. "Fineee! We're good as long as you're not a douchebag like your brother and you don't drop me into this pool!" I yell out to him, hoping he won't drop me in.

"Great! I'm glad we got that settled!" he says, sliding me down his body. We're standing almost at the edge of the pool and he's grinning down at me.

"You're lucky I love you," I say, looking up at him while giving him an eye roll. "But try it again and your balls won't like the outcome."

He chuckles at me, knowing I'm joking. I never could stay mad at him for long. I'm just about to move away from the pool and head back inside for my drink when a hand wraps around my throat a second before I'm shoved backward and straight into the pool.

I splutter, and water gets into my nose and throat. I'm sinking to the bottom. Fuck! This is what I get for not learning to swim. I try to swim to the surface but it's no freaking use because again, I can't fucking swim.

Just when I think I'm about to pass out from the lack of oxygen in my body, I feel hands wrap around my waist and someone pulls me up. Once we get to the surface, I splutter and cough out some of the water.

I see it's Gray who went in after me. Looking up, I see it was Mason who pushed me in.

"What the hell is your problem? Are you trying to fucking kill me?" I yell, feeling pissed off.

"Not yet, but maybe soon. You've only been in Gray's company for a minute and you're already rubbing yourself on him like the seasoned whore you are! What? Are you planning on fucking both brothers?"

Every word out of this asshole's mouth just makes me want to punch him in his pretty-boy face. Everyone is silent, watching our interaction.

"And what if I was? I don't see how any of that is your fucking business. I'm a free agent and can fuck whoever the hell I want. Besides, Gray is probably better than you in the sack, since you keep throwing out small-dick energy anytime I'm next to him. His must be bigger," I seethe. *Spoiler, he doesn't have a small dick, but he needs that ego to go down for sure.*

"It is my business when you're trying to fuck my brother with that loose cunt of yours. Lord knows we could probably double team you and your cunt would still be loose!" he spits harshly at me. I'm taken aback for a second. My cheeks heat with embarrassment. It fucking sucks being insulted like that in front of your friends. "And don't act like you don't already know what my dick looks like because it tore up that loose pussy of yours on too many occasions," he says smirking.

"Who the hell invited this ogre over?" I ask, directing my question to Riley because honestly, I can't think of a comeback for that asshole right now.

"Erm, blame Beck! He heard we were having a girls' day today and decided he needed to have a boys' day too," she says, looking as uncomfortable and pissed off as I am.

"Gee thanks, fuckface!" I spit at Beck while standing on the edge where Gray placed me to sit after he got me out of the pool.

"My pleasure, babe! I love watching you two deny that you still have feelings for each other," he says. I flip him off.

"This isn't funny, and that ship has fucking sailed. He could have fucking killed me!" I practically yell at him.

"Unfortunately, you wouldn't have died. Didn't Grayson save you? Always acting like a fucking victim," Mason chimes in.

"What the fuck ever, nobody asked you! And you know what, you're not even worth my time," I say before stomping my way inside to get changed into my clothes so I could leave.

I knew I should have left as soon as I saw Mason was here too. His actions were so predictable, and it proves that we can't be in the same space without going at each other's throats.

Once I get to Riley's room, I head straight to her shower and quickly rinse my skin off. As soon as I'm done, I step out. Just as the shower door closes behind me, I'm slammed back into it. My head collides with the door just as I feel a hand latch onto my throat, keeping me pinned in place.

"Real original, asshole," I say as I look up into stormy green eyes.

Eyes that have captivated me since before I knew what hormones were and how they affected you by making you stupid for the opposite sex. Mason is definitely sex on legs with dark hair and thick brows. He has a straight Roman nose and a jawline so straight it looks like it could be carved from stone. His lips are full and pink, so I can't help staring at them right now. "Do you see something you want?" he asks after catching me looking at his lips. Of fucking course, he noticed.

"Nahh! Been there, done that!" I say with a smile. I know it'll piss him off.

"Why the fuck are you still here?" he spits at me as he squeezes tighter before moving closer, so close, the entire front of his body is touching my still naked one.

Finally, remembering I'm still naked, a shiver runs through my body. Of course, the asshole caught that because he never misses anything.

He nuzzles my neck and inhales while dragging his nose down the length of my throat. "Mmm, you smell the same... like lies and deceit."

"Well then, maybe you should leave me alone," I mutter.

"Not quite yet, I made you a promise," he says.

"And what's that?" I ask, even though I already know where this is going.

"I'm going to break you bit by bit until you're nothing but pieces no one will want to pick up."

I push my body closer to him and rub my nakedness

against him. I'm surprised to find he's already as hard as a rock. Hmm, guess douchebag isn't as unaffected as he'd like me to believe.

"This doesn't feel like hate to me," I say seductively.

"Any cock would get hard for a whore that's rubbing up on him, but make no mistake, I fucking loathe you more than anything in the world," he says in a husky voice. He might hate me, but he's turned on and it looks like he still wants to fuck me.

"Ah, but you still want to fuck me, is that it? Is that why you followed me up here?"

"If I wanted to fuck you, then your legs would be spread already with my cock buried deep inside you."

"Uh-huh, keep telling yourself that. Do you want to get it out of your system or something and then we can pretend like the other doesn't exist?"

"Nah, I'll pass. I don't make it a habit of fucking whores. Just want you to know since you didn't listen to my warning, I'm going to enjoy taking away everything you love one by one," he says casually with no emotion. I wonder what the hell happened to him to turn him into someone so cold.

"Get the fuck out!" I snarl at him. He looks at me smiling with satisfaction because he got to me.

He pulls me closer to him before slamming me back into the glass. My head and back collide with it. I let out a grunt because it hurts. "With pleasure. I can't stand being in the presence of trash any longer."

He walks out of the bathroom leaving me standing there wondering what the hell just happened. If I thought I was coldhearted enough to play in the big leagues with Mason, then I was mistaken. I'm nowhere near that level of cold.

As much as I try not to let his words bother me, they cut

deep, especially when he calls me all those derogatory names. I can't believe we used to say 'I love you' to each other when nothing but hate spills out of our mouths now.

Taking another moment to compose myself, I walk back into Riley's room and quickly get changed back into my regular clothes. I already feel a headache coming on with how hard he slammed my head against the wall, plus I can already feel the signs of nausea coming on.

I've suffered with terrible anxiety for so long it's definitely made some changes to my body, and nausea in confrontations is just one of them.

I head out the door as soon as I'm done and leave without saying goodbye to anyone. I'm too drained from all the confrontations with Mason.

I head straight up to my room when I get home and take my medications before sliding under the covers where thoughts of my uncertain future plague me until I eventually fall asleep.

FOURTEEN

Winter

I LOOK at myself in the mirror for the millionth time this morning. I feel completely out of depth with myself given that I don't know who the girl is that's staring back at me.

She looks put together in a way I know the real me isn't. Right now, she looks different, and I'm not sure if that's a good thing or bad.

The woman looking back at me in the mirror is dressed for success and she looks like she's ready to take on anything and anyone who stands in her way.

The saying 'fake it 'til you make it' has never been more accurate before than in this moment right now.

I opted for a business dress that ends a little above my knees, and I have on a pair of black, red bottom heels. My hair is in a bun with some tendrils hanging loose. Light makeup and red lips complete my look for today. Outwardly, I look like I should be on the cover of some magazine while on the inside I'm nervous and on the verge of freaking out.

I mean, who wouldn't be nervous if they learned out of the blue that they were responsible for millions of people's lives, right?

Today is going to be the first day where I make an appearance at Crowne Enterprises. I have no clue how this

is going to go, but the determination to kick ass is prominent even if my brain is coming up with millions of reasons
why this is going to be a bad idea.

I've already emailed Chase about setting up a press
conference today, so I'll have that to look forward to in
addition to the other items on my list of things to do
today.

Getting rid of all my thoughts, I try to focus on the positive. Once I'm finished getting dressed, I grab my stuff and
walk down the stairs and into the kitchen to grab a cup of
coffee before I'm ready to leave.

It's only eight AM and I need to be there by nine, so I
have time. Not that it really matters what time I get there
since I'm the boss and all that, but setting an example on
punctuality is a good start, right?

When I step into the kitchen, I see that my mother is
already up and drinking her own coffee. She's still dressed
in her robe, which brings me to the assumption that she
woke up specially for me.

I really could have gone the whole day without seeing
her. It's just what every girl wants to see before her big day
—a mother who doesn't give a shit.

"You look fat in that dress," are the first words she says
to me when I'm grabbing my coffee. I get the sudden urge
to want to bash her head into the table or something. I
continue ignoring her because I know she's trying to get a
rise out of me.

This isn't the first time she's made stupid comments
about me, my weight, or even my appearance, if we're
being honest. She takes every opportunity she can to tear
me down, and for someone like me who suffers daily with
too many thoughts in my head, it's not a good place to be.

I'm probably a few meals away from having an eating

disorder, as well. I've tried to lose weight just because her words have gotten inside my head.

"Gee, thanks! You know just how to make a girl feel special. It's always so refreshing to hear your unwanted opinions of me, Mother," I say in a voice dripping with sarcasm.

"You know, your life would be so much easier if you just gave me control of the company. You could study without the distraction or the stress and your life would be so much easier."

I think back to the note that my father left me and shake my head. She still doesn't know about it, and I'm not about to tell her. It said to do everything in my power to not let that happen, and who am I to refuse my dead father's wishes?

"Sorry, but you already know that I can't. The instructions in the will were very precise and I can't do anything to change it," I say.

"Hmm, I'm sure if we really wanted to, we could find a way."

"I'm not changing my mind, Mother, and that's final."

I barely hear her mutter, *"That's what you think,"* before she says, "Break a leg or something today." She gets up and walks out of the kitchen while I stand staring at her retreating form.

Somehow, I know she doesn't mean that in the good luck sort of way. Coming out of my trance, I gulp the rest of my coffee and am about to wash my cup when the maid appears out of nowhere.

"I'll clean up, Miss," she tells me.

"Thank you, and like I said, just call me Winter. What's your name?"

"Mira," she says.

"Got it," I tell her. I hate the fact that I didn't even know her name before now, but I'll definitely attempt to get to know the people around me.

I get ready to leave. I really don't want to stay in the house any longer. My day feels like it's already heading toward disaster because of my mother's presence. I don't want to be in a shitty mood, especially when I'll be spending the entire day dealing with people.

I grab my stuff and once I make it out the front door, I see Martin is already waiting for me. Ahh, a man after my own heart! My brain functions in a way that chaos would ensue if I were late to something, and Martin is always ready whenever I am.

I can't help the flutters erupting in my stomach the closer I get to the car. I'm not sure if this is a bad omen or not, but the feelings won't go away. It's like my mind and body know that today will be a disaster.

"Good morning, Martin," I say beaming at him. He's one of the people in my life who I can always count on and for that I'm grateful because there aren't that many anymore.

I can't count on the guys anymore because they've taken sides and my girls are the only other people who actually care.

It's times like these when I wish I had a sibling, but from the way my mother treats me, I figure they dodged a bullet by not existing.

"Good morning, Miss Crowne, are you ready for your first day at the office?" he asks as he opens the car door for me.

"How many times do I need to tell you to call me Winter?" I ask, rolling my eyes at him. "I'm as ready as I'll ever be," I say in answer to his previous question. Martin is also one of the few people who is already privy to the 'me taking over as the boss' situation.

As we take off for the Crowne headquarters, I get lost in my thoughts again of everything that happened yesterday while I was over at Riley's. Since I didn't have my phone, the girls were the ones to show me the articles that were already up after that disastrous party on Friday night.

Looks Like the Kings and Crownes Still Hate Each Other.

Is This a Lovers' Quarrel?

Do Mason and Winter Hate Each Other? Or Do They Secretly Love Each Other?

If They Are Getting Cozy with Each Other, What Does This Mean for the Future of Their Empires?".

Those were just some of the headlines, and most of those stupid articles were full of pictures of me when I was yelling at Mason on the dance floor. *Yeah, that was not one of my finest moments.*

My least favorite was ***Love Triangle? Do Both Brothers Have a Crush on Miss Crowne? We Don't Think a Love Triangle Will End Well for These Three.***

They filled those articles with pictures of me and Gray when we were having a heated discussion while dancing, and of course next to that was a picture of Mason looking over at us with hate-filled eyes.

I know none of that hatred was directed toward his brother, it was all aimed at me. If Mason had to die for anyone in this world, it would be for his brother.

I had to get my PR company to take care of it and try to get as many articles as they could taken down. Ever since moving back to Ravenwood, I feel like there's been one issue after the other I've had to deal with and it's making me lose focus.

I'm just hoping that today doesn't suck and I can get through it in one piece. A few minutes later, Martin's voice pulls me out of my musings, letting me know that we're here.

"Thank you. I'm not sure what time I'll be done today, so I'll just call you when I'm ready," I tell him.

"No worries, Miss Crowne, enjoy your day. I know you'll kill it."

I nod to show that I heard him as I get out of the car. I'm glad that one of us is positive in my abilities today.

I walk through the lobby and head straight for the elevators. None of the security officers try to stop me. I'm guessing they already know who I am, which is a good thing because I'm not in the mood to deal with that.

Once I get to the twenty-fifth floor, I walk down to my office. I'm taking what used to be my father's office. No one has touched his office since he left for London, and the current acting CEO has a different office on this floor.

I drop my bag onto my desk and walk to stand behind it, looking out the window at the view. It's a stunning view of Ravenwood's business district.

A knock sounds on my door a few minutes later, pulling me out of my trance. I turn around just as a guy enters my office and shuts the door behind him.

"Good morning, Miss Crowne, I'm Chase, your executive assistant," he says in way of greeting.

"It's nice to finally meet you," I tell him. Based on first impressions, he seems nice, but I guess we'll have to see how that goes.

"It's nice to meet you too, Miss Crowne. I just wanted to let you know as per your request, Mr. Carson will not be meeting with you yet. He agreed to wait until your meeting with him later today."

I nod. "Do you have my schedule for today?"

"Mind if I come around your desk to show you how to work the system and pull everything up?" he asks.

"Nope, go right ahead," I say as I take a seat and then push it to the side to give him space to access my desk and computer.

"How long have you worked here?" I ask to pass the time and get to know him a little. I don't want to seem like an uptight bitch who doesn't care about her employees.

"Three years. I started as an intern when I was in my final year at Ravenwood U and after I finished, I was offered a permanent position here," he says.

"That's awesome! You must have impressed them during your time here. I can't wait to work with you," I say genuinely. His personality shines through like a beacon of light, and I've only just met the guy.

"Okay, so here is your schedule. It shows your monthly schedule since you have a lot of responsibilities to take care of. For today, you have your meeting with Mr. Carson so he can begin showing you the ropes. You have some papers that need looking over and then at two PM, you have the press conference you asked me to schedule. At four PM, you have a meeting with Mr. Antonio Bandini."

Damn, okay, that all sounds like a lot, but I need to do this. "Is that all?" I ask in a joking manner.

"Don't worry, I'm sure you'll have this down in no time," he says. "I'll leave you to get settled and get used to your system. Call if you need any help. Is there anything else I can get for you?"

"Some coffee and a new phone, please. I lost my old one."

"Got it! I'll get your phone and then I'll come back around one thirty to get you for the press conference," he says before walking out of my office and closing the door behind him.

I take a minute to let out a breath before going onto my computer and checking out the programs and what does what to see if I can understand anything at all.

A few minutes later, Chase walks back into my office with my coffee before leaving again to get my phone.

The programs that the company uses are not so bad, and I get acquainted with the basics of things quickly. After that, I spent the next hour going over some reports that needed my immediate attention due to the fact some paperwork had to be put on hold after my father's death. I'm getting more accomplished than I expected, so I'm taking this as a win.

"Ah, you're a godsend!" I say when Chase comes back in with my new phone.

"Don't forget you have to meet with Mr. Carson in an hour," he says, and I nod my head. He takes that as his cue to leave and walks out of my office since I don't need any additional help right now.

I look over at the clock and see that it's already eleven. Okay, so I have an hour before my meeting and all the other meetings for today before I can call it quits.

I set up my new phone and then text the girls.

ME: Hey bitches! I finally got my new phone.

Riley: Who is this?

Avery: Yeah... we don't know who this is...

Luna: OMG, how did you get our numbers? O.O

Me: I fucking hate you bitches sometimes, you know that!

Avery: LOL, don't lie! You know you fucking love us!

Riley: You wouldn't know what to do with yourself without us!

Luna: Agreed! :p

Riley: How's your first day going so far?

Luna: Give us the details, bitch!

Avery: What she said!

Me: It's actually not so bad! I've been reading through some reports and I have a few meetings later. Also, the press conference is at two... so don't forget to watch. LOL

Riley: Wouldn't miss that for the world!

Avery: Me neither! We all know how much you hate being in the spotlight, so this should be fun. LOL.

Luna: What they said! But we'll be watching and trying not to laugh :D

Me: Ugh, I hate you guys. LOL. It's like you bitches enjoy my pain or something!

Sᴏᴍᴇʜᴏᴡ, the hour flies by while I've been talking to the girls and before I know it, Chase is sticking his head through my door telling me it's time for the meeting.

I tell the girls I need to go before getting up off my chair and walking over to where he's standing.

"Are you standing in on this meeting?"

"Yes. As your EA, I'm usually in all the meetings with you to take notes in case you need them later," he says.

That makes sense and is convenient because Lord knows I'm forgetful sometimes. Once we get to Mr. Carson's office, I knock before we enter.

"Winter, my dear, it's so good to see you again and see you doing well," he says as soon as we enter. All I can think is that jokes on him. I'm not even close to doing well, but I give him a smile in return.

"Thanks," I say. "So, are you ready for me to annoy you in all our future meetings while you're showing me what I need to know?" I ask jokingly.

He's been close friends with my father for years, so I know I can trust him with getting me ready for my takeover. He's also like another father figure to me, so I know he won't be some stuck-up tool.

"Yes, I'm ready and not to worry, I know you're a brilliant young woman and you'll get this in no time. As for your annoying quality, I've had years to get used to it," he says chuckling.

"Ha ha, so funny!"

"I thought so. See my game is still good." This time I'm the one rolling my eyes. "I believe you'll be able to take this company to greater heights."

I feel like crying because it feels good to have someone else besides your friends believe in you. With that, we get down to work with him explaining the basics of what I need to know

FIFTEEN

Winter

THE MEETING with Mr. Carson ended up going better than I expected, and before I knew it, it was over after an hour. He said he didn't want to overload me too much on my first day here, which I appreciate because hell, I'm not super-woman or anything.

Once I'm in my office again, I use the few minutes to freshen up. As soon as I'm done, Chase walks back into my office letting me know that it's time to go down.

The press conference is being held in front of our building, so that's another thing that's good about today.

Once we get to the elevators, Mr. Carson is already there waiting on us. We all step into the elevator to head down to the lobby.

Once we're there, I see the outside is filled with people already and my anxiety threatens to rise with every second that passes. I did not expect this many people and reporters to turn out today, if I were being honest with myself.

The turnout is probably this big because people are nosy. No one knows what it's about, and everyone wants that information badly. I'm sure they know it's about Dad's death and the future of this company.

Gahh! Right now, I wish that someone else could have done this for me. But it's like I can hear my father's voice inside my head saying there's no one else who can do this but me.

With that thought in mind, I let my determination set in and we walk outside to get this over and done with. Chase is by my side and he gives me my notes with my speech. Mr. Carson is the first one to go on stage to speak.

"Good afternoon, everyone, thank you all for being here. We know you probably have questions as to why we've asked for this conference. First, let me just say that Crowne Enterprises has been like a second home for me for the past thirty years, working here and then as acting CEO, but alas my time is ending. I'll be retiring soon but there will be someone in my place who I'm one hundred percent confident will take this company to greater heights."

At his words, the crowd bursts into murmurs and questions all at once. Wow, eager little beings. Self-doubt really is a bitch and I'm having a healthy dose of that right now. I take in a deep breath as Carson continues. I school my features into my resting-bitch-face look because again... fake it 'til you make it, right?

"Please hold all your questions until the end. Now, without further ado, please help me welcome Miss Winter Crowne to the stage," he says, and the crowd goes silent. I have a feeling they know that whatever is happening next will be big. So yeah, all their attention is on me.

I take a deep breath and exhale before I walk up to the stage. Chase whispers, "You'll kick ass." I give him a smile in thanks.

"Thank you, Mr. Carson. Hello, everyone. First, I'd like to say thank you all for being here today. Second, Mr. Carson has been the acting CEO of Crowne Enterprises in North America for the past few years and the work he's helped my father accomplish has been exceptional. I couldn't be happier with all the progress we've made throughout the years. Third, and this is the main reason we've asked you here today, is to let the public know Mr. Carson will retire soon and as the sole heir to Crowne Enterprises and all of its subsidiaries, I'll be stepping up as the new CEO in the coming weeks after his departure from the company. The floor is now open to questions. One at a time, please," I say. That went better than I expected. I didn't even trip over my tongue once. *Progress! Maybe I am cut out for this gig after all.*

As soon as I finish speaking, the crowd erupts with questions. They're all speaking at the same time and I can barely make out what they're saying. Ugh, it's like they don't understand English because clearly I said one at a time.

"If you could all shut up, I'll gladly answer any questions you may have along with Mr. Carson." It goes quiet in an instant. That probably wasn't the best or professional way to get them to shut up, but right now I can't bring myself to care. I'm ready to get this over with.

Who knew things like these were exhausting? My father and mother made it look easy. They never shied away from the spotlight and it's in this moment, I realize that said spotlight isn't for everyone.

I look over at the crowd and then get the ball rolling by choosing the first person to ask their question.

The first reporter is up. "Do you think you can handle all the responsibilities of running a billion-dollar company?"

"Yes, because I was always meant to be the CEO after my father. This was... is my legacy after all. I'm just taking over sooner than I ever expected I would."

The second one goes next. "Why isn't your mother here supporting you?"

Fuck! It didn't cross my mind to ask her to come. I didn't even think that people would have even expected her to be here. Clearly, I'm not thinking like a businesswoman, and I'm already failing at this gig.

"She had prior engagements. I'm the one who will take over as the CEO, so she wasn't required to be here."

The third reporter asks, "What makes you think you deserve this position?" And there it fucking is. I knew people were going to question this, but I need to nip this in the fucking bud.

"What makes you think you have the right to determine whether or not I deserve this position?" I ask. The stupid sexist asshole goes quiet along with everyone else. I can tell my question to him was unexpected, and he looks stupid trying to come up with an answer now. "Let me be frank, this was my father's legacy and now that he's no longer here to run it, it's become my legacy. That's why I deserve this position. I don't think anyone else would have the best interests of this company more than I would."

He looks like he's about to ask another question when I say, "Next." He does not look pleased, but I don't care because fuck him and his dickish self.

The fourth reporter inquires, "What's the relationship between you and the Kings? Do you have any plans of merging the companies together?"

"My relationship with the Kings is none of your concern and no there are no plans of merging the companies together. Why would we?"

The fifth question is asked, "We figured the companies would merge because of the rumors surrounding—"

This one doesn't get to finish her question. In the blink

of an eye, chaos erupts while I'm left standing there frozen to the spot. I have no idea what is going on and my brain is taking too long to play catch up.

I'm barely aware of the sound of gunshots, but that can't be right. Why the hell would there be gunshots here?

Something whizzes past my head, and a moment later, I feel something wet splash on me. The wetness rolls down the side of my face and I bring my hand up to touch my cheek. When I pull my hand away, it's stained red. Everything feels like it's moving in slow motion right now.

In a daze, I fully turn around to look behind me and the sight makes me want to lose the contents of my stomach. The security guard that was standing behind me has half his head blown off.

I hear the sounds of more bullets going off, but I'm too disoriented to even move. A second later, a huge body slams into me, taking us both down, as the glass behind me shatters with what I'm assuming is another bullet.

Holy shit... was that meant for me? I would have been shot if this man hadn't slammed into me.

"Stay down," the man who is currently holding me says in a deep masculine voice just as I begin to panic and hyperventilate. It sounds like he has an accent and I try to focus on his voice so I won't totally lose it.

I look over to the side and see that Mr. Carson and Chase are fine. They're crouched down behind one of the tables that were set up out here.

The sound of sirens can now be heard. I try to stand up to see if they hurt anyone else, but the guy stops me from moving any further.

"Don't. We don't know if the shooters are still around or not," he says in a firm voice. It doesn't even look like this had any effect on him. Meanwhile, my heart is beating erratically like it's about to jump out of my chest.

"I-I need to get out of here! I need to make sure that everyone is okay... I need to do something!" I say as tears stream down my face. At this moment, I'm so confused as to why someone would start shooting at a press conference.

"Calm down, I've got you. Worry about yourself first. The police are almost here," he says, grabbing my face and turning it toward him so that I can focus my attention on him.

Holy hell, what a face! He has got to be one of the most gorgeous specimens of a man I have ever laid my eyes on... well, besides Mason and the guys. Yeah, I know, this isn't the time, but it's either focus on him or freak the fuck out, and I'd rather not freak out more than I already have.

He's definitely older, but he has an exotic look to him, blue eyes with a sharp jawline and dark hair. He looks tall from his crouching position and his lean body is clad in an Armani suit that fits to perfection. He definitely has money.

"Who are you?" I ask, trying to focus on him rather than my shaking hands.

"My name is Antonio, but we'll discuss things later," he says as he gets up and looks around.

At the same time, a few officers and Chase rush toward me. My adrenaline level is off the charts right now, and I can't concentrate on anything.

"Come on, let's get you up to your office and out of the public's eyes so you can calm down," he says.

"What about all the people?"

"I'll come back down and help Mr. Carson deal with the police and everything once I have you settled upstairs."

"Yeah... um yeah, sure, let's go." I barely manage to nod.

I think I'm in shock because I can't even process what

the hell just happened out there. I'm not even aware that tears are still streaming down my face until Chase hands me a tissue as we make our way back to my office.

"Thanks," I say to him, still sniffling.

Once we get to my office, Chase asks if I need any help. Wanting to be alone so I can catch my bearings, I tell him no. He heads back downstairs to help Mr. Carson with the aftermath.

I feel like it should have been me down there, but I'm thankful I have people that can help. I'm not in the right state of mind to do anything. I'd probably just be in the way.

I walk over to the side of my office and open the door that leads to the small apartment. It comprises a bedroom, bathroom and a small living room with a small kitchen off to the side. I doubt my dad ever used that kitchen, so I don't see the point of actually having one there.

My dad added the apartment for when he was working here before we left for London. Sometimes he'd stay late at the office, sometimes even overnight, especially when he had a heavy workload.

Now I'm thankful for it because I can shower and get this blood off me. Thank God, I had the foresight to let my stylist add some business dresses and suits here in case I ever needed it.

I walk straight into the bathroom and strip off my clothes before stepping into the shower. As soon as the water touches my skin, the tears begin to fall. Why the hell is this happening to me?

If I were superstitious, I'd say that wasn't a good sign at all. Since stepping into Ravenwood again, everything has been a disaster.

I scrub my skin until it's raw to get the blood off of me.

It feels like it's still there, no matter how many times I've scrubbed my skin.

Somehow, this feels like it's all my fault, even though logically I know that none of this was.

A few minutes later, I finish up in the bathroom and walk into my room to grab a fresh change of clothes. As soon as I'm finished dressing, there's a knock on my bedroom door.

"Come in!" I yell through the closed door and a second later it opens. Chase pops his head into the room.

He inspects me and I can tell that he sees that I've been crying. My eyes are probably red and puffy by now.

"Are you okay, honey?" he asks, coming further into the room.

"I honestly don't know. That was a first. I've never been shot at before."

"I'm so sorry that happened to you. We've never had an incident like that ever before..." I know he's probably trying to make me feel better, but it does the opposite.

"Guess I'm just lucky then," I say sarcastically.

"The police, along with Mr. Carson, are in your office ready to speak with you whenever you're ready."

"Thanks. Can you tell them I'll be out in a second?" I ask. I need a moment to compose myself.

He nods and walks out of the room and back into my office. I use the time to take my anxiety medication. If I don't, I probably will have an attack.

I hate taking them during the day because it makes me drowsy, or sometimes I have trouble concentrating. That's why I only take them during the day if I absolutely have to, and right now, I absolutely have to.

Once I'm done and I feel like I've calmed myself down enough, I step out of my room and head back into my office.

The officers, Mr. Carson, and Chase, along with Antonio, the man from downstairs who practically saved me, are all in the office sitting in various seats throughout the office.

"I'm sorry for the wait gentlemen, I um... I had to get a change of clothes since my other ones were covered in blood," I say as a way of explanation for keeping them all waiting.

"It's no worry at all. We completely understand the situation. My name is Detective Jackson," he says before pointing to his partner and adding, "and this is Detective Thomas."

"I know this would be a traumatizing situation for anyone, but we have some questions to ask you," Detective Thomas says.

"Sure, go ahead."

"Do you know who would want to kill you?"

I sit and stare at him. What? Kill me? I mean, my mother probably wouldn't mind if I were dead, but she wouldn't stoop so low as to try to kill me, right?

"Umm, no. I don't know. I only moved back here last week, and I've hardly left my house so I... wait, do you mean that whoever was shooting was trying to kill me specifically?" I ask just to be clear.

"Yes, that's exactly what we're saying. No one who was there was hurt except for the security guard that was behind you. We're thinking that the shooter was aiming for you and missed," the other officer informs me.

I gulp. I don't even want to think about why someone would try to kill me in public like that.

"We're opening an investigation to see what we can find, but we wanted to come up here to make sure that you were fine," one of them says before they get up, intending to leave.

"We'll be in touch when we have more details." They walk out of my office, leaving me alone with Chase, Mr. Carson, and Antonio.

Mr. Carson takes the reins and introduces Antonio properly to me. "Winter, this is Antonio Bandini. You were supposed to have a meeting with him after the press conference today."

"Oh, yeah, right. Hi, it's nice to officially meet you," I say.

"I just wanted to come up and tell you we can reschedule our meeting for another day. I know you just went through a lot, *cara mia*," Antonio says. I have no idea what *cara mia* means, but it sounds good rolling off his tongue.

"No, it's fine, you're already here," I say. Why let him make another trip when he's already here. I nod to both Mr. Carson and Chase to let them know it's fine.

Looking at him, I see that he's more handsome than I gave him credit for earlier.

An hour later, we've concluded all our business regarding the process for getting the land inspected for the new high-rise apartment building Crowne Enterprises will be working on, and he's ready to leave.

"Would you be interested in going to dinner with me tomorrow night, *cara mia?*" he asks, and I blush like a freaking schoolgirl. I want to smack myself in the face.

"What does *cara mia* mean?"

"Come out to dinner tomorrow night and I'll let you know."

"I could just google it, you know?"

"But what would be the fun in that, *cara mia?*"

"Fine, you saved my life today, so I owe you for that," I say relenting. "But I have school tomorrow, so it will have to be after," I tell him.

"I'll pick you up from school then."

"Great, I'll see you tomorrow." We exchange numbers and then he leaves. I haven't felt this kind of attraction to anyone in ages, and I'm sort of excited.

My hookups in London weren't based on whether I was attracted to the guy or not. It was just a way to fill the void that Mason left behind, and now it looks like I may have a chance of finally moving on from him.

I attempt to get back to work, but I can feel the medication working and I'm getting drowsy by the second. Deciding it's best to call it quits for today and go home to get some rest, I call Martin and let him know he can come pick me up. My nerves are shot after such an eventful day.

SIXTEEN

Winter

I wake up with a start, gasping for air. My sheets are tangled around me and I'm sweating from the nightmare I just woke up from. Last night was a nightmare in itself because all I kept seeing every time I closed my eyes was the security guard lying there in his own blood with half his head missing.

Apparently, that was more traumatic than I thought it would have been. I thought I got out unscathed, but the memories and nightmares of yesterday say differently.

As soon as I got home yesterday, my mother was the first person I saw. She didn't even ask me if I was okay after, you know, almost being shot execution style.

Not going to lie, her lack of emotion really cuts deep. Every time I think I'm over wanting her to care, something happens that makes me see how much she doesn't.

Knowing that I will not sleep again, I just lie here staring up at the ceiling. I think about all the things that have happened to me since returning home, and I just wish I could go somewhere else, where no one knows who I am and I don't have people hating me just because I exist.

An hour later, my alarm goes off. I look at my phone and remember that today is my first day at Ravenwood U. Yay! I wish I were happier for today, but with everything that happened yesterday, I'm still not settled.

There are dozens of missed calls from the girls and Grayson. *At least some people still care.* Shit... the girls are going to kill me for not replying, but after I got home yesterday, I grabbed another quick shower and then went straight to bed where I collapsed.

I just ignore the texts for now because I'll see the girls in school later. At least I have that to look forward to.

I crawl out of bed and start getting ready for school. When I get to the bathroom, I look in the mirror. Geez, I look like I was run over by a bus or something.

There are bags under my eyes, and I look like I haven't slept in years. I just sigh and continue getting dressed.

I'll have to be excused for the way I look because I almost died yesterday. I won't worry about anyone today besides myself.

An hour later, I'm done and walking out of the house to the car. I'm letting Martin drive me today because Antonio will pick me up for our date. I dressed nicely today. Hopefully, my appearance lasts all day long.

"How are you feeling today, Winter?" Martin asks as soon as I get to the car.

"I see you've finally learned," I say, giving him a big smile, referring to him finally calling me Winter. "I'm a bit shaken up still, but fine," I say as I get into the back of the car.

"I'm glad you're okay," he says bending down to look at me before straightening up and getting into the car himself to take me to school.

I feel a bit excited because in addition to my studies here, I'll have the use of the University's lab.

Money speaks, I guess. They only said yes because

Crowne Enterprises is one of their major contributors, and I know they don't want to get on my bad side in case I stop their donations. I roll my eyes at the thought because that's all these universities care about these days.

But whatever, I'm just glad that I'll get to continue to work on the formula for the antidepressant pills I've started working on since I was back in London. I'm halfway through with the correct formula and I'm excited. Hopefully soon, I can begin producing the pills and then have them ready for the trial stage.

So far there's been a lot of trial and error, but I've kept going because I know this will make a difference in people's lives if I eventually get it right. This is one of my passions.

My thoughts go back to yesterday and I make a mental note to call the detectives later to see if they have any information about the shooting.

I've never been one to think about death often, like it's never been something I feared before, but actually coming close to it yesterday was very disconcerting.

I'm not sure how the first bullet missed me, and then Antonio saved me from the second one. If he wasn't there, then I would have already been on my way to the afterlife. *I wonder if they have food there?*

Based on my mother's actions yesterday after I got home, I'm sure she would have been overcome with joy if that bullet had found its way inside my head. I mean, what kind of monster doesn't ask their kid if they're okay after almost dying?

I'm one hundred percent sure that she along with everyone else in this town saw the press conference and I'm sure there might have been something on the shooting too. She definitely knew. Ugh, I don't know why I keep expecting her to magically change her ways and start caring about me.

I haven't checked any of the gossip sites because I'm not ready to relive one of the worst moments of my life yet. I know this is going to be the talk of the town for a while too.

When we pull up in the parking lot of the huge and imposing campus, I see the girls are already here and judging from their facial expressions; I know I'm in for the questioning of my life.

Who knows, I might even be in for an ass kicking as well because you just never know with my best friends. They are hella crazy on the best of days.

"I have a date tonight, so you won't need to pick me up," I tell Martin as I exit the car.

I'm assaulted with "What the fuck bitch?" from all three of them as soon as I walk over to them.

"We tried calling you like a million times last night!" Avery screeches out.

"You had us freaking worried, bitch!" Luna finishes.

"You didn't think about picking up the phone and telling your best friends that you were still alive?" Riley asks with a hint of anger in her voice.

It really is annoying when the three of them gang up on me together, and I'm guessing this is probably what it would feel like to have a mother fussing over me–annoying but welcomed all the same.

"I'm sorry, guys! I was out of it last night," I say rubbing at my forehead. I can feel the telltale signs of a headache forming.

"Sorry? Oh look, she's sorry, guys! That's all the bitch has to say after not answering her fucking phone for hours!" Riley announces, like that wasn't what I just said. "You were almost freaking shot yesterday! And we saw that shit live on the news! What the hell happened?" she asks sniffling.

Shit, I didn't even think about this from their point of view. Looking at all three of them, I see the various expressions of worry they're all wearing, and I feel guilty for waiting this long to talk to them. I walk closer to all three of them and pull them into a group hug.

"I'm so sorry, guys. I'm honestly not sure what the hell happened. The police are investigating and after the incident, I had a meeting with the guy who saved my life. By the time I got home, I was so exhausted I just crashed and that's why I missed all the calls," I say, trying to explain and hoping they'll forgive me faster.

"If something like this ever happens again, I'm storming your freaking house!" Avery says.

"Gahh, it's no big deal. I swear I'm fine. Besides feeling shaken up at the fact I was almost shot, my anxiety started acting up, so I really couldn't have functioned properly even if I wanted to. But everything is fine now. Please forgive me?" I give them my best puppy dog eyes that always work on them.

Just like I hoped it would, it works, and they stop yelling at me. Unfortunately, their yelling from before has gained the attention of people in the parking lot and I look around noticing that everyone here is staring at us.

I'm sure most of them saw the shit on the news too, and that's why we have even more attention on us now. Everything that happens in this town is grounds for gossip. I keep looking around the parking lot when my eyes suddenly clash with stormy green ones.

Of course, he'd be out here too. I can't catch a bloody break. Whoever said it was right: *when it rains, it pours.* We've gathered all the guys' attention and Mason is looking directly at me with an expression filled with hate as usual.

It's funny that even from here I can tell what his hatred for me looks like. Okay, not funny but heartbreaking and tragic. I can't wait for the day when he finally gets his stupid head out of his ass.

Something tells me if that ever happens, it'll be when we're broken beyond repair. Just that thought is enough to mess with my head on the days when I feel vulnerable.

Movement catches my eye and I scowl when I look at him and see that he has that stupid girl from the party draped all over him. I don't even know why I care. It's not like I even love the guy anymore.

Yeah, and pigs fly, Winter. Oh, cruel fate, how dare you give me the love of my life only to ruin it by taking him away and then make me have to watch him love someone else.

At this rate, she could probably star in a soft core porno with the way she's grinding up against him. He moves his hand down to cup her ass and squeezes, all the while still staring straight at me. *God, I hate this asshole!*

This must be what hell is like because if it weren't then it wouldn't hurt so much. I rub a hand against my chest and of course he notices if the widening smirk is anything to go by.

Do you ever forget your first love? The first person who made you feel everything good in the world? Or rather, the better question is, how do you forget about them when you have to see them every single day?

Everything about him makes me want to smack him across his stupid face. Deciding I'm done with the pathetic stare-off we have going on, I'm the first to turn away.

"I have something for you," Riley says, digging into her

bag and pulling out a container with chocolate cake and handing it over to me.

I squeal and throw my arms around her. "It's like you love me!"

"Yeah, yeah, whatever! Pull that shit again and I'm kicking your ass to the curb!" she says grumpily.

I look at my besties, ready to give them some gossip so they can forget all about my actions yesterday. "I've got some juicy info that you guys will definitely want to hear!" I say to get their attention.

"Spill it, hoe!" Riley is the first to respond.

"I have a date tonight!"

"What?" They all screech at the same time, causing me to wince. It's so loud that all the guys' attention is on us again. I groan when I see Grayson walking over to us.

"Why do you girls insist on being so fucking loud?" I ask in a groan just as Grayson walks up to my side.

"Hey, babe," Grays says.

"Hey, Gray," I say as he pulls me into a tight hug. With the way he's hugging me, I'm staring at the guys from over his shoulder. Mason is now looking over at our little group with an even bigger scowl on his face. I give him a sweet smile before flipping him the bird. I hug Gray tighter.

If I didn't already know he hated me, I would have thought he was jealous or something about the way his brother is hugging me. Now it's my turn to smirk because he can't figure out if I'm into Grayson or not.

I'm not, but he doesn't need to know that. Grayson has always been one of my best friends and nothing else. He's never been interested in me that way either, which is a good thing. As much as I despise douchebag, I don't want anything to come between them as brothers, especially me.

"I'm glad you're okay. What the hell happened yesterday?" Ugh, and there Gray goes, ruining the moment.

"Please, no more questions on that subject," I groan out. "The police are investigating." The thought of yesterday brings back the moment of feeling that guy's blood all over my skin. I have the urge to itch my skin because of the phantom feel of still being covered in blood.

"You should let go of her now before you catch an STD!" Mason yells out to his brother, loud enough for everyone in proximity to hear. The stupid-ass bitch next to him laughs like that was the funniest thing she's ever heard in her life.

"I'm not the one two seconds away from starring in free porn," I yell back.

Grayson chuckles next to me. "Do you have a death wish or something?"

"Please! I'm not scared of that asshole."

"You should be," he says.

I choose to ignore that statement because Riley butts in, "Come on, tell us about your date and forget about douchebag Mason!" she whines from next to us.

"Fine. He's sooo hot! Like Mr. Tall, Dark and Handsome. I think he's Italian! After my freak-out yesterday, I was on the verge of drooling after meeting him officially."

"Where did you guys meet?" Luna asks.

"He was the one who tackled me to the ground so I wouldn't get shot. I mean, that's good material for the grandkids one day. I'll tell them how he saved me from almost dying," I say, sighing dreamily.

"Aww, how romantic. He's like your knight in shining armor," Avery pipes in.

"Mason will not like that one bit," Gray pipes in.

"Why are you even here? Go back to where you came

from. No one gives a hoot about douchebag over there," I say.

"I'm just trying to save you from being killed," he responds. I roll my eyes at him and because I'm so mature, I also stick my tongue out at him.

"Oh yeah, that part was caught on camera yesterday," Luna says.

"Really?" I ask, stunned.

"Yes, and I'm pretty sure the entire town has seen it," Riley says. "It was so hot watching him protect you like that. Gah, I wish I had my own knight."

I roll my eyes again. Living through that was not romantic at all. I was fucking scared to death.

"I'm sure if you ask Royce nicely, he'll volunteer." She rolls her eyes at me before looking over at Gray.

"Say a word about what she just said, and I'll hang you by the balls!" He snickers and raises his hands up in a surrendering motion.

I look at the time and see that class is about to start soon so I motion toward the front door letting them know it's time to go inside. When I get to my class, I see Grayson following me and when I take a seat; he takes the one right next to me.

"What are you doing?"

"I have this class too," he says, looking at me like I'm the crazy one here.

"Did you take this class just to torture me?" I ask. I wouldn't put it past them for this to be one of Mason's games since he loves playing them so much.

"Why would I want to torture you when I love you so much? Are you sure you're okay, though? I'm here if you need to talk."

I'm not sure what Gray's game is. I have no clue if he's

being genuine or not right now. For all I know, he could be spying for his brother. Yeah, we used to be friends, but things have changed in the time I've been away so if he means well, I'm still not about to spill any of my secrets to him.

"Thanks, Gray," I say even though I know I won't be getting close to him. My phone pings with a text that distracts me from having to respond further, and I fish it out of my bag before looking at it.

ANTONIO: *Hello, cara mia, are you ready for our date tonight?*
    Me: Mmm maybe ;p
    Antonio: Ah, I see you like playing games, cara
    Me: Not really, but I am excited to see you again.
    Antonio: Much better and likewise
    Me: I have to go. My class is about to start. See you this afternoon.

I CAN'T KEEP the grin off my face, which definitely does not escape Grayson's notice.

"Mason will be pissed after he hears you're going on a date. There's no telling what he'll do."

"Well, too bad! Mason isn't my boyfriend, and he doesn't get a say in what I do or who I date. Besides, he's made it perfectly clear he doesn't give a fuck about me, so why would he care about me going on a date?" I growl at him.

"Don't say I didn't warn you." He sighs before opening his book as our lecturer has come in to start class.

The day goes by fast, and I have to say, my first day

wasn't too bad. I walk out of the building where my last class of the day was held and begin my trek to the parking lot. I groan when I see the guys are still here and are all standing next to Mason by his car.

At least I know which one is his. It's a matte black Bugatti Veyron. Of course, the asshole would have one of those.

I thought they would have been gone by now, but nope, they're still here. I look over to Grayson and he just lifts his shoulder in a shrug. I know he told his brother what was going on. What a traitor! See, I knew I couldn't trust him.

Just then, a black-tinted SUV comes rolling into the parking lot and stops a few feet away from me. The driver gets out of the vehicle before going over to open the door.

Antonio steps out of the vehicle and walks over to me. As soon as he's close to me, he pulls me in for a hug and drops a kiss on the top of my forehead which causes a flush to appear on my cheeks.

"*Cara*, you look beautiful as always," he says in greeting.

"You don't look so bad yourself," I say in a joking manner, and he chuckles.

"How are you holding up?" he asks, concern lining his voice.

"I'm okay, it's no big deal," I say, trying to brush it off, but he's not having it one bit.

"It wasn't no big deal. I saw how shaken up you were yesterday," he says while holding my chin up to look at him directly.

"Please, can we not talk about that right now?" I plead with my eyes and he must know how desperate I am to let go of that subject because he relents.

"Are you ready to leave or do you need anything else from school?"

"No, I'm ready to go," I say.

I chance one more look at the guys before getting into the car. I can practically feel the stares burning into my back. As they always do, my eyes go straight to Mason and even from here, I can see the muscle in his jaw ticking.

He has an angry expression on his face, but what else is new? We're done, so I have no clue what his problem is. Is this the typical *if I can't have you, then no one else can* type of bullshit behavior?

This is the first time since our breakup that I've actually felt like I wanted to move on, and I will not let him ruin this for me.

As soon as I'm in the SUV, we drive off, making our way back to the downtown area of Ravenwood. We pull up in front of one of the expensive restaurants. It's a good thing I dressed in something five-star worthy this morning since I knew I wouldn't have time to go home and change.

Antonio places his hand on the small of my back as we make our way into the restaurant. His touch feels nice, and I can't help the little smile that spreads across my face. It's been a minute, but I'm finally feeling a little happiness at being back home.

"Welcome, Mr. Bandini," the maître d' greets us as soon as we make it through the door. He shows us to our table. Our table is in one of the rooms that the restaurant offers for privacy. There are always high-profile people here with the need for discretion. This is actually one of my favorite places, so he gets bonus points for that.

"So, thank you again for saving my life yesterday. I owe you big time," I say to get it out of the way. I'm not sure if I ever thanked him for what he did yesterday.

"You don't need to thank me, *cara*, I couldn't let anything happen to such a beautiful woman while I was there, now could I?" he asks with a smirk, and I blush.

Wow, smooth talker much?

Ugh, what the hell is wrong with me? And when the hell did I turn into this pathetic, blushing schoolgirl?

"You're such a flirt." I laugh.

"Not when what I say is the truth, *cara*."

"How long have you worked with the company?" I ask, trying to change the topic. He smiles at me, letting me know he knows exactly what I was doing. Even his smile is nice because of his straight white and perfect teeth.

"A little over a year," he replies, going with it, for which I'm glad.

We order our food and continue chatting throughout dinner, getting to know each other. I find out he's thirty-two, which puts him at ten years older than me. Wow, I have my own age-gap thing going on.

By the time we're done with dinner, I'm feeling much better. I haven't felt this way in a long time, and he makes talking to him so easy. I feel the stress of the last two weeks leave my body, leaving me feeling light.

I don't know if it's a good idea mixing business with pleasure, but I don't want the feeling I've had all night to end. By the time we leave the restaurant, I feel like I'm on cloud nine and it feels as though nothing in the world can touch me anymore.

I should have known that feeling wouldn't last.

SEVENTEEN

Winter

WHEN WE GET BACK to my house, he gets out of the car to walk me to my door. Gah, what a perfect gentleman!

"I had a nice evening with you, *cara*, I hope we can do it again soon."

"I had a nice evening too," I let him know.

He gives me a kiss on the cheek before he walks back over to his car, and I walk into the house with a smile across my face. I think it's the first genuine one I've had in a while.

I call out to my mother, wondering if she's home, but she doesn't respond. The house is quiet so I'm guessing she went out to wherever it is she goes. I have no clue what she's up to, which reminds me; I need to do some snooping.

I walk up to my room and take a shower before heading to bed. I open my balcony door to get some fresh air because the night air is always calming, and I need that right now.

I feel rejuvenated but also exhausted at the same time if that makes sense. I'm still not one hundred percent back to normal after yesterday, but I'm trying. Thankfully, school wasn't that bad today.

I hear my phone buzzing and thinking that maybe it's Antonio, I quickly grab it. Only it isn't him and the messages make the hair on my body stand on end.

. . .

UNKNOWN: *Tsk-tsk, if you don't stop being a whore I'll be forced to do something about it.*

Unknown: **image**

The picture is one of me and Antonio at the restaurant.

Unknown: **image**

This next one is of us outside the house.

Unknown: **image**

The last one is of me in his arms when he gave me a hug and a kiss on the cheeks before he left.

Unknown: *Better drop him before I'm forced to hurt him. Even if you're a whore, YOU BELONG TO ME!!!! I have plans for you. Your life is not your own anymore.*

Me: *Who the hell is this? This isn't funny, Mason!*

Unknown: *If you don't obey me, you'll find out exactly who I am when bodies drop and it'll be all your fault.*

I try blocking the number, but since it's an unknown one, I can't do anything about it. A shiver runs across my body. What the hell? This has got to be douchebag Mason because it can't be anyone else, right?

I mean, he wouldn't actually kill someone, right? I slide down further into my bed and pull the blankets up to my chin. Trust that asshole to want to ruin the bit of happiness I've found after ages. *Well, he promised to ruin me.*

I close my eyes and try to forget about everything, including him. I will not play his idiotic games. I must have eventually dozed off because the next thing I know, I'm woken up by the smell of smoke.

My eyes spring open. My room is filled with smoke. I rush out of my bed and onto my balcony. All the blood drains from my face.

Nooo! My tree house is on fire!

I rush out of my room and down the stairs before rushing out the back door. I grab the hose and try to turn it on, but nothing happens. Motherfucker! Of all the times not to work, it just had to be right now.

I move again, intent on running closer to put it out with something, but I have nothing. My mind spins. I don't know what to do right now.

Without even thinking, I run up the stairs and just as I make it to the top, there's a blast from inside. I try to backtrack as my brain is now comprehending that this isn't safe. I slip and go tumbling down, feeling my ankle twist with the fall.

I'm not even sure why I thought running up there would have done anything except put me in harm's way. I thought I could get to the switch on the side of the treehouse that activates the sprinklers inside, but I was too late.

I land on my back and stare up at the tree house, the flames in the front now. Hands grab me under my shoulder and pull me away.

"What the hell are you thinking, Winter? You could have been killed in there or seriously injured!" Martin yells at me. I don't think I've ever seen this man raise his voice or lose his cool before, and of course it takes an idiot like me for that to happen.

"Please, do something! You can't let it burn!"

"I've already called 9-1-1," he says to me. "Let's get you back inside until they get here."

I try to get up, but there's pain in my ankle when I put pressure on my foot. I sink down onto the grass again.

"I think I twisted my ankle when I fell," I whisper just as sobs rack my body.

How the hell did this happen? I can't even describe the

pain I feel in this moment. That tree house meant the world to me. I haven't even been inside of it since I got back home, and now it'll be gone.

I cry harder when I realize I had a lot of childhood memories and tokens in there. Everything filled with value is gone. Pictures of my father and I and so many other things that he gave me over the years as a child. All of it destroyed and I'll never be able to get them back. The pain of that pierces my heart more. I don't understand how the hell this happened.

I'm still in a state of shock even after the paramedics get here. They wrap my ankle and then place it in an ankle brace while the firefighters try to put out the fire. Thankfully, it's just a minor sprain and nothing too serious.

I'm sitting on the couch in the living room a while later when one firefighter and an officer come into the room.

"We've put the fire out, and we did a sweep to see if we could determine what started it," he begins.

"Do you know what happened?" I ask with a quiver in my voice. Just thinking about it has me wanting to cry again.

"From our initial search, it looks like someone deliberately set the fire."

"What?" I gasp. "Why would someone do that?"

"That's what we'll need to find out. Do you have any enemies? Do you know who would want to set your tree house on fire? " the officer asks this time.

I give a sarcastic laugh at that because I do, and the only person on that list is Mason. But I can't tell them that unless I have proof, right? For now, I just go with a diplomatic answer.

"I just announced I'm taking over my father's company

and while in the midst of doing so I was shot at. Now someone burned down my tree house... so I guess, yes?" The last part comes out as a question. I don't want to believe he hates me so much that he'd burn down our place.

"Well, we'll speak to the detectives involved in your previous case and see what we can find out."

"Thank you," I tell them as they both get up to leave.

I have no idea who is messing with me, but I don't feel safe anymore being back here in Ravenwood. If it turns out to be Mason, I can't be held liable for killing him and burying his body where no one else will be able to find him!

I sigh and head up to my room after everyone leaves, and the house is calm again. There's still no sign of my mother, and I wonder where the hell she is. She's always conveniently missing every time something goes wrong in my life.

I move into one of the guestrooms for tonight because mine still has a smokey smell. As soon as my head hits my pillow, the tears flow out again. I don't know how to cope because it feels like I'm losing my father all over again.

My phone buzzes next to me. I pick it up and freeze when I look at the text messages. It's from that unknown number again. Fucking hell... this is kind of getting scary now, and as I open the messages, I see that I'm right.

UNKNOWN: *Aww, look at how pathetic you look.*

Unknown: **image**

I gulp because this picture is one of me sitting on the grass crying earlier.

Unknown: *This is just the beginning... If you don't*

comply with my demands soon, then you probably won't make it out of this alive.

Me: Who the hell is this?

Unknown: Someone who is waiting to take it all from you! There are many people who want you right now and the price for you is high.

Unknown: Buckle up, sunshine, you have no idea what's coming your way.

THE MILLION-DOLLAR QUESTION IS, is this my mother or Mason? Or is this someone else entirely?

I know Mason and my mom both hate me, but they wouldn't go this far, would they?

If it is someone else entirely, then why are they doing this?

I'm scared and I'm not sure who to trust anymore besides my friends.

I eventually fall into a restless sleep where I see nothing but the faceless people out to hurt me in my nightmares.

THE NEXT MORNING, Martin drives me to school again because I don't think I can drive with a sprained ankle. When we get to Ravenwood U's parking lot, he gets out of the car and comes around to help me get out.

"You're making me look like an invalid, Martin!" I whisper-yell at him. The man just chuckles.

"I'm just doing my job, Miss—"

"Call me miss one more time and you're fired!" I cut him off before he even gets the words Miss Crowne out of his mouth. He rolls his eyes at me like it's difficult dealing with me or something.

Your tree house burns down in one night, and the man thinks it's okay to revert back to Miss Crowne.

I don't have a clue why, especially when I'm such a delight to work with. With the brace on my foot, thankfully, I won't be putting too much pressure on my ankle and I can just limp my way to class.

Riley is the first to see me and rushes over. My best friend, bless her heart, always fucking catches the douchebags attention and this time is no different.

Why the hell are they just always there? Like it doesn't matter what the hell we do, somehow, they're always freaking close by. Which when you think about it is sort of creepy.

"What the hell happened to you?" she rushes out as she gets closer.

"Got into a fight with my burning tree house last night. Spoiler—it won," I say, trying to lighten the mood.

Yeah, it didn't work 'cause she's looking at me like I grew three heads or something.

"Someone set the tree house on fire last night," I clarify, and she gasps just as Luna and Avery come over too.

"What the hell? Who would do such a thing?"

"I don't know. The police and arson unit are going investigate. But if I had to guess on who, only one person comes to mind," I say looking over directly at Mason. The girls all follow my line of sight to look over at him too.

"That sucks ass. I know how much that tree house meant to you," Luna whispers next to me.

"You don't seriously think he would stoop so low, do you?" Riley asks.

"I honestly don't know him anymore. I don't know what he's capable of, to be honest. He hasn't exactly been welcoming since I got back here, you know?"

"I never would have thought that the two of you would end up like this," Avery says.

"You and me both, babe. But I have to say he's looking guiltier by the second. No one else would know where to hit to torment me like this."

We're still looking over at him and he's smiling down at that girl who is all over him again. Doesn't matter how many times I see that sight; it always cuts deep. I'm the one who is supposed to be like that with him. As if he feels our stares on him, he looks over in our direction and our eyes lock.

He gives me his usual smirk, though this one looks smugger than his previous ones. Like he knows a secret I don't. I'm the first one to look away because I can't bear to look at him anymore.

The pain from last night is still too fresh and I can't deal right now, especially when he takes so much pleasure in my pain.

The girls and I head inside before separating and heading to our own classes. I forgot that my class today is the one with Grayson in it, and I groan when I see him come in and head straight for the seat next to mine.

I ignore him because there's still a lot on my mind. I need to figure out why Mason took all those pictures of me and why he'd send them like that. Plus, why would he threaten to kill people? Though this could be someone else entirely because Mase is not a killer, right?

Ugh, so many unknown variables. I'd say this is like a chess game and whoever is playing against me has a high chance of winning because spoiler alert, I know nothing about chess.

Apparently done with me ignoring him, Grayson starts talking to me just as class is about to be over. He finally asks what I'm sure he's been dying to ask this whole time.

"What the hell happened to your ankle?"

"Nothing."

"Come on, Winter, talk to me," he says.

"Why? So you can go tell your asshole of a brother everything I said?" He looks affronted for a minute and when he goes to reply, I cut him off.

"Look, we both know whatever this is that's happening between me and him, you'll always take his side because he's your brother. So, you don't have to act like you care about me because if push came to shove, I'll be the one left to face things on my own while you'd be by his side." He goes to interrupt again, and I cut him off for a second time. "It's fine, Gray. I don't blame you for that, but I don't need to feel like I can depend on you when I know I can't."

With my last word, I get up and hobble out of class. I don't want to deal with this conversation anymore. I'm too unsettled to actually think straight right now.

As if this day couldn't get any worse, as soon as I'm out the door, the sight in front of me makes me gasp. The hallway is filled with pictures of me stuck to the walls.

The first ones I notice are those of me from last night on the grass crying and then it goes on to the ones of me falling down the stairs of the tree house. It's a huge collage of just me along the walls of the hall.

The next set of pictures are the ones of the press conference with me just standing there covered in blood, with the security guard right behind me on the floor. Whoever did this is clever because this set is arranged to show exactly how and when the guy was shot.

After the last picture, there's one that reads *murderer* and another one with *he wouldn't have died if it weren't for you*. The final one—the one that's stuck to the wall in more places—is the one with me covered in blood and that one reads *you don't belong here anymore*.

I feel sick to my stomach. Someone is actually insinuating it's my fault that guy died. Like how the hell would I have known some crazy person would shoot at a press conference?

I'm so stuck inside my head, I don't realize that everyone is out of class and the hallway is full of students looking at the same thing I am. I hear the whispering around me and my stomach twists.

I need to get out of here, but I can't move. I'm too disoriented, and my brain can't work fast enough to let me know what to do.

Someone bumps into me, snickering the words, "You killed him." They throw vicious comments on how I look ugly crying while also being a dumb bitch for trying to run up the stairs of a burning place and then falling flat on my ass because I'm too fat to hold my weight up.

I mean, that's not true, but it's one of my major insecurities. It's the one thing my mother always harps on about. People and their vicious tongues never know the damage they can cause, and yet, they never stop to think about how their words could affect someone.

I feel tears sting at the back of my eyes, and I spin around intending to run toward the bathroom. Crying in front of them is not an option. I stop in my tracks when I see Mason and all the guys, including Grayson, standing there lounging against the wall.

I just stare at Gray, realizing that everything I said to him in class was true. I can't trust him.

I march up to them with tears and anger threatening to take over. I stop right in front of Mason and demand to know what the hell is going on.

"Did you do this?" I ask. I look at all of them pointedly, but no one answers. Mason just shrugs and then a thought finally slides through my brain.

The picture of me crying looks like the one from the text message last night. It's not the same pose which means he took a lot of them. Horror washes over me and a second later so does the pain at the realization of what he did.

"Yo-you set the tree house on fire..." I barely manage to whisper out because my throat is clogged up making it hard to breathe.

He doesn't answer me. He just pretends like I'm not talking to him. A second later though, he gives me a smirk and from the look in his eyes, I know. I know that Mason was the one who set our tree house on fire.

That was our place. We had so many memories there and he just got rid of them like it was nothing to him, nothing to me, and nothing to us. If I didn't believe that he hated me before, then I certainly have no delusions now.

"How could you?" I ask, as the tears I've been trying to hold back finally stream down my face.

Again, he doesn't reply, and I lunge for him, hitting him in the chest before I feel someone grab my hair and yank me backward. Because I wasn't expecting it, I fall backwards and land awkwardly on my ankle before falling onto my ass. Pain shoots through my foot and it makes me cry out.

The person then kicks me in the face while I'm on the floor. A second later, I can feel the blood dripping out of my nose and the split in my lip.

"Stay the fuck away from my man, you fucking whore!" she screams at me.

When I look up and see that it's his girlfriend, it's like something flips inside of me and I lunge for her. I take her off guard. She wasn't expecting it.

I forget about my ankle and hell, even the fact that my face is on fire as I throw myself at her. I grab her by the face and rake my nails down her cheeks, feeling satisfied when I see the pools of blood following my marks. I grab her hair and pull, managing to pull out some of her extensions, and she lets out a shriek.

She's about to lunge for me again when Mason grabs her around the waist and Grayson grabs me around mine, holding me back.

I try to struggle out of his hold to get to her, but he's holding onto me with an iron grip. I can't move an inch.

"Get her out of here," Mason tells Gray, referring to me, and a second later he throws me over his shoulder and begins walking away. I pound on his back trying to get him to put me down, but he doesn't pay me any attention.

"I need to go to the bathroom," I mutter, knowing I will not win right now. He changes direction toward the bathroom. Once we get there, he finally places me down on my feet.

"Yeah, you wanted to be friends and act like you cared, right?" I spit out as soon as I'm facing him again.

"I am your friend! Did you not just see me get you out of that situation?"

"Did you know Mason was the one who burned my tree house down?" He looks away from me for a second, and I know all the guys knew. I huff out a dry laugh.

"I should have known..." I turn around and walk away, leaving him standing there. Once I'm in the bathroom alone, the sobs that were threatening to come out release and there's absolutely no way to hold any of it in.

He hates me so much and every day I feel it directed toward me. It feels like it's burning me alive. How can someone destroy all the memories you had with them without feeling any remorse for it?

EIGHTEEN

Winter

WHILE I'M SITTING on the toilet crying, I hear my phone buzzing on the floor. Thinking it's one of the girls because they probably heard what happened by now, I dig through my bag until I find it.

"Motherfucker!" I curse as soon as I see the message on my phone.

I wish this asshole would just leave me the hell alone. Like my humiliation wasn't enough for him already, he just has to rub more salt into my wounds.

UNKNOWN: *image*

The first image is me looking at Mason with nothing but heartbreak on my face. I feel pathetic just looking at myself in that picture. How can someone who you used to love, who you gave your entire soul to turn around and hurt you like this?

Unknown: Tsk-tsk, what do we have here?

Unknown: You're mine and no one else gets to have you!

Unknown: *image*

The second image is the one of me breaking down

and crying in front of everyone because it became too much for me.

Unknown: Aww, she looks so pretty when she cries.

Unknown: I can't wait to be the one to make those tears run down your pretty little face.

LOOKING at those messages just makes me cry harder. I'm so confused. I don't know who's messaging me. Just when I'm thinking it's Mason, these new messages throw me for a loop. He wouldn't send me messages of things he was there for, right?

I exit out of the messages and bring the phone to my ear. It rings once before he picks up.

"Hello."

"Hey, Martin, can you come get me? I'm not feeling so good today."

"No problem, sweetheart, I'll be there soon."

"Thanks," I say before hanging up.

Once I hang up the phone from Martin, I turn it off and walk out of the bathroom. It's just my luck that the hallway is still filled with people. As soon as I step out of the bathroom, the whispers begin again.

I ignore them and make my way out the doors with my head held high. I will not let any of these assholes get the better of me. That's the only thing they're good at—gossiping and bringing people down.

Once I'm in the parking lot, I see Riley, Luna and Avery already there waiting for me. My girls know me, and I've never been happier to see them then right now.

"We heard what happened and I'm so sorry," Riley says as soon as I reach them.

"Thanks," I say, sniffling. "Why the hell does he hate me so much?"

Luna moves in and hugs me, which brings the other two into a group hug as well. "Honestly, we have no clue," she says.

"Yeah, Beck never said anything either when I asked him what the hell was going on with Mason and you after you guys broke up," Riley says next.

A few minutes later, Martin pulls up and I get in the car while the girls all follow in their own cars. When we get to my house, we all walk up to my room to hang out for the rest of the day. I wouldn't have been able to get anything done, anyway.

I open the balcony doors for fresh air and as soon as I see the tree house, tears spring to my eyes again. I still can't believe Mason was the one to destroy what used to be our place. *Yeah, yeah, I know I said that before, but I'm really hung up on that fact right now.*

"Mason was the one who destroyed the tree house..." I start and then trail off because I have no idea what else to say. There is no excusing what he did, and I'll never be able to forgive him for this.

"What are you going to do?" Avery asks.

I think about it for a few minutes when an idea pops up and I grin at them. "I have the perfect idea if you guys are game. It's not fair for me to lose the things I love, so why not give him a taste of his own medicine? Hit him where it hurts, you know?" I ask as the idea takes root in my head.

AFTER WHAT HAPPENED on Tuesday night with the tree house and then everything at school on Wednesday, this week has not been the greatest. Since that day when everything went down, the whispers haven't stopped, and people have taken every opportunity they could to say something nasty to me.

I try to not let their words bother me, but I'll be the first to admit that it's hard. How are you supposed to walk around like an emotionless vessel when people's fucking words can tear you apart, making it feel like a blade against your skin destroying you?

It's finally Friday, and I'm just glad to have somehow made it through this week in one piece. The messages haven't stopped, and they've gotten a little more aggressive. I don't know who to turn to for help with this.

Should I even tell anyone? I mean, so far it's just harmless messages and some pictures so I don't think I need to involve anyone else, at least not yet. I hope it stays that way, and I don't come to regret my decision of not telling anyone.

Tonight, the girls and I have big plans and it's time for some payback. My plan for payback is genius, and I'm literally so excited to teach that asshole not to mess with me. I'm going to hit him where I'm sure it'll hurt.

This entire week has been nothing but one mess after the other. After the girls left, I gave the police officer a call and told them that Mason King was the one who set the fire to my tree house. They said they would look into it.

Somehow, I have a feeling that nothing is going to happen there. As if my day wasn't bad enough, when my mom got home, we got into a huge fight because apparently someone videoed the whole incident with Mason and me and then the fight between me and his dumb bitch of a girlfriend.

The rags got a hold of everything including the posters calling me names and me crying on the night of the fire, and you know what; I was trending.

It's been a PR nightmare. I don't care what they say about me, but I know the people at Crowne Enterprises probably saw it as well. I can't help but feel like I'm failing this company already. That thought alone has made me feel like shit this week because it means I'm failing my father.

To say she blew up would be an understatement. She went one hundred times past exploding.

That's the main reason I decided to get some revenge. I'm in the office today to keep up with my responsibilities. So far, things have been great with a few bumps, but I'm getting the hang of it. It's been uneasy here too because I see all the looks directed my way when they think I'm not looking.

But I've kept my head held high and act like it doesn't bother me in the least what the papers are saying about me.

When I'm done for the day at work, I head home and a few minutes after I get there the girls show up. We hang out in my room until it's time to get dressed.

We know the guys are having a party at Mason's house tonight and even though that's the last place I want to be, I don't have any other choice. Especially if I want my revenge. It's the perfect night to cause some mayhem.

We all get dressed in black jeans and some fancy tops before pulling black hoodies over our outfits. After we're done, we head out the door and into Riley's car. She's our designated driver tonight.

"You know, you guys don't have to do this, you can still back out," I say one last time, so they know what they're getting themselves into. I mean, I'm not letting them do anything besides be the lookouts. This is going to be all on me.

"We've got your back, babe. It's only fair he pays for what he did because that was a really shitty thing to do," Luna says.

"Yep, we've always got your back," Riley and Avery both reply.

When we get there, we can hear the loud music coming from inside the house and thankfully no one is outside. It's so loud I don't think anyone could hear us out here.

We grab the jars with the gasoline before making our way to the front of the house. I instantly see his car and it's parked on the lawn further away from the house, away from everyone else's cars.

I guess the asshole doesn't want anyone to scratch his baby. Too bad it's about to be more than scratched. We move quickly over to his car and begin throwing gasoline all over the outside.

Too bad it's locked. After we're done with that, Luna and Avery run back to Riley's car to hide the jars before coming back over to us. I grab the string we had dipped in gasoline and tape it onto the front of the hood before lighting it.

As soon as it's lit, I tell them to run. We all take off running toward the house and around the side of it to the section that has the pool in the backyard. There's a pool section on one side and the garden is on the other side. This house is freaking huge.

We slow down when we get close to the backyard and then casually walk in. There's a section that has an empty table and lounge chairs, and we beeline over there and grab some drinks on the way from the outdoor bar.

As soon as we're seated, we drink and act like we've been there all night. Thankfully, no one out here pays us any attention. About fifteen minutes later, there's a commotion in the entire place and everyone outside quickly runs to the side of the house to make their way to the front.

If I had to guess, I'd say they found out about the burning car. I can't keep the smile off my face. We've drunk so much since we got here that I need to pee, so we head inside to find the bathroom.

When we get to the hallway, we see the front door is open and everyone is outside. Because I can't help myself, I walk outside to see what it looks like and yep! Mason's car is engulfed in flames.

A second later, everyone who was close to the car runs away and then there's an explosion. Oops! Shit, I didn't think that through. I didn't realize that there would be an explosion after I lit the thing on fire. Thank God, it doesn't look like anyone got hurt. At least I hope so.

A few minutes later, people come inside again. I look over to the car again and see that a few people are hosing down the car. They must be the staff. I quickly rush to the bathroom to pee before heading outside again.

I wish I could see the look on his face right now but then again probably not. I'm sure he's super pissed, but that's what he gets for messing with me in the first place.

We continue drinking, and we're having a great time. We stay outside the entire time because, you know, we don't want to get caught by the douchebag extraordinaire.

An hour later I need to pee again, and I tell the girls I'll be back in a few. Riley offers to come with, but I just motion for her to stay put. It's packed inside so if I just sneak in and out I should be good.

I make it to the bathroom and quickly pee. Once I'm done and heading back to the party, a sense of deja vu hits me. This is the same spot I was in at the last party when I overheard my mother. *Fucking hell, I still need to do some digging.*

With everything going on in my life right now, I keep forgetting that I need to snoop where she's concerned.

I'm just about to pass the door to where she was the last time when it suddenly opens, and I let out a squeak thinking it's Mason. Nope, it's much worse. It's his father.

His eyes zero in on me before narrowing. I'm just about to move past him and not even say anything when he grabs me by the arm and pulls me back into the office. *What the hell is it with these assholes trying to manhandle me?*

"What the hell, asshole?! Let go of me!" I yell out. He's got a firm hold on me and we're in his office, but he still hasn't let go of me yet.

H lets go of me before slapping me across the face. *Fucking hell, this man has a hand on him!* He grabs me around the throat and squeezes so hard I feel my air supply being cut off. And nope, this is not the sexy kind of choking either.

"Do you think my son's life is something that you can play with?" he asks in a sneer.

"I have no idea what the hell you're talking about," I gasp between the limited amount of air I'm getting right now.

"Oh, I heard about your little statement to the police pointing out that Mason did something he didn't." I look at him with wide eyes and of course he notices.

"Ah yes, I know all about your stunt. Nothing goes on in this town that I don't know about. Ever heard the phrase *snitches get stitches*? I'd hate for you to be found in a ditch or something," he says casually, like we're discussing the bloody weather.

"Well, I know for a fact that your asshole son is the one who set my tree house on fire. He practically admitted it in school!" I yell at him. Screw this asshole. "He's probably just another dick like you and that's why he did it."

Have you ever been in a situation where you know you should have kept your mouth shut, but that realization came like a second too late? Yeah, well, that's me right now.

He squeezes my neck harder before bringing his face directly up in front of mine before dishing out his threat.

"Oh, little girl, the things I have planned for you," he says, and to my horror he brings his hand down to rub my neck before making his way down to my breast.

I shiver in disgust as he gropes me. When I try to struggle away, his other hand clamps down on my shoulder. My fight-or-flight instinct kicks in and without thinking, I bring my knee up and smash it against his balls.

"Fuck you and fuck your bloody son, you perverted asshole!" I spit out at him.

He wasn't expecting that move. He lets go of me just as quickly and lets out a roar before grabbing onto his junk. Fucking hell, if I wasn't dead before, I'm going to be dead now. I'm pretty sure I just painted another target on my back where he's concerned and I don't know who's worse, Mason or his father.

Not even waiting to give him a chance to recover, I run out of his office as fast as I can with tears streaming down my face. My throat feels raw, and it has me wondering if he crushed my windpipe or something.

I'm practically running down the hallway and I turn back to see if he's following me, but he isn't which is a miracle. I think it's time I left this party.

I spin back around and crash face first into a wall of muscle. Because the gods hate me, or this could be karma, I don't even have to look up to know who is standing in front of me. One, his smell is ingrained into my soul and two, I can practically feel the unrestrained rage coming off him in waves.

"Mason... I—" That's all I manage before I look up at him. He is pissed the fuck off. I don't think I've ever seen this much rage on him. *I mean, the fury on his face is so prominent. If I had the choice between being in a room with him or his perverted dad right now, I'd choose his dad.*

"You're going to fucking pay for that stunt you pulled tonight!" he spits out at me.

"I-I don't know what you're talking abou," I say, trying to play it off cool, but even I can hear the tremor in my voice. I'm shaking because of what happened in his dad's office and now I'm shaking harder because he looks like he'd love nothing more than to kill me.

I take a tiny step back from him but of course he notices. It's like my movement has flipped a switch inside of him. He stalks closer to me and wraps his hand around my already bruised neck. He notices my neck and sneers at me.

"Looks like you like it rough, huh, whore? I have just the thing to keep whores like you occupied."

He drags me back the way I came from. I'm worried he's taking me back to his father's office, but then he passes it and I let out a tiny breath of relief that doesn't last for long.

He stalks all the way to the end of the hall where the elevator is and then pushes the button. Once it gets here, he shoves me in roughly and I almost trip on my way in.

I give him a glare, trying to look tough, but I'm really about to pee my pants right now. "What the fuck is your problem, asshole?"

He slams me up against the elevator wall and wraps his hand around my neck. Fuck! Now he's just adding to my already bruised neck. It hurts and my voice is already coming out hoarse.

"You fucked up tonight and you're going to pay for that. Everything I did to you before is nothing compared to what I have planned now," he whispers in my face. I gulp. Holy shit, that's a scary threat, especially coming from him.

When the elevator stops, he drags me out. When I see we're heading for his bedroom, it's like my fight-or-flight instinct has finally kicked in again knowing I'm in worse danger now than I was before with his father. I struggle to get away from him but it's no use. His grip on me is iron clad.

He opens the door to his room and shoves me roughly inside. This time, I trip and fall to my knees. I look up at him as he locks the door shut behind him before turning back to me. The next words out of his mouth make mine go dry.

"Strip..."

NINETEEN

Winter

"Wha-what?" I ask. I think I just heard him wrong. Okay, it looks like I'm way tipsier than I imagined. But nope...

"Fucking strip before I do it for you!" he seethes.

When I don't make a move and just sit there staring at him, it feels like his anger goes up a notch. He stalks over to where I'm still sitting on the floor and hauls me up by the front of my shirt.

He's in my face yelling, "Did you think you'd be able to get away with that stunt you pulled tonight? You're in for a world of hurt, you fucking bitch!"

"What the hell is wrong with you, asshole?" I scream at him. "You're the one who wanted to play, didn't you? What, you can't take the heat when it's directed back at you?"

He doesn't answer, but instead throws me onto his bed roughly. I try to crawl away, but he yanks me backward and a second later his hand is undoing my pants before moving to rip my shirt off of me. *If he wasn't such a douchebag, I'd think that was hot, but right now I can't help but think how wrong this feels.*

I'm in my bra and panties when he moves to take off his shirt. Wow, he's changed, that's for sure. His chest and torso are filled with tattoos. *So not the time, Winter!*

Because I was the dumbass who stopped to ogle him,

he's now crawling onto the bed toward me. I've finally caught onto my senses.

"What are you doing?" I shriek.

"Getting payment for my car you destroyed. No one messes with me without paying the consequences," he says with so much anger in his tone it makes me flinch.

It appears every word that comes out of his mouth just gets angrier and angrier, and I know I'm not making it out of here tonight unscathed.

"I have no idea what you're talking about! I came here for the party just like everyone else," I say with a slight tremble to my voice, even though I'm trying to stay strong.

"Tsk-tsk always such a fucking liar. Let me help you along a little yeah, since your stupid brain is taking too long to catch up. There are cameras everywhere on the property," he says with a raised eyebrow. I feel the color drain from my face. "Ah, she's finally catching up."

"Mason, don't do this, please!" I plead while scrambling to get off the bed, but he just yanks me back to him. I struggle harder, but he straddles my legs, keeping me in place.

My struggling does nothing to deter him and I can feel him getting hard. I freak out. Even though I've thought about what it would be like to have sex with him again; it was not like this, never like this.

He's so much stronger than I am and fighting him is useless. He's still pissed off for what I did to his car, and I know I haven't felt the brunt of it yet. I gulp because I don't think I'm getting out of here until he's done with me.

"I'll never forgive you if you do this," I say with tears streaming down my face. I know exactly where this is going and there's no stopping him.

"Does it look like I give a fuck what you think? I fucking hate you. I don't give a shit about you or your feelings."

"You accuse me of being the same thing, but you're the fucking liar! I know you still give a shit even if you try to hide it."

An furious expression crosses his face and in one lightning quick move, he flips me onto my stomach and grabs one of my wrists before pushing it toward the headboard where he fastens it to a pair of handcuffs before moving onto the next.

He moves and ties some kind of silk tie to my ankles on the bottom of the bed. I'm restrained and spread eagled, just waiting for him to do whatever it is he plans on doing. He moves to straddle my ass this time and I hear the unmistakable sound of a switchblade popping open.

"What the hell are you doing with that?" I ask while struggling more. He doesn't answer but instead moves to cut off my panties followed by the straps of my bra. I'm completely naked and vulnerable to him.

"Mmm, such perfect skin," he murmurs in my ear. "I've always wondered what it would look like if it wasn't so... perfect." As soon as the last word is out of his mouth, I feel the blade of the knife on my spine. He drags it down and a second later I feel the unmistakable sting of my flesh being cut.

Fuck! That hurts. He moves onto another spot, and I feel another nick and I scream out. He leans down and I feel his tongue lick the blood that's seeping out of my back. His tongue feels good, but this is so wrong. We shouldn't be doing this. We hate each other.

I moan with how good it feels, though his next words are like the bucket of water I need to snap out of my stupid haze.

"I've always wanted to know what a whore's blood tastes like if I'm the one causing them pain. Now I do," he says with a sneer before moving off of me. His words shouldn't hurt. I should be used to them by now, but they still do.

I turn my head in his direction and see that he's taking off his belt. Ah, fuck! He's not about to do what I think he's about to do, is he?

He catches me watching him and smirks. If I were free right now, I'd probably kill him. He moves back onto the bed right behind me and now I can't see what he's doing anymore.

I hear the whoosh and don't have the time to prepare before his belt lashes me across my ass. I let out a scream. It's like he put all his strength into that hit.

"Someone has to teach you a fucking lesson because clearly there's no one to do it! Oh, that's right, your dad's dead." How fucking dare he bring my father into this bullshit he has going on.

"Fuck you, asshole! Maybe if you didn't start your war with me, then you'd still have your precious car, but you're the dickwad who started this shit!" I yell out as another smack lands on me, this time on the back of my legs.

"You're the reason this whole fucked-up mess started. I fucking hate you with every fiber of my being. I wouldn't be in constant hell every day if it weren't for you!" he says in a more pissed-off tone than before.

I should be used to his nasty words by now but somehow my brain never catches up to what's going on when it comes to Mason. Every word out of his mouth right now is like a whip branding all the hits to my soul and it makes me cry even harder.

If I thought he had a heart left under all that coldness,

then I was sorely mistaken. The man behind me lets out all his frustrations on my body with his hits. The screams that leave me feel like they're coming straight out of my soul and I feel a tiny piece of me starting to break.

"Scream as much as you want, no one can hear you," he says calmly, not at all affected by my pain or tears.

He lays the fifth strike right on my back where the cuts are, and I scream out again. He stops and runs his hands across my ass and back where it stings. His touch is soothing even though I wish his hands weren't on me.

He moves his hand lower until they're between my legs and he snickers.

"You're fucking wet?" he asks as he lets out a laugh. "See, my assumption about you being a whore wasn't too far off. You must like it really rough if you're wet right now. Where was this side of you when we were dating? Were you saving it for only when you were being a cheating skank?"

I feel so ashamed of myself right now. Why the hell am I wet when all he's doing is spewing nasty words to me? Tears stream down my face. I don't know what the fuck is happening to me. I'm not supposed to be weak when it comes to him. I'm supposed to hate him as much as he hates me.

I really am fucked in the fucking head.

"Maybe I should get a taste of what I've been missing for the past two years," he says. I hear him taking off his pants.

"Mason! Stop! Don't do this!" I scream when I feel him push open my legs more. "Please, I know you still care about me somewhere in there!"

"I don't fucking care about the fucking bitch who ruined me!" he screams just as I feel his thick cock plunge into my pussy in one hard thrust.

I let out another scream and try to wiggle away from his brutal pumping, but it's no use because of the tight grip he has on my hips.

"You were right that day over at Beck's. Maybe I do need another fuck to get you out of my system." He moans while still thrusting into me violently. "Yeah, that's right, baby, clench on my cock like a whore in heat."

I freeze because I didn't realize I was clenching his cock with my pussy.

"You're so fucking wet," he murmurs in a voice filled with ecstasy. "I thought you were supposed to hate me, babe. What happened? Were you just pretending because secretly you still want my cock?"

God, I can't bear to listen to his words anymore and I try to run away inside my head. I'm about to do just that, when I feel his hands on my clit rubbing. A few minutes later, I'm coming on his cock just like the whore he accused me of being not two minutes ago.

He lets out a roar and spills his cum inside me a minute before he gets off me. I'm left lying there still bound to his bed, lying spread open on my stomach with cum dripping out of my pussy. I've never felt dirtier than I do at this moment.

"You look fucking pathetic," he says when he comes back over to me.

"Fuck you, asshole!"

Tears spill down my face now, and a minute later, I stiffen when I feel him touch me. Before I can even move or do anything, I feel a prick on my neck and then everything goes black.

As consciousness slowly sets in, I let out a groan. The pain stabs me in the head and in my body.

Where the hell am I? And why did I drink so much? My eyes slowly open and I spot Mason next to me in the bed. He's still asleep.

Oh God, please don't tell me I had sex with this asshole last night. I will be pissed with myself.

I try to move but pain shoots through my back which causes me to wince. The memories of last night come rushing back a second later, and horror washes over me at what he did to me.

I look over at him again and he looks so peaceful in his sleep, like he could do nothing wrong. Well, the devil was also a liar, and he hid his true nature behind something good-looking.

I slowly sit up with every intention of leaving but freeze as I take in the bed before me and the state I'm in.

I'm naked and so are all five of them. Horror washes over me before pain unlike anything I've ever felt consumes me whole. I've had people hate me and betray me before, but I never thought they would ever betray me like this.

I feel the symptoms of a panic attack coming on and I feel sick to my stomach. I barely manage to jump out of the bed before rushing into the bathroom off to the side of the room.

I barely get in there before the contents of my stomach come spilling out. *No, no, no, nooo...* I keep chanting in my head as the vomiting continues.

When I'm done, I rinse my mouth and grab the t-shirt on the floor of the bathroom, not caring who it belongs to right now. My entire body aches and the only thing consuming my mind is the need to get out of here.

My breaths are coming out in gasps now and I know I

need to leave before I have an actual panic attack. I espe-cially can't let it get past that because it's not safe for me.

I make a dash out of the bathroom intending to leave but come full stop in the room when all five of them turn to face me. They're still naked and I feel the first set of tears run down my face.

"Did you guys—" I cut off because I can't even finish my thought, but I need to know. I don't even know what knowing will do in this situation right now. Would it be better, or should I just stay in the dark and leave?

"Di-did, you guys ha-have sex with m-me?" I finally stutter out because I figure I need to know if they betrayed me and violated me because of him. I wrap my hands around myself as my breathing picks up.

I can already feel the stabbing pain in my head. I close my eyes, willing the pain away, but it's getting worse if that's possible. I'm sweating and feeling dizzy. My heart feels like it's about to beat out of my chest while I wait for someone to answer me.

It feels like ages but might only be five seconds since I've been standing here waiting for an answer. Is it time or is it my brain slowing down?

Mason is the first one to answer me, because of course he is. "Use your fucking brain, Winter. We were all naked when you woke up, weren't we?"

I don't want to believe him, I can't. I can't believe that he'd do this to hurt me while also hurting my friends. And that's when it hits me, if the girls ever found out about any of this, they will hate me even though I had nothing to do with this.

Everything is getting the better of me now and the panic takes over the longer I stand there waiting.

I look over to Royce and plead with him to tell me none of this is true. "Please tell me you wouldn't do this to Riley!"

I look over to Beckett and then Nate frantically. "Please tell me you guys wouldn't do this to Avery and Luna either! I'm sure you all know by now they've had crushes on you for years!"

Finally, my eyes land on Grayson, and my voice cracks as I rasp out, "Please tell me you wouldn't hurt me like this..." Pain shoots through my chest.

It's the kind that lets me know I'm in trouble already if I don't get out of here and calm the fuck down soon. None of them answer me, but they all watch as I slowly fall apart in front of them.

"Fucking answer me!" I scream when I can't take the silence any longer.

"Of course, we had sex... actually it was a gang bang, but your pussy wasn't that good. It was really stretched out after the five of us had our turns. I mean, we've shared before and the girls have never been that stretched out before..." Mason is the one to answer. None of the others are saying a word.

"Pass me the remote, Gray," he says to his brother, and of course Grayson does what he's asked.

Once he has the remote in his hands, he flips on the huge flat-screen television he has mounted on the wall. I don't know why I'm still standing here, waiting for the other shoe to drop.

As soon as it turns on, a slideshow of pictures plays on the screen and I sob. They're from last night. There are different pictures from various angles which show me and each of the guys and then all of us together with their hands and mouths all over my body.

I close my eyes to block out the images playing across

the screen when I hear him again, "Guess you're my bitch now. I own you and you'd do well to remember that if you don't want those pictures finding their way to the girls or the press."

I'm still crying and it's as if his words are the last nail in my coffin. The stress of everything that happened since I woke up slams into me full force. *Yeah, yeah, I already regret not leaving when I had the chance.*

My body convulses, and I fall to the floor, hitting my head. I can feel my body twitching and feel the spit coming out of my mouth like foam. My body keeps twitching. This is the point where my brain is still semi-conscious, but it's fading.

I know it's only going to get worse from here. I've suffered through a few of these before. After the Mason shit two years ago, I was under what the doctor called severe mental stress and that's what caused my seizures in the first place.

I lie there in pain while my vision goes in and out, my body convulsing and then the numbness takes over and everything goes black...

TWENTY

Mason

"Guess you're my bitch now. I own you and you'd do well to remember that if you don't want those pictures finding its way to the girls or the press," I say to her emotionlessly.

Every time I look at her all I want to do is hurt her. My hatred for this woman has grown exponentially in two years, and sometimes it's hard to believe that there was a time when I actually loved her.

Seeing her here in tears, wondering if she actually slept with us and then seeing the proof herself is like a balm to my aching soul. Horror washes over her face as the slideshow plays, and I love every minute of the crestfallen expression that now covers her beautiful features.

Even while sobbing so hard, she's still beautiful. *Whoa there, Mase... get your shit together! We hate her.*

Last night was the most fun I've had in years. I was fucking pissed for what she did to my car, and I fucking made sure she paid for her little stunt.

Besides it being my baby, it costs a cool 1.9 million and even though I can afford to get a new one, it's the principle of making the bitch pay, you know?

My thoughts go back to last night before the guys came in. I was so fucking hard while I whipped her ass to teach her a lesson that I had to have her.

She was fucking wet and coming on my dick. I don't know if it was the fact that I hate her or what, but that was kind of the best sex we've ever had. Guess she really was holding out on me.

I thought having her one last time would quench my thirst for her and get her out of my system, but no, I still want to fuck her again.

I hate her and I still want her to pay for what she did. Just because she let me back into her pussy didn't mean I wouldn't punish her still. I had plans and that included the guys. They knew the score, so after I gave her the drugs, we did what we had to do.

And that brings us to now. We're all watching her freak out and I can't help but taunt her about fucking us all. I continue watching her. I can't keep my eyes away from the train wreck of what is slowly her falling apart.

She has all my attention and I'm like the moth who is ensnared with the flames of their death. I don't have a clue why I'm so obsessed.

Our story will turn out differently though because I happen to love the flames, it's where I thrive. But I can't say the same for her. She should have already known not to fight me because I always win.

People tend to get burned in my rage once they cross me, and when that happens, I'm all too happy to let out the barely restrained rage I have living inside me. Everyone gets the same cold man once they've done something to deserve it, and since it's *her,* she gets an extra dose of venom.

I look over to her again, and she's full-on crying. She's gasping with the force of her sobs, and the sight of her tears does nothing for me. I don't even feel sorry for her. Now that I've done what I set out to do, I just want her out of my sight.

When things start to take an unexpected turn, however, I realize that I'm also the fucking liar I'm always accusing her of being.

Her body shakes and at first, I think it's because she's crying, but a second later, her body convulses and shakes even harder before she falls to the floor. It looks like she has no control over her body and she's not able to stop her fall.

She hits her head, and her body continues to twitch. When I see what looks like white foam come out of her mouth, it's like that finally breaks me out of my trance and I rush off the bed and run over to her.

That spurs everyone else into action and they all rush out of the bed and come over to her.

"What the fuck is happening to her?" Grayson stutters out. From the tone of his voice, I know he's about a second away from freaking out.

"I don't fucking know!" I say, my heart hammering inside my chest. I want to fuck with her, but I don't want to kill her. *Yet.*

"Fucking hell, Mason! I told you we shouldn't have done that!" he says, grabbing his hair while pacing the room.

"Now is not the time for freaking out!" Nate snaps and then instructs everyone to get their clothes on.

"We need to get her to the hospital," Royce says, and they all quickly get dressed.

I do the same before picking her up into my arms and rushing to the elevator. The guys all follow and then we're in the garage. Grayson opens the door for me, and I get into the SUV with her still in my arms before we take off for the hospital.

I don't know if picking her up was the right move, but I

didn't want to leave her there. I just hope I didn't cause any internal damages.

Beck drives like a bat out of hell and before we know it, we're pulling up to the emergency room. Gray flies out of the car and rushes into the ER. As I'm getting out of the car, two nurses rush out with a gurney.

They quickly take her from my arms and place her onto it before rushing into the ER room with it.

We wait for an hour before the doctor comes out with some news. He knows better than to try that doctor/patient privacy bullshit with me because we give this hospital a lot of money. He lets us know she's fine and resting now.

"She had a seizure. It's the type that is caused by extreme mental distress. From her chart we pulled, it started happening about two years ago. Not to worry, she's absolutely fine now."

"Okay," I say because I have no clue what else there is to say.

"We'll be keeping her overnight, just in case there are any other issues."

"Sure thing, doc. Is she allowed any visitors?"

"Yes, but make sure that she stays calm. We don't need another episode like that to happen. More than one in just a few hours could cause serious damage."

"Yeah, I got it, doc."

"Are you actually going to see her?" Gray asks.

"No, I don't think any of us should. I'll just peep into her door and see if she's good before we leave."

"Does this change things?" Beck questions and I know what he's asking. He wants to know if I'm done torturing her, if I'll stop humiliating her any chance I get.

As much as I'd like to say that this changes things and I'll let her off the hook, I'm too much of an asshole to let things go. I'll back off for a while, but I'm in no way done with her.

I can't be because then I wouldn't know what to do with myself. She's still a fucking addiction even after all this time, and if I want to get over the spell she still has on me, then I need her pain. Nothing else will calm the monster inside me.

If nothing else, today showed me I still fucking care somewhat and I can't have that. She destroyed me, and I don't know if I'll ever be able to get over that.

"No," I tell them before walking off.

I walk to her room and stand just outside her door, peeping in through the glass. She's just lying on the bed staring out of the window, not moving a muscle. It's like she's completely lost.

I don't know how long I stand there looking at her before I finally catch myself. I walk away because I don't give a shit about her anymore.

Yeah, yeah, I'm still a fucking liar.

I SLOWLY WAKE up to the sound of a beeping machine. I don't even have to open my eyes to know where I am.

After spending countless days in a hospital before, I know exactly what it's like just from instinct now.

When I finally do open my eyes, I see that I'm alone in the room, which I'm thankful for. It takes a minute to remember why I'm here.

I remember feeling the signs of a panic attack coming on after seeing all those pictures and videos with the guys. It became too much that my stress levels passed the level it wasn't supposed to pass, which brought on the seizure.

I can't believe that shit happened in front of the guys. Who the hell knows how they're going to use that against me?

Tears form in my eyes because everything is shit now. I don't know how I'll be able to face my best friends after what I've done. I never thought the guys would go this far just to help Mason ruin me and my friendship with the girls. They'd hate me if they ever found out.

I can't believe the guys would even take part knowing how the girls feel about them. They might not have really said anything, but even having been away for so long, I can see how they all are around each other. The guys know how the girls feel about them.

I'm sure they also feel something for them too, right? I mean, they're always protective of their girls, respectively. I don't know why they would fuck it up by doing that with me and then having evidence of it too.

Tears roll down my face when I think about what happened last night. How do you get rid of pain when someone is always hurting you at every opportunity they get?

I'm just lying there lifelessly and staring out my window when I hear the door to my room opening. I haven't moved a muscle in hours. Why bother when I don't have the motivation to do anything, much less try to get better?

That's how I know things are going from bad to worse. I can feel my depression settling in. The last time I went through this, I had my father to help bring me out of it; now, I have no one. The thought of having no one by my side hurts more than anything right now.

"Hello, Miss Crowne," the voice says, bringing me out of

my thoughts. I turn around to look at the doctor before responding.

"Hello, and please call me Winter," I tell him.

"Okay, Winter, I'm assuming you know why you're in here?"

"Yeah."

"Okay, well I won't go over everything with you because based on your file I know you've dealt with this often, but we're keeping you overnight just to be safe," he says in a friendly but professional tone.

"Yeah, fine, that's okay." I don't bother arguing because I just don't care right now.

I sigh and lie back down in the bed as he leaves the room. I fall asleep and a few hours later, I'm woken up from my nap when the nurse comes in with my medication and dinner.

I don't really feel like eating even though I'm sort of hungry. Yeah, my depression is already here without a doubt.

Ugh, why couldn't I just be normal? Since my life hasn't once gone the way I wanted it to, you'd think God or whoever is in charge of the world would give me a break or something.

The nurse leaves me after she's made sure that I have everything I need, and I'm thankful she didn't talk to me. I'm liable to just start crying now for no reason if someone tries to ask me any questions.

My mother hasn't tried to contact me for the few hours I've been in here. Does she even know I'm currently lying in a hospital bed alone? Does she even care?

I haven't seen any of the guys either since I woke up, though that's for the best. I don't want to see any of them at the moment or rather at all.

I'm still torn up about everything they did to me, and I hate the fact that I'm letting them consume my thoughts when they should have no space in there.

Sighing, I take a few bites of my food because if I don't get some nutrients into me, then I'll be no good to anyone.

I wish my life had a do-over button. I'd wish to never meet Mason. Maybe then, my life wouldn't be such a mess and I wouldn't have to constantly have my guard up.

TWENTY-ONE

Winter

I wake up in my hospital bed still alone on Sunday, and I'm not surprised that no one came to visit me. I don't know if the girls know what happened. I'm hoping they don't. Even though I wish they were here with me, it's for the best they aren't. I don't think I can face them right now.

Not after what I did and how I betrayed them. That's like the first rule of girl club, isn't it? Don't sleep with your besties' ex or crush. My fucking ass broke that rule. *Yeah, just give me the worst-best-friend-ever award.*

I spend the rest of the morning lost in my thoughts, thinking about how my life has turned into one big cluster-fuck. I still wish I knew why he hates me so much and why he's intent on destroying me.

If I take the events of yesterday into consideration, I'd say he's doing an amazing job so far.

Around noon the doctor walks into my room to check on me. Once he makes sure that everything is good for now and I'm not in any immediate danger, he gives the okay for my discharge.

I don't have my phone or any money, so I'm not sure how I'll get home. I'm thinking about it while getting dressed and Antonio comes to mind. Since our date, we've been talking and texting but haven't had a chance to see each other again because we've both been busy.

Now seems like a good time as any, so hopefully he doesn't mind seeing me or coming to pick me up. I could call Martin to come get me, but I don't want him to see me like this again.

I use the phone in my hospital room and since I never memorized anyone's numbers except for Mason's, I have to call 411. There is no way in hell I'm calling that asshole.

Once I get through, I ask to get Chase's number and it takes a few minutes before I get it. I hang up and then dial him, I would have called Antonio directly, but I have no clue if he lives here or if he just comes here when he has business. Chase is the best bet.

"Hello, this is Chase Bishop. How may I help you?"

"Hey, Chase, it's Winter."

"Hey, boss, what can I do for you?"

"Can you get me Antonio Bandini's cell number?"

"Sure thing, boss. Do you want me to text it to you?"

"Erm no, I'll wait on the phone. I don't have my cell right now."

I sit on the bed and wait while I hear what must be Chase typing away at his computer. A few minutes later he comes back on the line giving me the number I requested. After I hang up with Chase, I give Antonio a call and he answers on the third ring, thankfully.

"Hello?"

"Antonio?"

"Ah, *cara*, I was wondering when you'd call again. I haven't heard from you this weekend and got no response when I tried to contact you," he says in that sexy voice of his.

"Um, I have a favor to ask... can you pick me up from the hospital? And can you also bring me some clothes and shoes please?"

The flirty voice he had a few minutes ago turns serious as he speaks again, "I'm on my way, *cara,* and sure. Which hospital and what room?"

"Ravenwood Private and room 211," I say, giving him my clothes sizes before hanging up.

I move from my sitting position and lie back down on the bed to wait. I have nothing else to do and I'm exhausted. Half an hour later, the door to my room bursts open and Antonio's tall frame is in the doorway.

"*Cara!*" he says, rushing over to me. "What the hell happened? Why are you in the hospital?"

I gulp because I don't really want to talk about this. So I just give him the cliff notes version. "I-I um, I was under a lot of stress from work and school and I got sick..." That is close to the version of what happened. *Okay, not really, but I'm not touching that with a ten-foot pole right now.*

He must sense that I don't really want to talk about it because he drops it. He helps me get out of bed and walks me into the bathroom to get dressed. Once I'm done, we walk out of the room. I already signed my release papers and got my medication, so I'm all good for now.

He throws his arm around my shoulders and pulls me in closer to him as we walk out the doors. When we get to the front, he tells me to wait there while he goes to get his car.

I stand there and shiver as I feel the telltale sign of being watched washes over me. I look around. At first, I don't notice anything or anyone out of the ordinary, but then I see someone in the shadows. It's a guy, and he's on a motorcycle. I can't see his face because he has on one of those helmets that covers your entire face, and the visor is down.

I know he's looking at me even though I can't see his eyes. When he sees me watching, he revs his bike before taking off.

I gulp. It has to be the person who is sending me all those texts and pictures. A minute later, Antonio pulls up and gets out to help me into his car.

"Are you okay, *cara?* You look a bit shaken up."

"I'm okay," I say. I don't want to bother him with the fact that I have a potential stalker.

"Okay, where to, *cara?*"

"Do you want to hang out for a while before you take me home? I'm not really in the mood to go home right now."

"Of course, *cara mia*, but first let's get some food into you."

"That sounds awesome!" I say, cracking a smile.

I barely eat during our late lunch, but thankfully he doesn't say anything about it. He just keeps me company all day while we just spend some time doing nothing.

The day with him is one of the best I've had in a while, but even that couldn't stop my thoughts from running wild inside my head, wondering what happens next where my life is concerned.

I tried to ignore everything happening around me, and the one time I decide to fight Mason, I end up in the hospital. With this stalker escalating, I'm not sure what to do.

Mason's father cornering me in his office and letting me know about naming Mason as the one who set my tree house on fire means that the police are working for him so I can't trust them anymore.

Now I doubt I'll get any information about anything,

especially the shooting that traumatized me. I just want to break down and cry. This town is causing me to slowly lose my mind.

But I need to get through this. Somehow, I need to figure it out. I will not let anyone break me.

———

It's not until seven p.m. when I make it home and once I do, the sight I never expected in my house is there as I pass by the dining room.

I halt abruptly, taking in everything in front of me. Clearly, I've gone bloody bonkers.

The dining room is set and the four people sitting there are the ones responsible for my constant misery. I look at my mother, Mason, Grayson, and their dad sitting at the table chatting away.

Does no one even notice I'm missing? Even though it shouldn't, it causes an ache to spread through my chest. Nobody cares... least of all the people in this very room. Wow, it really is soul crushing when you realize nobody actually cares about you, especially when a part of you has been hoping that they do in fact care.

None of them have noticed me yet because they're having their own conversation. It's like I don't even exist. I'm not in on this little, whatever it is, they have going on here and that just makes me angry. I've spent hours in the hospital because of these assholes and no one bothered to visit me.

"What the fuck is going on here and why the fuck are they in our house?" I screech out, causing every eye in the room to land on me.

"Where the hell have you been?" my mother asks instead of answering my question.

"Why don't you ask those two assholes over there!" I hiss out, pointing to the two douchebags.

"Young lady, I don't appreciate you talking to my sons like that," Alister King grits out with anger in his voice.

"I really don't give a fuck what you appreciate."

"Someone needs to teach her some manners," he hisses out to my mother.

"Winter, shut the fuck up and go get changed and then come back here. We have some news to announce," she says.

I'm so pissed it's like I'm blind to nothing but the rage inside of me. Before I can even think about what I'm doing, the words are spewing out of my mouth, "What the fuck? No, I'm not coming down back here because I don't give a shit about what it is you have going on here. I've been in the hospital for two days and you didn't even bother to check on me to see if I was okay or not. You didn't think that something must have been wrong for me to not have come home?"

"I thought you were out whoring yourself around," she says with a shrug, and I feel the telltale sign of pain shooting through my chest because of her vicious words.

"Wouldn't be far from the truth," I hear Mason mutter.

I feel the tears threaten to come out when I look at her and she just has a bored expression on her face, not giving a damn about anything that happened to me.

"Well, it's not like you're dead, are you? And you're just in time for our news," she says, digging the dagger further into my chest.

I'm literally speechless right now. I haven't looked at

Mason or Gray since I started talking. Out of everyone in this room, they've done the most damage to me and I can't bear to look at them.

"You know what, fuck you and everyone in this room!" I scream at the top of my lungs.

Alister moves so fast I didn't even have the time to notice he moved out of his seat. I feel the sting of a slap that twists my head to the side and I instantly feel blood dripping down my chin from my split lip.

"Listen here, little girl, your mother and I are getting married, and you'd better show some respect!" he growls. I look over at Mason and Gray but neither one is looking in my direction.

"Fucking cowards!" I spit at them. That gets them to look up but they both have a bored I-don't-give-a-fuck look on their faces, not caring that their father is manhandling me.

I let out a laugh. It's finally sinking in that they don't give a fuck anymore if they're letting their father hit me without doing anything to step in.

"What the fuck did you just say?" Alister seethes out.

"I said they're fucking cowards and now I get it. The apple doesn't fall far from the tree—"

He slaps me again before yelling, "I can't wait to get married to your mother just to straighten you out!"

"I don't care what the fuck you do, because you and your pathetic sons will never be anything to me!"

I look over at them again and see Mason clenching the table and Gray holding him back. I'm under no illusion that he wants to help me because he's done everything in his power to cause me untold misery since I came home.

He's probably just pissed that I'm calling him a coward

in front of his father and probably wishes he could come strangle me right now.

He grabs me around the throat this time and I'm prepared. I knee him in the balls and he promptly lets go of me. This is the second time I've kneed him in the balls and if his expression is anything to go by, it's that I better sleep with one eye open because sooner or later he'll retaliate.

"You're going to fucking pay for that, you little slut!" he roars out, but I'm already halfway down the hall, running up to my room.

As soon as I get to the safety of my room, I lose it. I let out a scream and start destroying everything in sight. I throw every vase against the wall, flip over all the side tables and everything else I can get my hands on.

I can't stop moving because if I do, all these feelings inside me will get too much to deal with. I pace the room and will myself to calm down, so I don't end up in the fucking hospital again.

While pacing, I trip over one of the side tables I knocked over and land on my hands and knees. The broken glass of the vase slices my hands and knees and when I try to get up, the glass goes into my feet as well since I took off my shoes when I got to my room.

I'm bleeding all over the place now and I stand staring at the blood on my hands and feet. I don't know what it is about the sight of my own blood, but I break all over again as tears stream down my face.

I'm so engrossed in my own misery that I don't hear the door to my room opening.

I'm not aware of anyone else until I feel hands wrap around my waist, lifting me and then moving me away from the broken glass.

I'm snapped out of it and my tears stop for a minute as I

look up and see Mason is the one holding me. Grayson is standing a few feet away from him. I lose it all over again.

Without even thinking, I punch him in the face. Fuck, that hurt but I've never felt more satisfied in my life. Then I hit him in the chest because I can't seem to stop myself. He doesn't even flinch, and that just pisses me off more.

"Get the fuck out of my room! Why are you two even here?" I yell at them.

"I just came here to give you another friendly warning," Mason says.

"You can take your warning and shove it up your fucking asshole because I'm pretty sure you like it in the ass!" From here I see Grayson flinch at my words, and I turn my attention to him.

"Get the fuck out! I despise you more than this asshole!" I yell at him. "You wanted to be my friend and then stabbed me in the back," I say as the tears I've been trying to hold in start flowing down my cheeks.

"Winter—"

"No, don't fucking say a word. How could you? I expected that shit from cuntmuffin over there, but not you. Do you know how hard it is living with myself knowing what I did and how I betrayed my friends?"

He doesn't answer, but what else is there to say when you practically have the power to ruin someone's life further than how it's already ruined?

"I fucking hate the two of you for what you did!" I yell, my voice hoarse.

When I feel like a panic attack is on the verge of coming again, I abruptly stop. Both of them look completely confused with my abrupt change from screaming to not making a sound.

Yeah, I'd be confused as fuck too if someone went from

one hundred to zero in a second. But I will not hurt myself anymore so they can get the satisfaction from it.

"I don't care if our parents are getting married or not, I hate the two of you. You'll never be anything to me again. I will never forgive either of you," I whisper in a pain-filled voice before limping away and leaving them standing there.

TWENTY-TWO

Winter

AFTER THE DISASTER that was my mother and the Kings last night, I woke up this morning feeling drained but with a determination to push through even if it kills me.

I feel so lost. It's like I'm standing at the edge of a precipice and everyone around me is just waiting for me to fall off.

I don't have anyone to turn to anymore when things get too tough for me because I'm not sure how to act around my friends after everything that happened with the guys.

I don't know what games they're playing now, but I won't let those assholes win. When I got up this morning, it was with the intention of facing them head-on and letting them know that whatever they do; it does not affect me.

Easier said than done, especially when you're still hoping that the people who want to destroy you are the same ones that love you.

My mom and Mason's dad getting married is something I never saw coming, and that has put me out of sorts more than anything. What the hell happened to our families hating each other?

For years they've supposedly hated each other, and now they're getting married? Yeah, something is definitely not right, and I need to figure it out.

I'm worried about what this means for me. One, Mason is going to be my stepbrother and two, the way his dad looked at me, I wouldn't trust him as far as I could throw him. And let's face it, I can't throw him an inch.

He looks like he wouldn't mind hurting me, but also the way he looks at me gives me some very creepy vibes. I wouldn't put it past him to try something.

I know I'll need to be extra careful from now on. I'm literally living in enemy territory.

It's now I realize that my life is about to go from bad to worse because every single one of the four of them, hates me.

How the hell do you live with the people who hate you? And I say live with all four of them because my mother said we're moving in with the Kings this week.

I told her I'd rather stay on my own and get my own place, but she nipped that in the bud with her threats again.

I honestly don't understand why she still wants me living with her when she hates me. It could only mean she has plans for me and she needs me close to her.

Keep your enemies close and all that...

Back to Mason... I don't know how to feel about the fact that we'll be family? No, we're definitely never going to be family because there's too much bad blood between us. It's absolutely disconcerting thinking about him as my step-brother.

I mean, I've loved the guy for half my life, so thinking of him as family definitely does not get the juices flowing.

Gah, so much is happening in such a short amount of time, I don't know which way is up anymore. I've shoved everything that happened this past weekend out of my mind because if I think about it, I won't be able to function properly. Though that doesn't help with my guilt at all.

I need to talk to my friends soon before they find out about what happened from someone else. If they do, that will probably not end well.

I push that thought in the back of my mind to deal with later because I just got to my office and I have other things to think about.

I look through some of the personnel files my father had and find his private investigator to see if he can help me with what I need. I get the number and dial right away. I don't have time to waste.

I have a bad feeling that something bad is coming soon and I need to be prepared even though I have no clue what it is yet.

Being around the vipers, I'm deciding to trust my gut on this. The phone rings three times before there is an answer.

"Hello?"

"Hi, is this Chester Thomas?"

"Who's asking?"

"Winter Crowne. I was looking through my father's files and found your name. I was wondering if I could use your services."

"Sure, I'm always free for the Crownes."

"Whatever I ask of you, I'll need it to remain confidential... as in no one else can know what you're looking for," I tell him. I don't want this getting back to my mother.

"Absolutely, I was loyal to your father and now to you."

"Thank you," I say and then tell him exactly what I need from him.

After that phone call, I get to work and get ready for all the meetings I have today. I'm surprised that so far, I've actually got the basics down and every day is getting a little easier.

This makes me happy and I don't feel like a complete failure. I hope my father is proud of me for everything I'm doing so far.

After lunch, I get started on looking over some proposals and some of the numbers for the company's financials. I notice some of these numbers are off.

I spend the rest of the day going over them and trying to find out what's missing, but have no luck in sorting out the issue.

I make a note to get Mr. Carson's input on it tomorrow. I seriously hope it's not someone fucking with me.

I'm exhausted by the time I can leave the office. I call Martin and let him know I'm ready.

I seriously don't know how my father did this every single day and still had the energy to put up with me and find time to spend with me.

When Martin lets me know he's here, I make my way down. Once I'm in the car, we make our way to my new home.

Once we get there, the exhaustion fully takes over. All I want to do is fall onto my bed and sleep for at least an entire year.

I walk into the house and it's quiet. Well, it always is because this house is so big. It's like a ghost house. You'd never know if anyone is home or not.

After not seeing anyone else, which I'm thankful for, I make my way up to what is now my bedroom. True to her word, my mother made us move into the King's mansion. To say things have been strained and awkward would be an understatement.

This room feels all types of wrong. It's just a plain

bedroom, and it doesn't fit me at all. And because the universe hates me, imagine my surprise when I walked into my bathroom and saw that it's connected to Mason's room.

It freaking sucks that we have to share. This house is filled with rooms, so I have no clue why they gave me this one. Grayson's room is opposite mine, which I am not happy about either. I'm literally in between my two enemies.

I guess I didn't notice any of this the last time I was up here. I was in his bathroom puking my guts out after what they did, so I never noticed the other door. Not that it would have mattered even if I saw it, because never in my wildest dreams did I ever think I would be living here.

This place doesn't feel like a home and I will never consider it as such. Too much has happened between me and these people for me to not be on edge while living here.

I don't know why, but I keep getting the feeling of just waiting for the other shoe to drop. I have to constantly keep my guard up around everyone here because they all seem to have hidden agendas when it comes to me.

I still don't know what's really going on because I haven't been able to find anything on my own. Thank God, I contacted that PI today. Hopefully, he will have some answers for me soon.

I asked him to look into my mother and Alister and while he was at it, Mason and Grayson too. You can never be too careful.

I'm still not talking to the douchebags, but that doesn't mean they've left me alone.

I still get taunted by them.

I still get the mean words from my mother.

I still get the weird looks from Alister.

It's a constant everyday thing where I always have to

watch my back whenever I'm in this house. So far, this has been another aspect of my life that's been nothing but exhausting.

All I want is for the hostility and hate for me to end. But again, that would be wishful thinking.

Sighing, I get undressed and walk into the shower to wash off the exhaustion of the day.

I turn on the shower and wait for it to heat up before walking into it. I brace my hands on the shower glass with my head bent while I let the hot water cascade down my hair and body.

The hot water helps to ease my muscles a little, and I'm instantly feeling better. Too bad that feeling doesn't last for long.

My head is still bent when I hear the shower door open behind me. I don't even need to look to know who it is.

Fucking hell, I thought no one else was home.

"Get out!" I say, still not moving from my position or looking in his direction.

"This is my house, and I can be in any part of it. The better question is, why don't you get out?"

"Because I was in here first, asshole!" I say.

"That's not what I meant, and you know it!"

"Whatever. Just leave so I can finish showering," I tell him, hoping that he'll leave. But again, Mason never does what you tell him to.

"Why are you still here? I thought I told you to leave Ravenwood," he growls.

"I'm not leaving just because you said to. You've already destroyed the one thing that meant anything to me here, so I don't see what else you could possibly do."

"Oh, there's so much more I could do to you," he whispers close to my ear. I wasn't even paying attention to his movements.

He's moved closer to me and both his hands are on the shower wall next to mine and his body is melded to my back.

I can feel the hard planes of his abs on my back and it's all muscle. His arms are filled with tattoos and the veins protruding from his hands are hot as hell.

But I can't give in to whatever game he's playing because that's all it is. He finds great pleasure in playing with my emotions whenever he can.

Oh how I wish I was strong enough to not fall for it, but how do you resist the man you were in love with for years even when you know he's no good for you anymore? And all he wants to do is see you suffer?

I turn around and his erection presses into my stomach while I stare at his pecs. The tattoos here are even more stunning. There's a raven on his right pec and a crown on the left. I try to resist the urge to look down, but my eyes betray me. There's an enormous skull on his stomach with a crown on it, and its significance doesn't escape me.

Dead king? As in he's dead inside and his name is king? I have no clue, I'm just assuming.

He brings his hand up and wraps it around my throat before tilting my head up to look at him. He has a deadly and angry expression on his face, which definitely deceived his voice from when I wasn't looking directly at him.

"Every time I look at you, all I want to do is hurt you."

I feel myself getting choked up and internally curse myself for being such a weak bitch. "You're already hurting me. You've been hurting me every day since I've been here."

"It's not enough!" he suddenly yells out at me. "How can someone who looks so pure be so disgusting?"

"And yet you're in this shower naked with me. What do you want? Why do you hate me so much?"

As usual, that is the wrong thing to ask him because it instantly makes him angrier.

"Leave that guy you've been seeing. I won't ask you again," he says instead, throwing me for a complete loop with this swift change of topic.

"Good, you don't have to ask again, because I'm not going to."

"Don't fucking test me, Winter!"

"Why the fuck do you care who I'm seeing? You don't give a shit about me, so I'll ask again, why do you care?"

"I don't, but you don't deserve to be happy for what you did!" His words just make me angry because he keeps saying what I did but never actually tells me what I supposedly did.

"Then fucking tell me what I did, asshole! I'm fucking sick and tried of you insinuating I did something when I have no idea what you're talking about!"

"You're still going to fucking deny it and act like you don't know what I'm talking about?"

"I'm not acting. I. Don't. Know what you're talking about, you fucking bastard!"

He grabs me by the neck again and drags me out of the shower and into his room. He flings me onto his bed. I try to crawl away, but he grabs me by the legs and hauls me closer to him again.

"If you're not going to leave, then I'm going to use you until I get my fill. If you don't cooperate, then those pictures will circulate around to every media site so fast you won't know what hit you!" he growls out at me.

"Mason! Stop! I don't fucking want this!" I scream out at him.

"I don't give a fuck! You should have fucking left when I gave you the chance to do so!"

"Ugh, you know I can't fucking leave, you ass... aahhhh- hhh!!!" I let out a scream as he plunges his cock into me without warning.

It hurts because I'm not wet. I wasn't ready for this. I can't take him when he's like this. It cracks my soul wide open every time he fucks me, especially when he lets all his hatred for me show.

I'm on my knees and he has his hands pressing my head into his mattress, making it hard to breathe. All the while, I feel his hips pumping into me.

He smacks my ass, and I try to struggle away from him, but it's no use. He's stronger than me and is using his strength to keep me down.

He flips me over onto my back and is inside me again in no time. This time, my hands are free and I move them around him and rake my nails down his back with all the strength I can muster.

I smile with satisfaction when I feel blood on my fingers, but it's short-lived when he grabs my throat with one hand and both my wrists with his other. His thrusts become merciless as he pounds into me.

He bends down and puts his mouth onto my breast before biting down hard, and I can barely let out the scream because of his hand around my neck before he moves on to the next one. I know that's going to leave a mark.

He moves to my neck and leaves more marks on my skin, all the while not even breaking the momentum of his thrusts into me.

Tears flow down my face when I look into his eyes and see them filled with so much hatred even while he's having sex with me. He doesn't even care that he's hurting me right now.

I don't even know if he's feeling any pleasure or if he's doing this just because he can. Because he thinks that he's punishing me for something I did.

A few minutes later, he stops, and I feel the telltale sign of him coming inside me. He rolls off me and I'm left lying there with my legs splayed open while tears run down my face.

So many different emotions are running through me right now, I don't know which one to feel.

When his breaths calm down, it's like he's finally realized what we just did. Is he mad at me or himself? I have no clue.

"Get out of my room!" he says in a harsh tone.

I stand up with shaky legs. My pussy hurts because of how brutal he was with me.

"When you get your head out of your ass, I'll take great pleasure in hating you forever," I tell him as I race out of his room and into the bathroom again.

I feel so dirty because of the way he just used me and then discarded me. I walk into the shower and turn it on and scrub my skin raw until I can't feel him on me anymore.

After I'm done, I slide down the wall as the sobs I've been holding in finally spill out and I cry until I'm too tired to do anything else.

TWENTY-THREE

Winter

I WALK DOWN into the kitchen the next morning after a sleepless night and the first thing that greets me is the sight of Mason sitting on the counter shirtless, eating a bowl of cereal.

Damn, doing something so mundane should not look so hot but too bad because I'd love nothing more than to stab his ass and watch him bleed to death. Too much? Well, you'd feel the same way if you were around this asshole.

I don't say anything to him and just proceed to get my own food and coffee before I need to leave for school.

A few minutes later, Grayson comes into the kitchen, also shirtless. Ugh, why couldn't they be fat or something?

"Morning Win," he says, but I ignore him and continue eating. The faster I eat, the faster I'll get out of here.

"It looks like she woke up on the wrong side of her bed this morning," Mason says to Gray. I give him one of my signature death glares.

My mom walks into the kitchen next. Could my morning get any worse? Apparently, it can. We haven't spoken much since our blowup at their family dinner that I crashed when she announced she was getting married to Mr. creepy.

"The engagement party is next week, and I expect you to be there," she says, looking directly at me.

"I have to work."

"It's happening on Saturday."

"I'm doing overtime."

"I don't care. I expect you to be there," she says before walking out of the kitchen, leaving me alone with the two idiots.

"Grrr, I fucking hate everyone in this place," I mutter under my breath.

"It's not like anyone here likes you, so it doesn't matter if you hate everyone," Mason responds. Of course he's always the one with the shitty replies.

"Get fucked, asshole!"

"I did last night, and it wasn't even good," he says smirking.

Dear God, I wish murder were legal for like a day so I could get rid of him. His presence is unwanted on this earth.

Struggling to contain my anger, I get up and stalk out of the room intending to leave.

"Have a good day at school, babe!" he calls after me and I'm immediately suspicious. Since I've been back, he's made it his mission for me to constantly have bad days, so him wishing me a good one is shady.

Not having any time to dissect his words any longer, I walk out the door ready for Martin to drop me off at school before I'm late.

I can't risk it. I've already left school early too many times when people have been messing with me.

I'm so behind and I haven't even started with my lab work yet, which is pissing me off. If I wasn't so caught up in trying to survive this god-awful place then I'd have probably made some improvements already.

I sigh because it is what it is, and I can't get mad at the things I can't change. I need to up my game somehow. My plate is so full, and I feel like I bit off more than I could chew. But I can't give up because I have to get this done.

After my panic and seizure attack this past weekend, I really need to put more focus into my work if I want to get it into the trial process soon.

After we pull up to school, I get out and walk into the main building. I need to get to the locker room to get one of my books, and no it's not a locker room filled with boys. Get your head out of the gutter!

It's an actual room filled with lockers in case you need one and I do because it's easier to leave my stuff here since I go back and forth from the office to school during the week.

The first thing that hits me after I enter the room is the smell. It's gag worthy. I hurry to my locker to get my book for class and leave this room. The smell is detestable.

I open my locker and a spray of liquid bursts out into my face and my entire front. A scream rips out of me from the unexpectedness of it, and I take a minute to get my bearings in place.

I wipe my face to get the liquid out of my eyes and when I look at my hands, they're red. In an instant, I feel my stomach turn queasy.

The sight fills me with horror, and I can't keep the contents from staying inside my stomach any longer. I throw up right where I'm standing and then continue to dry heave when there's nothing left to come out.

There are fucking dead rats in my locker and there's blood dripping everywhere. I'm soaked in it, and that realization makes me instantly on the verge of gagging again.

This is so fucking gross! I scramble out of the room and burst into the hallway. Immediately, I hear the sound of whispering and laughing. *Seriously? Is this some dumbass's version of Carrie? How bloody unoriginal.*

I don't pay them any mind however because my only thought is getting into the bathroom to clean this filth off me. I shudder at the thought, wondering what kind of blood this is. *Gag!*

The significance of those rats isn't lost on me either. This has Mason written all over it, and now I'm wondering if it's because I said they were the ones who made me end up in the hospital.

I guess me ending up in the hospital because of him didn't cause his hate for me to waver one bit because we're back to the fucking pranks. Although, I don't think pranks is the right word for what he's doing to me.

I WOULDN'T PUT it past the asshole though and with the way Alister looks at me, like he wouldn't mind strangling me with his bare hands, I don't see the boys getting chewed out by him. He would probably just laugh and tell them what a good job it was while slapping them on the back. You know, with that weird hand-back-slap-thingy that guys do?

Or it could be more payback for his stupid car. Gahh, I literally have no clue anymore. As soon as I make it into the bathroom, I rush into one of the stalls and empty my stomach again. I'm not going to lie, blood is so not my color!

I'm sensing a pattern here and Ravenwood U is not agreeing with me being back either. It seems like I've practically spent most of my time in the bathroom here.

Once I'm done, I strip out of my shirt and start washing

it in the sink. Thank God, it didn't have enough time to soak into my bra. I never thought about bringing extra clothes here, but now I'm rethinking things.

Though if they did that with my locker, then my clothes would have been damaged too.

That means I have nothing to cover me and I'm not putting that fucking shirt on again. It might be clean now, but there's still a sort of metallic smell from all the blood. Just having it anywhere near me makes me want to puke again.

A few minutes later my phone vibrates, and I stiffen. Can this day seriously get any worse?

I sigh and open my messages. What do you know, it's a video of everything that happened in the locker room just now? Well, that didn't take long at all. I let out a groan because everyone is getting to witness my humiliation firsthand.

I call Martin to pick me up and with no other option left, I walk out of the bathroom in my leggings and my bra. My leggings are wet with blood too, but I will not give these assholes the satisfaction of seeing me strut through these halls in my bra and panties.

As soon as I'm out and into the hallway again, all eyes are on me. No one helps because they never do. They just take out their phones. I know they're taking pictures and videos to post online, they all think it's funny.

Trying to act unaffected, I walk out the doors with my head held high like none of this even bothers me at all.

When I get to the parking lot, the guys are lounging by their cars because, of course, they are. There are also photographers here, and they don't hesitate to take pictures. Ugh, this is so embarrassing.

I know these assholes are the ones responsible for the

press being here and not even thinking about it, I flip them all the bird.

Thankfully, the girls weren't here yet. Even if they were, I've done my best to avoid them ever since I woke up in that bed with the guys. I usually come in late or when I know they don't have class.

I have a flexible schedule with RU since I'm running Crowne Enterprises. That makes it easier to evade them when I'm on campus.

Today was the one day I came in early to grab my work and books and I'm guessing Mason knows my schedule for him to be able to plan this. I know it was him because he's the ringleader.

Mason smirks at me as he watches me try to hide myself. This is definitely going to be another PR nightmare. People will start thinking I'm some sort of floozy for always being in the spotlight for the wrong reasons.

I feel a lump form in my throat. How the hell are people in the business world going to respect me when shit like this keeps happening, branding me in a poor light? Maybe my father made a mistake leaving me in charge.

I look over at the guys again and Grayson is looking over at me with a pinched expression on his face, but I just turn away from them while I stand there in humiliation. None of them are ever going to help me, especially when Mason is around.

A few minutes later, Martin pulls up and I scramble to get into the car. As we're pulling out of the parking lot at the entrance to school, I see a figure clad in all black sitting on a motorcycle again and chills break out onto my skin.

That can't be the same person from the hospital, right? As soon as we pass him, though, we make eye contact. Well, I'm guessing we would if he wasn't wearing a helmet again.

My window isn't tinted, so I know he can see me just as clearly as I can see him.

After we pass him, I turn around just in time to see him take off in the opposite direction. I have no clue why, but I feel it deep inside me—he isn't the person who has been sending me those notes and pictures.

Honestly, I have no idea why I have that feeling when I've never even seen his face before, but my gut is just telling me it's not him. I mean, I've seen him a few times since I've been in Ravenwood and he hasn't done anything to hurt me.

Then again, it could be him, and he could be waiting for the perfect time to make a move or something. Apparently, my instincts have not been helping me lately.

If I wasn't certain before, I am now. Someone is definitely watching me, and I have no clue who it is.

It could literally be any number of people, but what's the purpose? My days are seriously getting creepier and creepier the longer I'm here.

BY THE TIME we make it home, I'm super pissed off because of everything that happened this morning.

No wonder that asshole was wishing me a good morning when he knew it wasn't going to be a good one because of that shit he had planned.

God, I hate the man he's become. He's nothing if not fucking cruel to me, and I'm just waiting for the day he finds out that I didn't betray him. I can't believe I thought we had a future together. Guess I was delusional even from a young age.

After I get home, I jump straight into the shower and

scrub my skin raw to get rid of the blood. *I wish it were his blood from me slicing him into tiny pieces and then throwing him in the Ravenwood river...*

Since I'm not keen on going to jail for this asshole, the perfect idea comes to me while I am murdering him in my mind in a million different ways.

I quickly got out of the shower and grabbed my laptop to do some quick research.

Two hours later, with the help of Martin, I've got everything I need. It might be considered juvenile, but I don't care. This asshole deserves some of his own medicine.

I walk into his room and set about doing what needs to be done before walking back into my room and relaxing for the rest of the day while waiting for the magic to start.

My mind goes to Antonio because I haven't seen him in a few days and Mason's threat for me to leave him is still on my mind.

He's a certifiable psycho and I have no clue what else he'll do if he finds out I didn't listen. But then again, he can go fuck himself. I'm not letting him mess up the happiness I've finally found after two years.

My phone buzzes and I see all the new articles popping up on the gossip sites—me in my leggings and bra, and the locker incident. I groan. That didn't take long.

It's a nightmare being constantly humiliated but as much as I try to fight back, they have the upper hand. It's all of them against me.

I must have fallen asleep because a girl's scream wakes me up and when I look out my windows, I see that it's already dark outside.

I know where it's coming from and I rush through my bathroom and open the door into Mason's room.

The sight that greets me makes me want to laugh and

cry at the same time. Mason and his fling or girlfriend or whatever are both standing buck naked and scratching themselves like their lives depend on it.

That's the sight that makes me want to cry because he fucked me last night and now he already has someone else in his bed. He really is a despicable pig! He must take after his father.

"Yikes! Looks like someone has crabs after all," I say. That catches both their attention. "Better get tested, sweetheart."

"What the fuck are you doing inside my boyfriend's room?" she screams at me.

"Oh, he didn't tell you?" I say in a sickly sweet voice. "I live here now."

"What the hell is she talking about, Mason?" she screams. It would carry more weight if it weren't for the fact that she's scratching like crazy. I can't help but let out the snicker.

I mock gasp and act like I just remembered something. "Speaking about testing... holy fuck, I need to get tested too because he fucked me bare last night and I seriously don't want to catch whatever it is you've both got right now," I say, and then walk out of his room.

She definitely looks like she wouldn't mind killing me right now if she had the chance. I'm not even in my room for a second when Mason comes storming through the bathroom and into my room.

He pushes me until he slams me up against the wall and wraps his hands around my neck, squeezing. "What the fuck do you think you're doing?" he seethes.

"Just playing the fucking game you started. What? Did you think I'd let you have all the fun?" I ask, smirking at him.

"What did you do to my room?"

"Just some good ole itching powder. I know, I know, it's childish, but it was perfect on such short notice. If I knew you would have your slut here tonight, I would've given your bed a little more pizazz!"

"You'll fucking pay for this!" he growls before stalking back out of my room and into his.

I grin. It might be small, but it's still a win.

TWENTY-FOUR

Winter

It's been two days since the blood incident in school and then the itching powder incident at home. I'm not sure how to feel right now.

Mason hasn't done anything to retaliate yet, and that has me on pins and needles. I know at some point he will. I just don't know when and the waiting game is killing me.

He's not one for not following through with his threats, and I know once I let my guard down that will probably be when he'll strike.

I'll probably just die from the nerves alone, waiting to see what he does. Every time I see him, he just smirks at me like he knows I'm freaking out because he hasn't done anything yet. I'm constantly waiting for the other shoe to drop.

I wish I could say that everyone at Ravenwood U left me alone after the last incident, but that would be a lie. My days at school are filled with snide comments that are thrown my way whenever I'm there.

People at the office are always giving me weird looks. I know they all saw the articles. Life has just been filled with crap lately. I mean, this is a small town, so I'm sure every single person saw those articles.

Trying to navigate through this new world sucks, and I

just want to go back to the days when I had nothing to worry about.

There haven't been any other notes or messages since the last one, but I'm under no illusion that they've just stopped. It would be stupid to think that. I have a feeling that the person is just biding their time. For what, though? I have no clue.

My PI still hasn't found anything on my mother yet. If she has skeletons in her closet, she's hidden it well.

I'm still hung up on her behavior. It's been like four months since her husband died and she's already planning her engagement with that asshole Alister.

Four months... wow, it feels a lot longer than that.

This week was spent with her going all crazy putting the arrangements in place, and for the safety of my life, I've stayed out of her way as best I can. With her mood, I don't want to be anywhere near her. I know she'd probably blow up on me any chance she got.

That has been the only thing to keep me sane through the shitshow happening this week. Though if she's out in public or around people, she tries to act like we're some sort of happy family. Like that's ever going to happen. I hate the four of them like my life depends on it.

As if they weren't douchebags before, they're even bigger ones now. Mason constantly dangles those pictures and videos over my head with the threat of showing it to my best friends.

Even though he hasn't done anything since the itching powder prank, he hasn't stopped threatening me with those pictures.

Yesterday while he was out, I snuck into his room to see if I could find the pictures to get rid of them, but no luck.

His laptop was locked, and I don't know his passwords. The old ones definitely don't work anymore.

I came to the conclusion that I'd just have to act like I'm listening to him until I can find a way to get rid of the evidence.

All of this has definitely put a strain on my relationship with the girls, and they've noticed. But how do you tell your best friends that you don't know if you slept with their crushes or not?

The pictures only showed them touching me and not actually having sex, but it is pretty damning when you look at it. I still don't know if they actually had sex with me and just decided to not take pictures of the actual act.

I'm sick to my stomach every time I think about all the unknowns concerning that night and the image of all of them touching me is too much to deal with. I really don't want my best friends to find out. If it's killing me, it'll be worse for them.

We're drifting apart. I've made every excuse under the sun to not hang out with them as much as I would've before. Truth is, I feel like a failure as a friend, and I feel too guilty being around them after knowing what I may have done even though it wasn't my fault.

Yeah, my glamorous life has gotten to the point where it's just exhausting. The only good thing is, I've managed to get lots of shit accomplished at work because I don't have a social life anymore.

All I want to do is sleep because exhaustion and depression are starting to kick my ass. I've tried to pull myself out of it, but the weight of everything currently happening in my life is just too much to bear.

No matter where I go, I can't get the feeling of being

watched to go away. I know it's more than one person watching me because it always feels different.

Don't even ask me how I know that, but you just know sometimes. Besides the helmet guy, I've felt the weight of someone else watching me and that presence feels wrong. I think that's the one with the malicious intent.

With hiding away from everyone to be alone, I've managed to start working on my project again. I've got to say using the lab and actually getting some of the work done is therapeutic. It's sort of helping to pull me out of my funk a little.

I've made some progress with the formula itself and have gotten the formula right, well, at least the part that I'm up to is right so far. That is a win in itself, and I couldn't be happier. Maybe things will hopefully start looking up from here.

I SHOULD HAVE KNOWN that happy feeling wouldn't last for long because of the douchebag that was currently out to get me at every turn.

I'm in the lab again today, hiding away from everyone because I love my own company more than I love being in the company of others.

I've had a routine this week—work, school, lab and then home. I've managed to talk to Antonio for a while too, but I haven't had the chance to see him since the last time we saw each other.

We've both been busy, so that's understandable. It's not because Mason said not to see him anymore. It's purely because we've been busy.

Great! You're a liar now too, Winter.

I groan. Okay; I haven't seen him because I don't want him to get involved with Mason and his shit. I'm sure he could hold his own against Mason if it came to that, but I'd rather not let it happen.

From what I've seen so far, Mason is a certifiable psycho, even if he hasn't been tested yet. I mean, after all the shit he's pulled on me since I've been back home can attest to that.

I groan again because I don't know why I'm always thinking about him. I hate him, yes, but I'm also torn between him and Antonio.

I could see myself loving Antonio, but I also still have unresolved feelings when it comes to Mason. I wish he'd wake up and see that he was wrong to blame me for whatever he's blaming me for.

Though if he did wake up and was aware that everything he did to me was wrong, would I forgive him?

I don't have an answer for that. Everything he's done has humiliated me in some way, especially in the public's eye.

It's been hard going to meetings and getting those prissy stuck-up assholes to listen to me. I've had to work harder just to insert my dominance and let people know that I'm the one running this gig and that has been exhausting too.

I guess you wouldn't have respect for your boss if you saw them half-naked in the media, or if you saw them being treated to a bloody rat prank filled with blood.

Pulling myself out of my thoughts because I need to continue working, I walk to the back of the lab to get some markers from the closet.

Writing down my formulas on the white board helps me to see where I'm going wrong and what I need to fix.

I'm walking out of the closet and not paying attention. I'm usually the only one who's ever in here.

The sound of the door clicking shut, however, finally grabs my attention and when I look up, all the douchebags are here. They're all standing and blocking the door. *Great!* I think to myself, *just when I was getting used to being alone, they have to spoil that for me.*

"What do you idiots want?" I ask, already irritated with the intrusion on my peaceful place.

"Remember when I said there would be payback for that stunt you pulled the other day?" Mason asks.

I gulp. Shit! I knew sooner or later he'd find some way to punish me for what I did. Though all I did was ruin sex for him for one day. If anything, I was probably saving him from an STD or something.

He moves away from the door and walks toward the front of the classroom where the desk is. Horror washes over me a second too late when he reaches the desk.

My notebook with my formulas and all the updates of everything I've done so far are on the table, and he starts flipping through it.

That is the only copy I have. I feel sick to my stomach. I have a feeling this is going to go in the direction I'm thinking of.

I begin to move to the front of the class to get my book, but Grayson and Beck each grab a hand, holding me in place so I can't move.

"What the fuck are you guys doing?" I scream at them. I try struggling, but it's no use, they have a steel grip on my arms.

Mason picks up my book and looks at it closely this time. "So, is this where you've been disappearing to every day this past week?" he asks casually, like he doesn't have half my life's work in the palm of his hands.

"Whatever you're planning on doing... don't!" I rush out since these assholes won't let go of me.

"What makes you think that you can tell me what to do?" he asks with an eyebrow raised.

In the next instant, he takes one of the Bunsen burners that's on the shelf next to the desk and he moves it onto the desk before lighting it.

I watch in horror as he lifts my notebook and places it over the fire. It slowly starts to burn from the edges.

"Stopppppp," I scream out as tears begin to trail down my cheeks. "Please stop! That's the only copy I have, and you know how many years I've been working on that!" I beg.

I've never begged him for anything, but I'm not above begging him to stop burning my book right now.

"Does it look like I give a shit? This is what you get for trying to play with the big boys," he says smirking while I start to feel numb.

I'm full-on sobbing now. The pain I feel right now is harsher compared to anything I've ever felt from all the things he's done to me.

I've worked so hard and so long on getting this project to where it is, and all it took was one asshole hell-bent on revenge to destroy my life's work.

Besides my father's business, this was the only other thing I've ever been passionate about and now, it's all gone.

"I told you to leave Ravenwood while you had the chance, but you didn't. This is the consequence for not listening," he says as he drops the book into the sink next to him.

Gray and Beck finally let go of me and I rush over to the sink as they all walk out of the lab, leaving me alone.

I pick up my book to see if I can salvage it, but it's completely burned, and nothing is visible to salvage.

I burst into tears again. I cannot believe he just did this to me after knowing how much this meant to me from the beginning.

He really doesn't care about anything that concerns me. He's just a coldhearted bastard.

I slide down the wall until my butt touches the ground and sob until I have no tears left. I have no idea how long I spend in the lab crying, but when I finally get myself under control, I look at my phone and see that it's been hours.

Slowly, I get up and grab my stuff along with my burned notebook and head out of the lab. I'm in a daze while walking to my car.

I feel the hairs on the back of my neck stand on end. It's the same feeling I get when I feel like someone is watching me.

Looking around, I don't notice anyone or anything out of the ordinary. I just keep walking to my car, but I make sure to walk a little faster.

When I get to my car, as if my day couldn't get any worse, there are some Polaroid pictures stuck to my windshield.

One is of the guys holding me, one with my book burning and then some with me on the floor crying. On the back of that one it reads *So pretty when she cries*.

This makes me break down again. I wish everyone would just leave me the hell alone. I should have known that brief reprieve wouldn't last long.

TWENTY-FIVE

Winter

THE DAY that I've been detesting is finally here. Today is the day my mother and Alister are announcing their engagement to the public during the party they have scheduled for tonight.

I haven't been looking forward to this day. I'm supposedly her "daughter" all of a sudden, and I have to attend this farce tonight.

I don't even want to attend this party. I'll probably hate every moment of it. At least I don't have to go too far tonight. I just need to walk from my room down to the ballroom since they're having the party at the King's mansion.

I'll keep calling it the King's mansion because this isn't a home and it'll never be my home for as long as I live. I feel so out of place here and it's probably because I feel so unwanted by everyone around me.

She's betraying all of my father's memories with everything she's doing, and it just makes me hate her more as the days go by.

I've invited Antonio to be my date for tonight. I don't want to suffer through this sham of a party alone. I'm sure it'll be like the first party I attended when we first came back here—all eyes on us. I know it'll be worse tonight because of the fact I'm the company CEO and everyone knows it now, and because of the way I've been making headlines lately.

All those prissy bitches who will be attending tonight will no doubt be judging my character, even though I had no say in what got uploaded onto the internet or the gossip rags.

I can already feel the headache coming on from what will no doubt be a rough night facing the vultures of high society again.

I especially don't want to be alone tonight knowing that all five of the assholes will be around as well. With Mason and Gray being here tonight, I'm sure the other three will no doubt show up as well.

I told the girls not to come because I'll leave early so I can spend some time with Antonio away from everyone else. At least that's the plan for tonight. They know how much I hate this engagement and don't even want to be here myself, so they agreed to stay home.

I never thought I'd say this, but I hate the three of them as much as I hate Mason and his brother. I never thought there would be a day when I'd hate Grayson too, but here we are.

I've spent the majority of this week in my bed and only leaving my room for food and to use the bathroom, but only when I was sure Mason wasn't around.

After what happened in school last week, I feel like I've just shut down. My depression is getting worse as the days go by, and I'm not sure how to get rid of it this time.

I've taken the meds my doctors have prescribed for me, but because of everything that's been happening, I feel as though they haven't been working as they should.

I was even more depressed and filled with anxiety compared to when I wasn't taking my meds.

All I want is to have these feelings to go away. They're constantly pulling me down to the place I don't ever want to be again. How do you stop pain when it's all you feel?

I'm still not over the fact that all of my work was destroyed and every time I think about it, I get pissed, which is always followed by crying. I hate being this weak and emotional, but it literally took years to get to the point that I was at and all of it was gone in a minute.

I let out a long sigh. I'll have to start from scratch because there's no other way. It'll now take longer to produce the stuff I wanted to for our pharmaceutical company, but somehow, I know I'll eventually get it done.

I'm looking at this setback as a way to make it better than it was before. Everything happens for a reason, right? Even if assholes are the reason...

I'm surprised my mother hasn't barged into my room yet to order me around. Even more surprising is the fact that Mason hasn't bothered me since everything in the lab went down.

Though I'm sure, as usual, that won't last for long. He's still hell-bent on ruining me. I'm not going to lie, he'll get there if this war between us keeps going on for much longer.

As much as I try to fight back, I wasn't built for a life of revenge and hate like they are. When I try to fight back, all it does is push me further onto his shit list.

I'm so tired of all the mind games and pranks. I wish I could go back to London and stay there without ever returning. I have a feeling life would be a hundred times better if I didn't have to constantly watch my back because of the bullies surrounding me.

I SPEND the rest of the day in my room until it's time to get ready for this stupid engagement party.

I figure I'd just show my face for a little while before sneaking out. I'm thinking I'll spend the night at our old mansion tonight. I miss that house already.

I haven't been back since mother made us move, so spending the night in my childhood home will be bliss.

At around seven p.m., I start getting dressed. The party starts at eight. I'm not keen on being there from the start, so I'll just show up when I feel like it.

By the time I'm actually done getting dressed, I can't for the second time since I've been here recognize the person in the mirror.

Though whenever I really look at myself, I never recognize the person staring back at me. I always feel like an imposter. Like this wasn't meant to be my life.

The dress I chose for tonight is a long black sequins dress with a side slit all the way up my thighs with an A-line spaghetti strap and a V-neckline. It's simple and I love it. It fits to perfection.

My long black hair is braided and pinned up in the back with jewels entwined into the braids and there are some loose curled tendrils spilling out across the braids. It looks amazing. Cute, but chic.

I opted for light makeup and red lips and of course my black, red bottoms. I'm definitely happy with the overall look.

It's about nine p.m. by the time I decide to go downstairs to show my face. I make my way to the elevator and once I'm on the first floor, I make my way down the corridor that leads to the ballroom.

I told Antonio to come at nine thirty. I knew I wasn't

going to come down early and I didn't want to keep him waiting too long.

Since we moved in, I've avoided the room because of all the bad things that have happened to me here every time I've stepped through this specific corridor.

As soon as I make it into the ballroom, people start to notice me. I'm instantly aware of the whispers and pointing directed my way.

I ignore everyone and go to sit at one of the tables at the front. Apparently, I need a front-row seat to this train wreck.

I'm not even there for five minutes when all the guys come over to sit at my table. *Fuck my life!*

Why the hell is it so hard for these assholes to leave me alone? I grab a glass of champagne from one of the passing servers. I'm not going to even look at them.

I concentrate on my drink and do my best to act like they aren't there. I hear them talking amongst themselves, but it's too low for me to hear what they're saying. Not that I care...

"*Cara,*" I hear from behind me a few minutes later, and I turn around to see Antonio. A genuine smile crosses my face. I swoon every time I hear him call me that since he said it means darling. How sweet!

"Hi," I say shyly. I don't miss the stares I can feel boring into me from across the table, and I know it's Mason without even looking.

"You look absolutely breathtaking tonight," he says, giving me a kiss on the cheeks. "Would you like to dance?"

"Absolutely!" I say before rushing out of my seat. I'd rather be dancing than sitting at this table with the guys staring at me like I'm some sort of carnival attraction.

We dance a few songs and even though I can feel the

eyes of everyone on us, I don't care and continue to have a good time.

"I've missed you, *cara*," he says while we're dancing.

"I've missed you too. Things at work and school have been crazy busy and I haven't had much time to do anything else," I say. It's not a total lie but I'm not about to tell him about everything going on in my life right now.

He pulls me in closer and holds me tighter while we continue to dance. I'm not going to lie, I feel the warmth in his embrace that I've been missing in my life lately.

Half an hour later, the music cuts off and I see my mother and Alister on the stage. Antonio leads me back to my table and thankfully the guys aren't there anymore.

"I'd like to thank everyone for being here tonight. The main reason for this party tonight is to announce the good news. Emilia and I are engaged!" Alister says, and then there's clapping.

I'm guessing everyone is excited about this shit then... *gag!*

The night goes on much the same and I'm bored out of my mind. Antonio leaves me to talk business with the people around the room. After a while, I decide to go out onto the balcony for some fresh air.

I'm there for two minutes when I feel hands grabbing me and pushing me back against one of the pillars. His hands go around my neck to keep me in place.

"Didn't I tell you to stop seeing that asshole?" he growls with anger in his voice.

"And why would I do that? We're not dating anymore so I can see whoever the fuck I want to!" I hiss at him. I'm tired of him thinking that he has a say in my life.

"Watch it! If you keep pissing me the hell off, I'm going to ruin you!"

I let out a sarcastic laugh. "You've already ruined everything so I don't see what else there is."

"Oh, there's so much more that I can do to you!" he says.

I wrench myself out of his grasp before spinning around and facing him. "Leave me the fuck alone, asshole!"

I don't even get another word out when he grabs me and pins me up against the pillar again and crashes his mouth against mine.

His kiss is hot, demanding, and filled with hate. His hands move to the slit in my dress and a second later his hand moves up my leg. I let out a moan.

He pushes his fingers into my panties, and then he's touching me. He roughly thrusts two fingers into me before he starts pumping them in and out.

I can't help the next moan that slips out of me and he smirks. "Wet for me just like a fucking whore, no matter what messed up shit I do to you."

His words are like a bucket of cold water splashed on me, and I come to my senses and push him away.

"God, I fucking hate you! If I'm such a whore, then why the fuck do you keep touching me?" I groan out in a voice filled with anguish. "Why the hell can't you just leave me alone?"

"Because you haven't paid enough for hurting me yet," he says.

"I-I didn't...." Not knowing what else to say, I walk out of there as fast as I can and head straight to the front door. I'm definitely not staying here tonight. I need some time alone to figure out what to do with this Mason situation. It's getting out of control.

I quickly get into my car and drive off. All our stuff is

still in my childhood home because I don't think she'd ever sell our house and I still have my keys to the place.

Once I get to the house, I park and then get out. I open the doors and head straight up to my old room.

I wipe off all my makeup and then get changed into a pair of sweatpants and a hoodie. I'm still in the bathroom when I hear the doorbell ring. What the hell?

No one lives here anymore, so the doorbell shouldn't be ringing at this hour. I gulp but slowly make my way downstairs to see who it is.

When I open the doors, there's no one there, but there's a package on the ground. I lift it up and take the box into the kitchen. It has my name on it, so I decide to open it. A scream rips out of me when I see the contents in the box, followed by the note.

I TOLD you bodies would start to fall if you didn't listen to me!!

You're already paid for, yet you keep letting these men touch you!

At least I know you'll be perfect for the whore position in the underworld!!

We're coming for you soon, baby.

What the hell does *'you're already paid for and whore position in the underworld'* even mean? These messages are really starting to freak me out more now.

There are also pictures with me and Mason against the pillar with his hand up my dress. The angle leaves nothing to the imagination of what he was doing. There are also some with Antonio and I on the dance floor.

Damn this asshole works fast, apparently. How the hell are they getting so close to me without me seeing anything?

The lights suddenly go off and another scream rips out of me. I rush out of the kitchen and run upstairs, back into my bedroom. I'm hyperventilating as I run. I'm scared.

I slam my room door shut, and it only takes a second to realize that I'm not alone in my room. Before I can get the door open again to run outside, a body slams into me and we both fall onto the floor.

I struggle as hard as I can, and this earns me a punch to the head. I instantly feel dazed, and my struggle eases up a bit. By the time I come to, I'm stripped and all I have on is my bra and panties.

I start struggling again and manage to knee my assailant in the balls, which gives me a second to get up and sprint for my door. I get it open and run toward the stairs. As soon as I get to the stairs, I feel hands push me and I go tumbling down.

I hit my head hard when I land at the bottom of the stairs and a second later, everything goes black...

TWENTY-SIX

Winter

WHEN I COME TO, I'm lying on one of the couches in the living room and I'm disoriented for a second before everything comes back to me. Instant sobs rack my body.

My head hurts from almost cracking it on my way down the stairs, and I realize I'm still in my bra and panties.

Someone was inside the freaking house and basically assaulted me! I shudder at the thought of them succeeding in what they came here to do, but then another thought circles my brain. Why didn't the person do anything while I was passed out?

Instinctively, I lift my hand up to touch the back of my head and instantly pull it away when I feel the sharp sting of pain from the bump that formed there.

"Why the hell are you crying?" Mason asks, and I let out a scream before scrambling away from him.

I was so focused and in my head that I didn't even notice anyone else in the room with me. I finally look around and notice all five of them here.

I narrow my eyes. What are the odds of them being here right after someone assaulted me? The timing is fucking suspicious, that's for sure.

The lights in the house are back on, so that's a good thing. "What are you guys doing here?" I scream out. Somebody better start answering my questions. I have no chill left for tonight.

"We came to check on you," he says.

"Yeah, and I'm the freaking Queen of England!" I hiss out at him.

"Your mom said she got an alert about the silent alarm going off in this house and since she and my dad are busy at the moment, she asked Mason and I to come check it out," Grayson supplies.

"Did you drink too much and pass out at the bottom of your stairs? Because that's how we found you," he says.

"Because everyone just drinks and passes out half-naked, right, stupid?"

"We've all got our vices," he says, shrugging.

"Yeah, and yours seem to be being an asshole all the time." I suddenly remember something important and freeze for a second.

"Oh, my God!" I scream and rush off into the kitchen. I don't even care that I'm half-naked right now. All I care about is looking for the package that was delivered earlier.

When I get to the kitchen, however, I don't see the package I left there earlier. Now, I'm freaking out more.

All the guys come in after me. I'm pretty sure I look crazy right now and on the verge of a freak-out. I'm panicking. The package that got delivered earlier had a fucking heart in it and now it's missing. I'm not sure if it was a human or animal's heart but I'm freaked out all the same.

"Where the fuck is it? Is this your idea of a sick joke?" I scream at them.

"What the fuck are you talking about?" Mason growls, but I'm in no mood for his shit.

"The fucking heart!" I screech. They all give each other a look, as if to say I'm acting crazy and irrational right now.

You'd be the same way too if you had a heart delivered to you.

"Calm down, babe," Royce says. "What do you mean a heart?"

"Somebody sent me a package with a fucking heart covered in blood! I really didn't think you assholes would stoop this low!"

"Why do you think we'd send you a heart? And where is it?"

"I don't know what you did with it! It was here and then the lights cut off and somebody was chasing me. They stripped me and when I got away, they pushed me down the stairs. I blacked out and now it's not here anymore," I say, pulling at my hair with tears streaming down my face. I'm frustrated.

I have no clue if that was a joke or not.

"We'll look into it," Nate tells me.

"Are you sure you're not just off your meds?" Mason asks.

"Get the fuck out now!" I scream at them. How fucking dare this asshole insinuate that I didn't take my meds after everything I just told them.

When none of them move, I get even more pissed off. I can't deal with them being here anymore.

"I'll fucking call the police if you assholes don't leave!" I scream.

"You're such a fucking bitch! We're just trying to help you," Mason growls out.

"Well, excuse me if I don't believe you and your fucking fake-ass help right now! If you don't get the fuck out of here, I will fuck you up!"

"I'm glad I don't have to deal with your crazy ass as a girlfriend anymore," Mason says before motioning for the guys to leave.

By now his words shouldn't have any impact on me, but God, do they ever. His words always hit straight to the fucking heart exactly where he intended them to.

I don't know what the hell happened tonight, but I'm freaking the hell out. I need to get away from here, at least for the weekend.

I don't know if I should report this to the police. I don't have the actual head anymore and now I'm wondering if I imagined the whole thing. I took my meds today and then I had champagne tonight so I have no clue what to believe anymore.

I try calling Martin to make sure he's okay, but I get no answer. After trying again a few times, I give up attempting to reach him and call my PI instead to look into the matter for me.

Ugh, I knew mixing my meds and alcohol would cause some damage, but I needed it to calm my nerves. Knowing that I need to get out of here if I want to save my sanity.

I pick up my phone and see a few missed calls from Antonio. Too drained to even explain all this to him right now, I send him a quick text telling him that Riley had an emergency and needed my help and that I'd call him tomorrow.

Next, I call the girls asking them to spend the weekend in Aspen with me. I hope they've forgotten I have been acting weird for the past couple of weeks but I should have known better.

They finally relent and respond with a yes when I tell them I'll explain my weird behavior once we're in Aspen.

I tell them to meet me at my old house in the morning so we can head to the airport from here.

I don't sleep a wink. I'm too scared to close my eyes. I

just hope this getaway helps to clear my head so that I can get back in the game when it comes to the company and my project.

———

THE FLIGHT TAKES a little over two hours from California to Aspen and by the time we get there, it's a little after noon.

We agree to meet in the living room once we're done taking our bags to our rooms and freshening up.

This house is my father's—mine now—I guess and I'm glad we don't have to spend the time in some hotel with other people. My anxiety has already been through the roof and I just can't deal anymore, at least until I recharge again.

The cabin is a huge wood structure that's very modern with ten bedrooms and just as many bathrooms. I have no idea why my parents needed such a big house when we rarely even came here in the first place.

It's basically in the middle of nowhere. All the other properties are closer to the skiing resorts.

I guess for what I need right now, I'm glad we're secluded. Sort of like we're in our own little bubble away from the outside world.

As soon as I get changed, I walk out of my room and into the living room only to see three sets of eyes looking directly at me. I took the longest trying to delay the inevitable. I let out a groan before plopping down onto the couch opposite them.

"Okay, time to spill, what the hell is going on with you?" Riley demands.

"Yeah, you've pretty much been M.I.A for the past few weeks!" Avery says.

"You've been pushing us away for weeks," Luna adds.

I knew sooner or later I'd have to tell them everything that is going on with me, though I'm going to omit some of the details. I'm still unsure of how they would react, and I don't want to hurt them like that.

So, I tell them about the constant back and forth between me and Mason, the things he's done, half of which they already know because it was all over Ravenwood U and on the internet. I also tell them about my notebook that he burned, which contained everything regarding the formula for my antidepressant pills.

That's when I broke down. That was the worst of what he's done. The next part is hard because I don't know if telling them about it will put them in danger or not.

"I think someone is stalking me," I whisper out. "I don't know who it is or why they're doing it, but some of the notes have been horrible. They made it seem like someone wants me for horrible things." Now I'm sobbing even harder with the weight of everything finally bearing down on me.

"Oh, my God! Why the hell didn't you tell us all of this sooner?" Riley practically screams at me.

"I don't know. At first, I thought nothing of it. I thought it was harmless but now not so much and I know Ravenwood's police force works for Alister. His entire family hates me, so I don't know what to do anymore. I feel like everything is falling apart."

Somehow, we're closer now and I'm lying on Riley's lap as she strokes my hair while I cry. My emotions are all over the place now.

"Everything hurts and I don't know what to do anymore. I love you guys but being back home has been nothing but hell. I don't know how much longer I'll be able to survive this," I say while more tears keep pouring out.

"We know, babe. I'm so sorry you're going through all of this," Avery tells me.

After that, we're all silent except for the sound of my sniffles. I guess I must have been more exhausted than I thought because I fall asleep to Riley stroking my hair.

I wake to the sounds of whispers coming from the kitchen and when I sit up from the couch, I notice it's already dark.

I get up and head into the kitchen but stop in my tracks when I see everyone in here, and I do mean everyone.

"What the fuck are you assholes doing here?" I yell at the five guys standing there looking at me.

"What does it look like? We're here for some downtime," Mason says.

"How the fuck did you even know where we were?" I let out a frustrated groan. I was stupid to think that I could have had some time away from these jerkoffs.

"Mommy dearest gave us the second set of keys when she knew that you were coming here," he says, smirking at me.

"Of fucking course, she did!" I spit.

I look at the girls, trying to tame my temper. I know this isn't their fault, but it sucks all the same. "I'm going for a walk to clear my head," I say as I walk out of the kitchen.

I grab my coat, and snowshoes before walking out the door toward the back of the property. It's a huge space and there's a nice view that always calms me down when I'm here.

I make it to the bridge that runs over the lake and when I reach the middle, I stand and look over at the view. The lake is frozen, everything is, and it makes for a nice, picturesque view.

I keep walking until I get to the other side of the bridge

and walk further in the distance past the lake. The walk is helping to clear my thoughts and I feel a lot better than I was a few minutes ago.

I hear the crunching of boots stepping on the fallen twigs but don't pay too much mind to it. I figure it's either one of the girls or one of the douchebags. No one ever ventures onto our property.

I guess this time, I'm wrong because a few minutes later, I'm grabbed from behind and slammed against the tree I was walking next to. I let out a groan and am about to scream when hands cover my mouth and a knife is pressed against my stomach.

The guy holding me is wearing a mask, so I can't tell who he is. When I try to struggle, he digs the knife into me and that makes me freeze on the spot.

"I've been waiting to come get you for a long time, Winter Crowne," he says in a menacing voice.

"Who the hell are you?" I ask with a quiver in my voice.

"That's not the question you should be asking. What you should ask is where I'm going to take you."

"Well then, where are you taking me?" I question.

"Someone paid a lot of money for Roman Bastianich to have his eye on you."

"Who... who is he?" I ask with a quiver in my voice. Somehow, I know that whoever this Roman is, he's bad news.

"The king of the underworld," he says happily.

Without thinking, and with him being distracted, I knee him in the balls. As if it were a reflex, he shoves his knife into my stomach.

He bends down and grabs his balls, which causes him to let go of me. I take the opening and run away, taking off in the direction of the lake.

He runs after me and the way we're situated, I'd have to run past him to get to the bridge. I'm not taking the chance of getting close to him again.

I run along the length of the lake and it's taking me further away from the house, but I don't have any other choice right now but to go this way.

The pain and blood loss from my stomach intensifies with each passing moment and I know if I don't get to the house soon, I'll either pass out from too much blood loss or I'll end up with this Roman guy.

I don't want to end up with some guy who is being called the "king of the underworld" That will not bode well for me.

The only option I can see right now is running across the frozen lake and then double back in the direction of the house, hoping to God, I don't fall and bust my ass.

I press my hand to my stomach to try and stop the bleeding as I keep running. The knife is still in the wound. I know you're not supposed to take out the object if you were ever stabbed because it'll cause more blood loss. I'm halfway across the lake when I hear him yelling after me. "Stop running or I'll shoot!"

I freeze for only a second before I keep going. I hear a shot ring out. I stop dead in my tracks and feel for any new pain but experience none.

Three more shots go off when I start to run again. The pain from my wound is unbearable now and as I set off running again, I feel the ice beneath me start to crack.

Oh no, no, no, no...

That's why I have no gunshot wounds. He wasn't shooting me; he was shooting at the ice. The lake hasn't been frozen for that long, so I know the ice isn't that strong yet.

I hear yelling from the direction of the path I took coming here just as two more shots ring out into the silent night air.

The ice beneath me finally breaks away and I let out a scream as I fall into the freezing water...

TO BE CONTINUED...

MORE FROM ME

Read my debut novel:

This Love Hurts

Coming Soon

Bleeding Crowne (Ravenwood Elites Book 2)

Coming Summer 2021

Bleeding Crowne (Ravenwood Elites Book 2)

Coming Summer 2021

Date TBD

Broken Empire (Ravenwood Elites Book 3)

Coming Fall 2021

Date TBD

Poisoned Throne: A Dark RH Retelling of Snow White

(A Twisted Tales Novel)

Coming January 2022

Add To Your TBR

HERE https://www.goodreads.com/book/show/57012832-poisoned-throne

THANK YOU

Thank you so much for reading!
If you loved it, I'd be eternally grateful if you would consider
leaving an honest review. I'd be happy with even a single sentence.
Your review would help get this book noticed by other readers.
Thank you once again.
Love Always,
Nikita
xoxo

ACKNOWLEDGEMENTS

I'm not good at these but I'd like to thank my PA Julia Murray as always for all the help with the book tour, graphics, teasers, beta reading and so much more! I love you and I couldn't have done this without you. I'd literally be like a headless chicken without you keeping me on track lol.

Secondly to my readers, thank you for reading my words. I love all of you who gave this book a chance. Xoxo

ABOUT THE
AUTHOR

Nikita is a full-time college student. In her spare time, when she's not procrastinating, she likes to
read or listen to music.

FOLLOW ME ON ANY OF THE PLACE LISTED BELOW:

Made in the USA
Monee, IL
02 August 2022

10697203R00168